TAINTED ASSET

KJ KALIS

This is a work of fiction. Names, characters, places and incidents either are the products of the author's imagination or are used fictitiously. Any resemblance to actual persons, living or dead, or locales is entirely coincidental.

Copyright © 2022 KJ Kalis
eISBN 978-1-955990-18-9
ISBN 978-1-955990-19-6
All rights reserved

Without limiting the rights under copyright reserved, no part of the publication may be reproduced, stored in or introduced into a retrieval system, or transmitted, in any form, or by any means (electronic, mechanical, photocopying, recording, or otherwise including technology to be yet released), without the written permission of both the copyright owner and the above publisher of the book.

The scanning, uploading and distribution of this book via the Internet or via any other means without the permission of the publisher is illegal and punishable by law. Please purchase only authorized electronic editions, and do not participate in or encourage electronic piracy of copyrighted materials. Your support of author's rights is appreciated.

Published by:
BDM, LLC

ALSO BY K.J. KALIS:

New titles released regularly!

If you'd like to join my mailing list and be the first to get updates on new books and exclusive sales, giveaways and releases, click here!

I'll send you a prequel to the next series FREE!

OR

Visit my Amazon page to see a full list of current titles.

OR

Take a peek at my website to see a full list of available books.

www.kjkalis.com

1

Travis kicked at a stray rock with the toe of his boot. He walked slowly between the outbuildings where his horses were being housed for the National Reining Horse Association Derby at the Oklahoma City Fairgrounds. It was nearly two o'clock in the morning on a balmy night in June. After a long day of showing, every bone in his body ached, a headache collecting itself at the back of his skull, ready to pounce.

A single light suspended from the top of a weathered telephone pole cast a yellow shadow over the edges of the buildings as he walked, the humidity of early summer in the Midwest carrying the smell of freshly cut grass, the sweet smell of oats laced with molasses used to feed the horses, muted by the acrid tinge of manure hanging in the air. Toads that had been croaking as he made his way between the buildings stopped, hearing the footfalls of a creature much bigger than they were, their noises starting again in his wake when they were sure he was gone. Off in the distance, he heard the call of a single owl, the haunting echo drifting off in the air. Travis glanced over his shoulder, staring at the shadows, wondering what other kinds of animals might be living in the fields behind the fairgrounds.

He and his assistant, Ellie, had been at the Oklahoma City Fairgrounds for nearly a week. It'd been a long trip, longer than most of the ones they made with the group of reining horses they had in training at Bishop Performance Horses. The trip to Oklahoma City itself had been relatively straightforward. After packing up the gooseneck trailer with all of the feed, tack, and equipment they'd need for a week, they'd gotten the horses loaded with little fanfare, all of them except for Joker. The spooky gelding felt the need to balk a couple of times before finally realizing all of his stable mates were already in the trailer and waiting for him.

The four-hundred-mile drive straight up I-35 into Oklahoma City was uneventful. They stopped every few hours to check the horses and get food and stretch their legs, finally arriving late in the afternoon after more than six hours on the road. By the time they got the horses unloaded, bedded down, fed, and watered, it was nearly dinner time.

And now, nearly a week later, the show was almost over.

By show standards, it had been a good one. Travis's horses had performed well, he and Ellie taking turns riding. Travis earned a spot in the finals for the pro division, and Ellie earned her own spot in the non-pro class. Two of the owners had flown out to see their horses compete as well, Georgeann and George Stevens, who owned Travis's favorite black gelding, Gambler, and the Hawkins family, who owned both Joker and Smokey. Travis had spent the better part of the week dodging them as well as a handful of women who had figured out he was single, attracted to his tall, dark good looks. They went so far as to follow him to the bar in the main arena one night when he just wanted to sit down and have a regular meal, rather than eating everything out of a takeout bag Ellie had bought for him. He ended up getting that meal to-go, too.

It was Travis's turn to stay at the barn that night, but he was having trouble getting to sleep with the constant chatter of teenagers traveling in packs, walking through the aisles, and nothing better to do as they avoided their parents. Traveling with hundreds of thousands of dollars of equine athletes and equipment meant that someone had to be watching them constantly. Travis and Ellie had been taking turns sleeping in the extra stall they'd rented at the fairgrounds, the other one heading back to the hotel just outside the fairgrounds proper, for a hot shower and soft bed.

It wasn't that Travis minded staying at the barn. Sleeping on a makeshift bed of hay bales was significantly more comfortable than many of the places he'd been forced to sleep outdoors during his time with Delta Force in the Middle East. It was the constant barrage of people talking and asking him questions, the drone of the announcers calling the classes and the winners that went on day by day, that was wearing thin. Travis was used to a much quieter existence.

But it was only for a few days. Or at least that's what Travis kept trying to tell himself.

There was only one full day left at the Derby, Travis realized as he walked between the long, dark buildings. Just one. He pulled off his baseball cap and ran his fingers through a crop of thick, dark hair. He'd taken a late night walk over the last few days, wandering to the back of the fairgrounds where nothing was happening, getting away from the constant thrum of voices and conversations and people coming up to him asking him questions. At the back of the fairgrounds, all was quiet. The only noise was the sound of his boots grinding on the gravel between the buildings and the animals and birds that lived nearby. The barns at the back of the fairgrounds were dark, dairy barns that were unused for the time being. All of that would change when the state fair kicked off, but by then Travis would be long gone.

Travis continued walking, staring at the ground, his hands shoved in his pockets when he heard a sound to his left, gravel crunching underneath boots. He stopped, listening. His stomach tightened. He narrowed his eyes in the darkness, listening, pulling his hands out of the pockets of his jeans.

Thirty feet ahead, a black silhouette emerged out of the shadows from the side of the barn as though someone had been watching for him. He licked his lips, waiting, as he glanced down at the ground. Without thinking, he grabbed a large stone gripping it tightly. If someone wanted trouble, he'd give it to them. He didn't have his gun with him, but he didn't need it. A chunk of rock would have the same effect in a pinch.

Travis narrowed his eyes as the figure made its way toward him, "Travis?" a female voice whispered.

Trying to make out the figure in the darkness, Travis didn't say anything, gripping the stone harder. "Travis? It's me, Catherine."

Travis blinked. He'd only heard that voice one other time. It was at The Sour Lemon in Austin, a restaurant that served as a hub for intelligence officers who were looking for some camaraderie and dealmaking over burgers and bourbon. There were restaurants and hotels like it all over the world. The Sour Lemon was the version near his home base of Burton, Texas. "Catherine?"

As the woman approached him, he saw her glance over her shoulder and then she grabbed his arm, pushing him toward the edge of one of the buildings, deeper into the shadows. It was so dark he could barely make out her face. Travis licked his lips, "What are you doing here?"

The glow from the single light at the other end of the building gave him barely enough light to make out her features. "I'd be happy to tell you, but could you please drop the stone first?" she whispered in a thick British accent.

"Sure."

The rock hit the ground with a dull thud, landing on a clump of grass. Travis looked at Catherine. The voice and the eyes were the same, but the face wasn't. She was dressed in a pair of jeans and a red shirt, a leather belt wound around her waist, and a light jacket on over her shoulders. Her thick blonde hair was braided around the back of her head, the tail of it hanging over her shoulder as if she was just one of the other riders at the show.

But she wasn't.

The last time Travis had seen Catherine, she was sixty years old with gray hair and wrinkles.

"What's going on? You look different. Are you in trouble?"

Catherine chuckled, a throaty, raspy laugh coming from deep inside of her, "You think I look different?"

"You could say that," Travis whispered.

"When I met you the first time," she said quietly, her voice barely above a whisper, "I was in disguise for another operation. Didn't take the time to take it off when I intercepted you at the bar. You didn't actually think all of those amazing special effects were created in Hollywood, did you?"

Travis shook his head, "Can't say I've ever stopped to think about it. Been a little busy with other things."

"So I've heard." Catherine glanced over her shoulder and then nudged Travis out of the shadows. "Let's walk. I need to talk to you."

Travis followed Catherine away from the edge of the building and back in the direction he'd come, toward the abandoned sections of the fairgrounds, far from prying eyes and other people. As they walked, the sound of the night creatures got louder, toads, crickets, and the occasional rustling of an unnamed critter in the grass. The only other noise was the sound of the gravel crunching under their boots, echoing off the sides of the buildings as they passed. Travis glanced at Catherine. She was exactly as he remembered from the single meeting they'd had when he was a brand-new agent for the CIA. She'd intercepted him at The Sour Lemon, passing on an assignment from his division chief even though she wasn't CIA. It was a test. Luckily, one he passed.

Travis glanced at her. Catherine was small, feisty. If he had to guess, based on her reflexes, she was probably better with a knife than she was with a gun. She was wily, with a big personality, a quick tongue, and an even faster mind. He could tell she was the kind of agent that had been in and out of some tough scrapes but had managed to get away by the skin of her teeth. He bet there were scars on her body and mind, some that he could see and some others that he probably couldn't. But, that was the life of work for the CIA, or in Catherine's case, MI6, the CIA's British equivalent.

"I'm guessing this isn't a social call," Travis said, glancing down at the dark ground and shoving his hands in his pockets again as Catherine walked next to him. "Can't say I was expecting to have a visit from one of my former colleagues this late at night or this far out in the country."

"Believe me, I wasn't planning on it either," Catherine said.

Quiet descended between the two of them for a moment. Travis furrowed his eyebrows as he glanced at her. It was as if Catherine had something to tell him that she knew he didn't want to hear. He scratched the underside of his jaw, feeling the rough stubble of a long day. "Listen, Catherine. It's nice to see you and all, but you know as well as I do this is no coincidence. How about if we cut to the chase and save both of us some time?"

He could see her smile in the darkness, the glow from the stars and the moon above enough to light the basic features of her face, "You're exactly as I remember you, Travis Bishop," she looked up at him. "Direct and to the point. You would've made a good MI6 agent."

"Except for the fact that I'm an American."

"Well, we all have our shortcomings," she chuckled. They walked for another few feet before she cleared her throat, "You're right. I'm sure my appearance here has been a bit of a surprise. You probably thought you'd never see me again."

Travis chuckled, "Honestly? If someone had asked me I would've told them you were dead."

"Dead?"

"Because you were so old."

Catherine elbowed him, "Very funny." Her face became still, as though the reality of what she was about to say was weighing heavy on her. Travis frowned, "What is it? Are you okay? Are you in danger?"

Catherine turned and looked at him, putting a hand on his arm, "I'm fine. Look, Travis, there's no easy way to say this." She glanced over her shoulder in both directions before continuing, "I'm here as a courtesy. I heard something that you need to know."

A knot formed in Travis's gut. Catherine's demeanor and the tone of her voice told him that whatever it was it was serious. "Spit it out, Catherine. Enough with the dodging. What's going on?"

"The CIA wants you dead."

2

"The CIA wants me dead?" Travis pressed his lips together. "What are you talking about? I've been out for more than five years. What could they want with me?"

"I don't know." She shoved her hands into her pockets. "As soon as I heard, I grabbed the next flight from London. I know we only met that one time, but it just doesn't seem fair for you not to know."

Travis's mind was reeling. Was Catherine being serious? Was this some joke that someone had put her up to? Nothing made sense. "I don't understand. How is this possible?"

Catherine sighed, "I don't know. The Director of MI6, his name is Archie Elliott. He pulled me into his office yesterday and told me he'd gotten a communiqué from one of our sources linked to the CIA, not actually from them, that a kill order had been put out on one of their own. When he told me it was you, I knew I had to do something. I felt like I owed you for taking care of that little errand years ago."

"Does he know you're here?"

Catherine nodded, "He's the only one."

Part of Travis wanted to ask Catherine how she'd found him, but the question itself was ridiculous. She worked for one of the most powerful spy agencies in the world. MI6 had as long of a history as the CIA did, if not longer. The two agencies had worked together through multiple world wars and had ended political skirmishes across the globe, all in the name of helping to advance peace and Western ideals as best they could, and preventing disaster where they couldn't.

Travis shook his head, "Do you know anything more?" Part of Travis wanted to believe that she had the wrong person. "Are you sure it's me? The CIA doesn't normally go after people who don't work for them anymore."

"Unfortunately, I'm sure it's you. I wanted to warn you. I know you've got skills you can use to defend yourself. I'm only telling you to be prepared, that's all…" Her voice drifted off. "Listen, Travis. I know you're an honorable man. I heard all about how you saved your president and the way that you drove that car bomb into Lake Pontchartrain during the Mardi Gras attack. I've gone through your record myself. I can't understand why there would be a kill order out on your life, but there is. Someone had to trigger it."

Travis gripped his hands into fists, "I have no idea. Like I said, I've been out for five years."

"I know. I'm sorry, Travis. I don't know what to say."

The two of them started to walk again, turning back the way they'd come. A knot the size of a boulder formed in Travis's gut. It hadn't been that long since he'd gotten caught up in a terrorist bomb plot in New Orleans, led by Rashid Sharjah. A few months before the Mardi Gras bombing in New Orleans, he'd stopped the assassination of the president. And now this? Something didn't make sense.

"I don't know what to say, Catherine."

"A thank you would be appropriate, I suppose," Catherine said, sounding decidedly British.

"In that case, thank you."

The two of them walked in silence for the next minute, options filling Travis's head, a habit he developed during his time with Delta Force and the CIA. Faced with any problem, his mind would quickly begin taking the problem apart and then figuring out the best way to put it back together to get things right again. Travis shook his head. If what Catherine was saying was true, the quiet life he'd been living at Bishop Ranch might temporarily be over, at least until he could figure out what was going on.

If he could do it before someone came to take him out...

3

Travis felt like a man drowning. Every breath seemed more valuable than the last. As he and Catherine walked back toward the stables where the horses from Bishop Ranch were spending the night, Travis wondered what to do next. Part of him wanted to pack everything up and head back to Bishop Ranch. At least there, he'd have his war room, complete with all of his guns and weapons. He'd have something of a tactical advantage. It might at least give him a fighting chance at defending himself.

But he knew, the reality was that if the CIA wanted to get to him, they could get to him anywhere. He could run to the ranch, but he couldn't hide. Not that he was a man prone to hiding. That wasn't his style.

An uncomfortable silence fell between him and Catherine as they wove their way through the dark buildings of the Oklahoma State Fairgrounds. Up ahead, from the slight rise where they walked, he could see the glow of the main arena lights lit up the distance, like the star at the top of a Christmas tree. The rest of the fairground buildings spread out around it were dimly lit, only sparsely placed overhead lights offering any break from the deep darkness that covered the fairgrounds.

Up ahead, the buildings narrowed, only wide enough for a golf cart or pedestrians to get through, the smell of piles of acrid manure filling the air, a line of green dumpsters with black tops shoved up against the concrete block building. Travis stared straight ahead, walking with Catherine, lost in his thoughts.

Over his shoulder, he heard a rustle and saw movement out of the corner of his eye. Travis's breath caught in his throat as a man dressed in black charged at him out of the darkness, the glint of a knife in his hand. Travis pivoted toward the man, squaring off with him, putting his right hand up in defense of Catherine, blocking the man from getting to her. Out of his peripheral vision, he saw her small form take two steps back and then disappear into the darkness.

Without time to think or call after her, Travis held his hands up in front of him glaring at the man, who had the blade extended toward Travis. He didn't say anything. A split second later, the man lunged toward Travis, closing the distance between them, the blade ripping through the flesh on his right forearm. Travis grunted. He didn't bother to look at the wound. He didn't have time. The man lunged at him again but missed. As the blade passed by Travis on his left side, Travis caught the man's wrist with his right hand, twisting it. The man yelped, the blade dropped with a clatter onto the gravel.

Travis didn't waste any time. He kneed the man in his gut, sending his attacker to the ground. Travis and the man grabbed for the knife at the same time, both of them getting a hand on the handle. The man twisted Travis's wrist and managed to push him back. Travis's eyes got wide as the knife blade got closer to him. The next time the man lunged, Travis grabbed at the man, covering his attacker's hand with his own. He pressed down as hard as he could, drawing the blade upward on the man's free hand, slicing the inside of his wrist, severing the tendons, making his fingers useless. The man cried out. As he did, Travis twisted the knife around and drove the blade upward into the man's gut, piercing the flesh and sending the metal deep inside of the man's abdomen. Blood immediately began to pour out, the man dropped to his knees and then onto his side with a grunt.

Travis staggered backward, his breath raspy, unconsciously grabbing for his right forearm. He watched as a pool of blood poured out of the man's abdomen, staining the chalky, gray gravel with crimson. The blade must have penetrated the man's abdominal artery. Travis stared at the body on the ground. If it was arterial bleeding, the man had probably less than a minute to live. Even the most talented trauma surgeon would have a hard time saving him at that point. Travis knelt over him, looking at him, "Who hired you?" he hissed.

The man gave Travis a weak smile, a trickle of blood rolling down the side of his cheek. He didn't answer.

"Who hired you? Tell me!"

The man still didn't answer, his eyes glazing over and then rolling back up in his head.

Travis leaned over, putting two fingers on the man's neck. The man's skin was still warm to the touch, but he was gone. Travis stood up, staggering a little, the adrenaline from the attack catching up to him. He glanced down at his arm, but it was nearly impossible to see the damage in the darkness. He looked over his shoulders in both directions. Catherine was nowhere to be seen. Where she'd gone, he had no idea. But he knew he needed to disappear just as she had.

Walking away from the scene as quickly as he could without attracting attention, he took the flannel shirt off that was over his T-shirt and quickly wrapped it around his arm, trying to make it look like he was carrying his shirt and not using it as a bandage for the wound on his arm. He could hear the whoosh of blood in his ears from the adrenaline of the attack, a trickle of sweat running down the side of his face. Catherine had been right. Someone was coming after him, but who?

More importantly, why?

4

It took Travis another four minutes of winding his way back and forth between the buildings to get to the trailer. He found the one belonging to his ranch perched in a long line of them, fumbling in his pocket for the keys. He opened the door to the equipment area, knowing there was a first-aid kit inside. As he pulled the door open, he heard a voice call out behind him, "Travis?"

For a second, he thought it was Catherine, or at least he hoped it would be. It wasn't. It was Georgiana Stevens, one of the owners who'd flown out to see her horse run in the Derby. "Travis? I wanted to talk to you for a second about Gambler."

Travis gritted his teeth together. It was bad enough that he was in pain but even worse that it was one of the owners that had found him. They always managed to call or interrupt at exactly the wrong moment. His relationship with the owners was much like the relationship between a shark and a pilot fish. The sharks needed the pilot fish to nibble parasites off their leathery skin underwater but in the process, the pilot fish were constantly annoying the predators.

That's a bit how Travis felt when it came to dealing with his clients. He needed them. Their investment in his training program paid the bills and kept the lights on, but their incessant questions, demands, and unfulfilled hopes and dreams made his life complicated.

"Georgiana, this isn't a good time. It's the middle of the night. Come and find me in the morning." Travis stepped inside of the trailer and turned the light on, opening a tack box and fishing the first aid kit out. As he turned around, Georgiana was standing just inside the doorway, blocking his exit. She hadn't left.

"Oh my God! You're bleeding. What happened?"

"Nothing. Where's George?"

"I left him at the bar." She glanced at Travis, "Here, let me help you."

Travis frowned as Georgiana stepped closer to him. The last thing he needed was George Stevens seeing Travis coming out of the inside of the trailer with his wife at two o'clock in the morning. Travis shook his head. How the two of them had managed to get together with their names nearly identical, Travis wasn't sure. "No, I'm good," Travis said, taking a couple of steps toward the door. "You shouldn't be in here."

"Why?" Georgiana frowned, "Are you worried about George?" She shook her head, "Don't be. He's on his fifth whiskey. He's not going to be leaving that bar anytime soon."

Travis elbowed his way outside, past Georgiana. No matter what she said, he wasn't spending any time in any trailer with any woman, except one of his choosing. And it wouldn't be a married one, that was for sure. Setting the first-aid kit on the step. Georgiana followed and then stepped in front of him, "Seriously, Travis. Let me help. I was a nurse before I married George."

Travis sighed. Georgiana wasn't going to take no for an

answer. "Let me take a look at that." She frowned. "Looks like you got sliced pretty good. Somebody get you with a knife?"

"Yeah, a drunk guy from a bar in town. It's no big deal," Travis lied.

"How's the other guy?" Georgiana smiled, leaning down and picking up a package of gauze. She tore it open and dabbed at Travis's arm with the soft fabric. Travis winced. "He's okay. I got the brunt of it," Travis lied again.

"Hold your arm up in the light so I can see better." Travis did as instructed. "It looks like you need stitches. I can wrap it up for you temporarily to slow the bleeding down, but you probably need to get yourself to an emergency room and let them have a look at it."

"Okay, will do." Travis had no intention of going to an emergency room. Any public places were going to be out of bounds until he had a better sense of the threat against his life. Crowds provided too much cover and too much distraction, not to mention the explanations that would be needed if he had to defend himself. No, he'd have to lay low until he figured out what was going on and how to stop it.

Humming to herself, Georgiana tore a few more packages of gauze open, laying them across the wound on Travis's arm and then wrapping it deftly with a rolled bandage. As she tied off the ends, she cocked her head to the side. "Looks like you got lucky. Just surface damage. Can you move your hand okay?" Georgiana's voice was soft as she cradled his hand in her own.

He pulled away. "Yeah. Seems to be fine."

Georgiana frowned as if it suddenly occurred to her why she was standing there. "I'm sorry you got hurt. Will you be all right to ride in the morning?"

Travis pressed his lips together and closed his eyes for a moment. Georgiana was trying his patience. His owner's compassion only went as far as it didn't impact the performance of their horse. People that invested in reining horses, but didn't ride them, were quick to make demands and even faster to jump ship from one trainer to the next, looking for the hot rider that could earn them the points and the reputation their horse would need in order to get into shows like the Run for a Million at the end of the summer show circuit in Las Vegas, an elite level, invitation-only, reining competition where the winner took home a purse of a cool million dollars to be split between the trainer and the horse owner. The money was only second to the bragging rights.

Travis narrowed his eyes and adjusted his baseball cap on his head, "Yeah. I'll be fine. I just need to get some rest. Like you said, it's a surface cut. That's all."

"You'll have that arm looked at?" Georgiana said, her eyebrows raised.

Travis grunted, "Yeah, that too."

As Travis locked the trailer door and walked back towards the barn, he could hear Georgiana behind him, "Oh, and by the way Travis I wanted to ask you..."

Travis kept walking.

Travis continued to the end of the line of the trailers and then circled back, waiting to make sure Georgiana had disappeared back in the direction of the bar where she'd left her husband. Sure, it was entirely plausible that George was in there drinking, but Travis had bigger things on his mind than having someone see the two of them leave the bunk in his trailer. It wasn't a good look, not one that his reputation could afford. The reining community was small, the top riders in the industry numbering fewer than a dozen, the rest of them, including Travis, trying to chase the top. The last thing he needed was some sort of a scandal with an owner, whether true or not, to damage his reputation.

Waiting as he watched Georgiana walk away, Travis looked

down at his arm flexing his fingers. Georgiana was right about one thing — he was lucky. The knife simply sliced the skin on his arm. There didn't seem to be any damage to the tendons, muscles, or ligaments that would prohibit him from operating his hand. He couldn't say the same about the man he'd left behind. Travis glanced in his direction, listening, waiting to hear sirens.

Travis waited another couple of minutes, watching for any sign that Georgiana was still lurking in the shadows. There was one more thing he needed to get out of his trailer if what Catherine had said was true.

Circling back toward the long line of sleek metal vehicles used to haul the horses, each one fancier and more elaborate than the next, Travis moved silently between the trailer next to his and the one he'd used to bring the horses in. By all standards, his was a relatively plain, gooseneck model with a combination bunk and tack storage area, hooks, and foldable saddle trees attached to the walls. He looked over his shoulder as he approached the door, double-checking the shadows. Travis didn't expect the man he'd stabbed to try again. That man had lost his life. But if there was one thing Travis knew about a kill order is that once it started, whoever placed the order would send assassin after assassin until the job was done. They would be like cockroaches coming out of the corners until the target was dead or the order was rescinded, if it could be....

Travis shoved his key in the lock and turned it, rattling the door handle to get the tack room door open. He stepped inside, closing it behind him. Flipping the small interior light on, he looked down at the plastic bag they carried for trash. It was filled with wrappers from the first-aid supplies Georgiana used, some of it tinged crimson with his blood. Travis stepped in front of a secured storage locker that had come with the trailer underneath the lower bunk. He lifted the mattress to expose the lid. When he'd bought the trailer, he noticed the locker itself was fine, made of metal with reinforced hinges, but the lock itself was something that a two-year-old and a paperclip could get open if given enough time. He'd spent one afternoon replacing it with a fortified version. Taking a key from his key ring, he inserted it in the lock and opened it up. Inside were the typical things to keep secured while at a horse show, extra cash, his wallet, and a couple of silver inlaid bridles that he didn't want to walk off. Pushing the bridles to the side, he exposed another locked box.

On the day that Travis had refitted the lock on the storage box, he'd added another secured compartment to the floor of the interior of the one that came with the trailer. This one had a combination lock and a fingerprint scanner, much like that lock he used on the war room back at the ranch. He keyed in the code and pressed his thumb to it, hearing the lock pop open. He lifted the top off, exposing a Smith & Wesson nine-millimeter semiautomatic pistol, already loaded and in a holster, five boxes of ammunition, and a K-Bar tactical knife with a seven-inch blade. In addition to those things, there was a flashlight, a long piece of paracord, and a tactical pen. From inside the box, he pulled out the gun, quickly unfastening the wide leather belt that he wore with the silver buckle. He stuffed the bloody shirt he'd been wearing in the trash bag, grabbing a light jacket from one of the hooks inside the tack room and laying it on the edge of the box.

Fishing the holster through his belt, he attached it to his hip, then checked his gun to make sure it was loaded. Satisfied, he stowed it in the holster, pulling the jacket gingerly over his injured right arm. Travis glanced down inside of the box, blinking. He stared at the assortment of other weapons that were inside the box. The only other thing he grabbed was another fully loaded magazine filled with nine-millimeter brass, hollow point, ready to fire.

As he locked up the remainder of his weapons and closed the storage locker, replacing the mattress on the bunk, he closed his eyes for a second. If they were coming for him, let them come. They'd have a fight on their hands.

In the meantime, he needed to find Catherine and get some answers.

5

CIA Director Tom Stewart broke down from a run to a walk as he heard his phone ring. He wore gray running shorts, a matching gray T-shirt, and a light jacket in the cool morning air, paired with high-tech, long-distance running shoes in a palette of lime green, citrus yellow, and gray. Feeling slightly annoyed that he had to break his stride, Tom pulled his phone out of the waist pack he wore, frowned for a second, narrowed his eyes, and then took the call.

"Yes?"

"I have a report, sir."

"Go ahead." Tom walked as he took the call, feeling his heart skip a beat as he listened. "What happened?"

"It didn't work. We took a casualty."

Tom's mouth hung open, anger surging through his chest, "What are you talking about? How's that possible?" he yelled, then realized he was walking down a running path in a park not far from his home and work in Virginia. He glanced over his shoulder. Luckily, no one was around.

The voice on the other end of the line stammered, "I have no idea, sir. All I know is when we didn't get word, our contact waited and then went to check the scene. It wasn't good. I'm sorry, sir."

A mouthful of bile surged its way up Tom's throat. He spit it out on the sidewalk. "Wait for further orders," he hissed and then hung up.

Shoving his phone back in his waist pack, he pulled out his bottle of water, took a sip to rinse the bile out of his mouth, and then started running again, trying to pick up where he left off.

It was going to be a long day...

Forty-six minutes later, another seven miles under his belt, Tom walked in the side door of the house he shared with Senator Shelley Stewart, slamming it behind him hard enough that their cat, a calico named Snickers, scuttled off beneath his feet. Tom walked over to the kitchen sink, pulled a paper towel from the roll and wiped his forehead, the beads of sweat still gathering on his brow. He'd given up trying to grow hair a few years before and now clipped what was left of the gray strands close to his head. He was nearly bald, but not completely. He kept a bit of hair on his head in the event that one morning he would wake up and find he had a full head of hair again. Miracles did exist, after all. He realized he would need one to get through the day based on the way it had started. Wadding up the paper towel in his hand, he realized things had a habit of rolling downhill. It looked like today was going to be a downhill day.

Walking over to the refrigerator, he opened it and pulled out a bottle of water infused with an organic vitamin blend that he liked. He'd taken up running ten years before when his doctor told him he was out of shape and that his blood pressure was through the roof, all things that Tom could have told him without a fancy medical degree and years of education. The doctor had suggested walking as a form of stress relief and exercise. After about a month of doing that, Tom got bored and upped the ante, adding a run-walk combination and then finally just running. Ten years later, he'd run in four marathons, finished three and completed numerous half marathons. After the last half marathon, Tom decided that was his sweet spot. Running just over thirteen miles seemed imminently more doable to him than a full marathon. Twenty-six miles was a distance out of reach, apparently much the way his target the night before had been.

Leaning against the sink, Tom cracked the lid of the water bottle open and chugged half of it down, feeling that cool liquid fill his stomach. Hopefully having something inside of him would settle it.

"Did you hear anything?" Shelley said, walking into the kitchen. She was wearing a rust-colored jacket with a white blouse underneath paired with a matching rust-colored skirt that went just below her knees, and a pair of brown closed-toe pumps on her feet.

Tom glanced at his wife from his position against the sink, narrowing his bulgy gray-blue eyes. No hello. No good morning. No, how are you? Over the last few years, the pleasantries between him and his wife had gone out the window, along with any sense of affection or any intimate activity behind closed doors. Their relationship was nothing more than a business transaction. They were roommates. Associates. Colleagues. Nothing more, nothing less. He glanced at the floor. Shelley was not going to be happy, but there was no way to hide the truth from her. "Yeah. They just called."

"And?"

Tom shook his head, "It didn't work. We took a casualty. "

Shelley slammed her hand down on their Italian marble kitchen island and let a string of expletives fly that would have made even the most hardened Navy sailor blush. Tom stood by and watched, waiting for the storm to pass. Shelley's personality resembled a tsunami — it crashed on the shore and then quickly pulled back out to sea, leaving peace and quiet, albeit a wave of destruction, behind her.

"What do you mean it didn't work? I thought that was one of your best guys?"

Tom shook his head, "I thought so too. I really thought he was the right guy for the job."

"What are you gonna do now?" she demanded.

Tom stared at his wife. When they'd met thirty years before, she was an aide to Congressman Murphy of Tennessee. Tom had been a newly minted CIA agent and was immediately smitten by her feisty personality and her long dark brown hair. He didn't even mind that she had a permanent limp, the result of getting hit by a car as a kid, one leg permanently shorter than the other. Tom would have liked it if Shelley had been able to join him on his runs, but the wear and tear on her back and hips from her uneven stride might have done damage to her body, especially with the kind of mileage Tom did every single week. A few years before, when they were in a calm patch, he'd suggested they see an orthopedic surgeon at Walter Reed, a friend of his who was willing to do them a favor. Over a drink one night, the surgeon had told Tom there was a way to insert a rod into Shelley's femur giving her the length in her leg back she'd lost as a teenager. "It would take some physical therapy to get her walking without a limp, but yeah, it's completely possible," the surgeon sighed, rattling the ice cubes in his empty whiskey glass.

Shelley wouldn't hear of it. The mere suggestion set them back a few steps in their relationship, as if Tom's idea, which was meant to be beneficial for her health, was a criticism of the way her body was. Shelley's limp was the least of Tom's complaints about how Shelley looked. She still had the same bushy brown hair that he thought was so cute decades ago, but her lack of movement had made her body soft. She wasn't overweight nor was she underweight. All of the running Tom did had made him lean and hard. Shelley was the opposite. Some men were attracted to that. He was not.

Tom took another swig of his water, hearing his watch beep. It was time for his sit-ups, push-ups, and a fair amount of stretching before he hit the shower and then went to the office. He pushed himself away from the counter, not making eye contact with Shelley. He could feel her eyes boring into him. As he made it to the other side of the kitchen, he heard her voice behind him, "I asked you a question. What are you going to do now?"

Tom whirled around, "I told you this before. I'll fix this," he said sternly.

Shelley threw her hands up in the air. She slammed her hand down on the counter again, rattling the crock that held the selection of spatulas, tongs, spoons, and scrapers they never used. "Tom, that's not good enough. You know the situation we're in."

Tom sucked in a breath, "Yes, I do. I'm well aware. That's why I'm trying to handle it."

Shelley started to pace, "This is all your fault. I hope you know that," she said, glaring at him over her shoulder. "Nothing is ever enough for you."

"Shelley, I don't want to fight this morning."

She narrowed her eyes, "Fight? I'm not fighting. I'm stating facts. You can't handle the truth!"

Tom stared at the ground, balling his hands into fists, before looking at her. "What is the truth, Shelley?"

"You're stupid and you're greedy. That's the truth!"

The words stung. It wasn't the first time Shelley had let loose a barrage of insults against him over the course of their marriage. No matter what he did, there was a better way and she was more than happy to share with him what that way was. It was like he had lived with his mother, except that his mom had been a much more gentle soul than Shelley was. Watching

Shelley go off on another one of her tirades, Tom shook his head. He knew how this would go. She'd scream and fuss and then burn out. The two of them would live in a cold, awkward silence for a period of time and then they would go back to where they had been before, acting like nothing had ever happened.

Except for the fact that Tom always remembered what happened.

He sighed, "The truth is I made a bad investment decision."

"With those crazy people? You think? It's not just your life and career on the line this time, Tom. It's mine! And I've worked for thirty years to get where I am. You and your get-rich-quick scheme have exposed us to a world of trouble, the kind that sends people to jail, not to mention destroying my career."

The contingent of women in the Senate wasn't a surprise to the small body of legislators anymore, but getting an appointment onto the most powerful committees that were still controlled by the boy's club of politicians in Washington, DC was. Somehow, through negotiation, threat, or sheer force of will, Shelley had managed to get herself a spot on the Senate Intelligence Committee, a choice appointment that gave her nearly the same level of access to information that Tom had in his position as the Director of the CIA. By Washington standards, Tom and Shelley were powerful, immensely so, with their fingers wrapped in all forms of espionage and intrigue at the highest levels. If hotspots or threats were developing somewhere around the world, it was likely that one of the two of them knew what was happening even before the president of the United States did.

Tom lowered his voice, staring back at Shelley. "I know you're upset. I understand why and I will take care of it."

"Really? I'll believe that when I see it!" Shelley bellowed, scooping up her briefcase, her car keys, and her cell phone as she stomped out the door, the frame rattling as she slammed it behind her. A second later, Tom heard her black Mercedes sedan start, the tires squealing as she pulled out of the driveway. Tom shook his head, wondering what the neighbors must think. "Just another fight at the Stewart household," he muttered as he walked to the shower.

6

A prickly stalk of hay poked Travis through his side as he rolled over, waking him. He blinked, his eyes dry from a lack of sleep. Sitting up on the bales of hay where he'd slept, he realized he'd slept with his hand on the butt of his gun. Wiggling his fingers, he felt a dull ache in his arm from where the knife sliced through his skin. Travis laid there for a second, staring up at the ceiling, the twitter of barn swallows somewhere overhead.

It was early. From somewhere off in the distance, he heard what sounded like a cart rolling down one of the aisles. He checked his watch. Five-thirty. The scene from the night before rolled through his memory like a train making a momentary stop at a station. Catherine emerging from the shadows. The threat on his life. The man with the knife. Georgiana tending to his wounds.

By the time he'd gotten his arm patched together, the adrenaline surge from the attack had worn off, and he checked on the horses, Travis had only gotten a couple of hours of sleep. Not that he needed much. After spending years with Delta Force and then the CIA, his body was trained to operate on whatever sleep was available. It could be no sleep, a couple of hours, or a full night's worth. It didn't matter. Whatever he had available was good enough.

It had to be.

Travis kicked off the cooling blanket for one of the horses that he'd used as his own overnight, he sat, hunched over, waiting for the last bit of exhaustion to pour out of his body.

He shook his head slowly as his mind started to replay the knife attack from the night before. He blinked, stopping the train of thoughts before it got out of control. He needed to stay focused. Today was the open finals at the Derby. He had one shot at getting more points and he needed to concentrate on the business at hand – the horses.

Pushing himself up from the hay bales, Travis stretched his shoulders for a second and then tugged the jacket he'd grabbed from the trailer down over the butt of his gun. Moving slowly, he peered out into the aisle. No one was moving around, although he could hear the hum of trucks and golf carts moving just outside the complex of barns. He would have a few moments of peace before the riders, owners, barn hands, and assistants all showed up to get the horses ready for the last day of competition. Travis sucked in a breath and then sighed. He felt a few butterflies gather in his gut. For some reason, showing the horses always put him on edge.

As he walked out of the stall, Travis stopped to think about that for a second. It wasn't the pressure of having to remember the pattern the judges had chosen for the ride. They were all similar — a series of circles, both large and small, some fast, some slow, flying lead changes as the horse changed directions, spins, rollbacks, and long runs leading to the iconic reining movement of a sliding stop. Memorizing things had never been a problem for Travis. His life and his missions depended on his ability to do so. That wasn't what made him nervous. And it wasn't the equipment. His equipment could be checked and rechecked to make sure that it would operate exactly as it should while he was showing whichever horse he was on. And it wasn't the horse either. Although he couldn't control their attitude for the day or how they were feeling as they traveled, whatever the horse couldn't give, he could. They worked together, each of them picking up the slack for the other.

No, that wasn't what made him uneasy. It was the spectacle of all of it.

In his years as an operator and an agent for the CIA, his job was stealth, cloaked. He moved in and out of situations, countries, through bodies of water, and even parachuted out of airplanes each time with the same goal — to get in and out without being detected, nothing more than a shadow.

And that was the exact opposite of showing a horse.

Unlike many of the other equine disciplines where there could be anywhere from ten to thirty horses in the ring all at one time, reining was a solo sport. There was only one horse and one rider in front of a panel of judges. It was more like figure skating than hockey. Each rider was judged individually, the crowd clapping and whistling when a move was done to perfection.

But all that attention wasn't comfortable, at least not for him. Travis felt like he had the red dot of a sniper's rifle on his chest the entire time he rode, all eyes in the arena staring at him. It was disconcerting, to say the least.

And based on what he'd seen and heard the night before, today's ride could be deadly.

His fear of being the only one in the arena and feeling like there was a red dot of a sniper's rifle aimed at him could be the real deal. His mind flashed to a scenario where he was stopping Gambler at the end of his run, the round from a sniper's bullet leaving the barrel just as he waved to the crowd and the judges, his body tumbling off of the spooked horse leaving him in a bloody pile in the middle of the arena. Travis swallowed and shook his head. That couldn't happen. He had to go forward. His mission was simple. Deal with the horses, then deal with the threat.

Stepping out into the aisle, Travis pushed the thought aside. There was no point in going down into a rabbit hole of what ifs. Sure, things could happen. He could get shot while he was riding in the finals, but it was unlikely. If a hit had been put out on him, the odds of it being a public spectacle were nearly zero. Too many eyes. Too many questions. Whoever had been hired would want to make sure that they got away cleanly. Trying to escape a herd of stunned and scared horse show goers and spooked animals wouldn't allow for that to happen unless a person was singularly qualified.

Travis stopped for a second, staring at the horses, pushing the thought to the back of his mind. He needed to concentrate on the horses. They had roused in their stalls, Smokey and Joker nipping at each other from between the bars. They were like two kids, bickering over some unknown injustice in their life. Travis shook his head and rolled his eyes, walking back into the stall where he'd spent the night. He pushed a grain cart out, filled with the supplies for the horses' morning feeding. As the cart moved and he rattled the metal grain scoop, the horses started to nicker from their stalls, wanting to be fed. As Travis rolled the cart down the aisle, avoiding too much pressure on his hand, he dumped the grain in the corner feeders of each stall, watching as they chewed happily. He knew he could have waited for Ellie to show up and take care of the horses, feeding them and watering them, but he was there and he was up. Based on how he was feeling, no amount of trying to sleep on the hay bales was going to get him any more sleep than he already had, especially now, given the fact that people were starting to arrive to take care of their animals and get ready for the day. He might as well get to work.

7

It took Travis roughly another hour to get the horses fed and watered and get their stalls cleaned, putting new bedding in each of them. After the open class ran later on that day, he and Ellie would pack all of the equipment they'd brought back into the trailer, connect the truck and trailer and get it loaded with the horses and then start the long trek home back down I-35 into Texas. With any luck, they'd make it home before midnight, but that wasn't a guarantee. His only hope was they could get on the road that day.

"Good morning!" Ellie chirped, walking down the aisle. She glanced at Travis, "You're up early." She was wearing a white t-shirt that had the Bishop Performance Horse logo on it, a pair of well-fitting jeans, and her scuffed boots. Her hair was plaited and dangled down her back.

Travis raised his eyebrows, as she passed. She smelled like shampoo. "Yeah, the accommodations are a little sketchy, if you know what I mean."

Ellie cocked her head to the side, "Did you get any sleep? Any problems overnight?"

Travis pressed his lips together and adjusted his baseball

cap on his head, "Yeah, I got some sleep. No problems to report," he said gently cradling his right arm.

"Good. Listen, I checked the schedule on my way in. Looks like they're doing all the non-pro and amateur finals this morning. Looks like the pros start to ride after that. So, if you want to head back to the hotel and get cleaned up, now would be a good time to do that."

Travis nodded. He could have been offended that Ellie was taking charge of the situation, but her military background, like his, had made her organized to a fault. While he was the face of the Bishop Performance Horse operation, she was the guts of it. "Yeah. That sounds good. I'll be back in a bit."

"I'll be here," she said, opening one of the stall doors and sliding inside. As Travis walked away, he could hear her murmuring to Joker, as if they were having a private conversation.

Travis quickly found the truck where Ellie had left it parked outside of the barn. He got in and started it up, feeling the cool air from the ventilation system blowing on his face. It felt good. The day was warming up already. Pretty soon he would no longer need the jacket, but that would expose the gash on his arm, not to mention the gun. He grimaced. It was a good thing that all the riders showed in long sleeves at least this once, he decided.

The drive to the hotel only took four minutes, the small brick building a block from the entrance of the fairgrounds itself. As Travis walked into the lobby, he saw a few other people he recognized from the show circuit, giving them a quick nod, the smell of their soap and freshly washed clothes trailing them as they walked by, the smell of eggs and sausage cooking somewhere nearby. His stomach grumbled. At least they'd had the benefit of sleeping in a soft bed and getting a morning shower. For some of the larger training operations, the pros never spent any time at the barn. They just showed up when it was time to ride and that was it. No sleeping on hay bales, no lugging tack. No driving a slow trailer hundreds of miles back to the barn.

Travis shook his head as he walked into the elevator. Maybe someday his operation would be like that, but it wasn't that way now. And if he didn't figure out whether Catherine was right about the hit put out on him or not, he might never know.

As the elevator doors opened on the second floor, Travis stepped out, checking the hallway left and right. If Catherine was correct, then another attack could come at any time, without warning.

The hallway seemed to be clear. There were no open doors or long shadows cast over the cheap gray carpeting that lined the floor. Off somewhere at the end of the hallway, Travis could hear what sounded like a blow dryer running. As he walked to his room, he heard the click of a door open next to him across the hallway. Travis flinched, immediately turning and grabbing for the butt of his gun. From inside, a woman and a man emerged, the two of them smiling. Travis nodded, relaxing his arm, "Good morning," they said in unison.

Travis nodded, using the key card to open his hotel room door, quickly closing it behind him and turning the deadbolt.

He walked through the room, scanning it for any signs of intrusion. One of the two double beds was rumpled, the other one neatly made. Ellie's suitcase was perched on the bed closest to the windows. It looked like she'd already packed and was ready to head out. That was good. Travis made a mental note to grab her suitcase and get them checked out of the hotel after he took his shower.

Other than Ellie's things, there was no sign anyone else had been in the room. Satisfied, Travis went into the bathroom, setting his baseball hat on the small bathroom vanity, pulling his pistol out of his holster and setting it next to the sink, keeping it close by. More murders happened in showers than anywhere else. Most people weren't prepared to defend themselves while they were wet, slippery, and naked. If what Catherine had said was true, Travis would have to be, no matter where he was or what he was doing.

Travis turned on the hot water in the shower and let it run for a second while he stripped off the dirty clothes he was wearing. As he pulled off his jeans, he realized how filthy he was — dirt and grit from the fight the night before caked on his pants, a thin layer of dust mixed with sweat covering every inch of his skin.

He stared down at the white gauze bandage wrapped around his forearm. He left it in place as he stepped into the shower, letting the water run over him. As the hot water soaked through the gauze his arm stung, but he ignored the pain. He put his head under the shower for a solid minute or two, allowing it to cascade down his back before scrubbing himself clean and stepping out.

Drying off and then wrapping a thin, white towel around his waist, Travis walked over to the sink where he'd left his hat and his gun. He brushed his teeth and then strode out into the bedroom, fishing a clean pair of jeans and a red t-shirt out of his suitcase, pulling them on.

Back in the bathroom, he unwound the bandages Georgiana had expertly wrapped over the wound, looking at the damage. Whoever his attacker had been had gotten a single slice into his forearm, exposing the blood-red edges of his skin. Any deeper and the knife would have penetrated the muscles of his arm. Travis sighed. He'd recently read a statistic that fifty percent of the people involved in knife fights died as a result of their wounds. Unbelievably, the statistics were much worse than a gunfight, where only twenty percent of people were casualties. He pressed his lips together. He'd been lucky. Things could have turned out much worse.

Travis tossed squares of wet gauze in the trash, grabbed a

couple of clean tissues out of the box mounted on the wall next to the mirror, and used the damp rolled bandage to rewrap his arm. Putting a wet bandage on an open wound wasn't ideal, but it would have to do for the moment. When he got back out to the truck, he had more first-aid supplies he could use to wrap it properly. Being in the military had taught him to make do. That's what he was doing. He quickly combed his dark hair and fished his belt and holster back through the loops of his jeans, shoving the gun back on his hip. He looked at himself in the mirror. Although he'd had very little sleep and was attacked only a few hours before, he didn't look much worse for the wear. A shower and clean clothes had done him good. His square jaw and brown hair looked much more presentable after a shower, even if he needed a shave.

Anxious to get back to the show, Travis walked out into the bedroom, striding over to the closet. He pulled out two shirts on hangers covered by filmy plastic bags. They were his show shirts. He added them to the pile. Walking through the hotel room, he put the last things in his bag and zipped it closed, grabbed Ellie's suitcase and his own, lining them up next to the door, glancing around the room to make sure that he'd gotten everything packed. With everything ready, he tossed his key card on the dresser, pulled on his jacket to hide his gun, grabbed the suitcases, and walked back into the hallway. The door clicked closed behind him.

Travis wheeled the suitcases to the elevator, ignoring the pain in his arm, and then went to the first floor. He gave the woman at the front desk a curt nod as he walked out to the truck. Unless something happened he didn't expect, he wouldn't see her again for a year, if ever.

After loading the suitcases into the back seat, he dug under the seat and found a first aid kit. Unwinding the damp gauze and tissues from his arm, he opened up a sealed packet of antibiotic gel, squeezing it over the wound. He found two oversized square adhesive bandages and smoothed them over his skin. After looking at the wound, Travis realized Georgiana was probably right — the skin was cut deep enough that he'd likely benefit from stitches. The reality was he didn't have the time or the inclination to go to the hospital. He'd deal with it when he got home. He was sure he could get Dr. Scott, the local coroner he'd helped with the Jake West case, or Dr. Wiley, his veterinarian, to give him a hand if he needed it.

Getting back in the truck, he started it up and headed back to the fairgrounds, passing the same couple he'd seen in the hallway by his hotel room as they left the building, arms wound around each other. He eyed them, but they didn't make a move toward him, too busy looking at each other. Their life seemed simple. His was not, especially not at that moment. Thoughts were circling in Travis's mind, the memory of Catherine appearing out of nowhere the night before and the searing sting as the metal blade from the attacker bit through his skin. Was there a chance Catherine was wrong? Was the attack just a coincidence? Travis rested his head on his hand as he stopped at the fairgrounds gate waiting to be let in. Was it possible her sources were incorrect? Espionage was much more of an art than a science, that was for sure. Agencies like the CIA and MI6 got things wrong all the time. Maybe there was a kill order out, but maybe it wasn't on him. Perhaps it was on someone else.

But that didn't diminish the fact that someone had come at Travis the night before and it was lucky he'd gotten away with his life. The man's face was burned into Travis's memory, the wiry brown hair, scruffy brown beard, and taut muscles, evidence of time in the gym, or more likely, out in the field.

As the guard at the gate waved Travis through, Travis gave him a nod, studying him carefully. If Catherine was right, then everyone he encountered was a potential threat. He felt the hairs on the back of his neck stand up. Everyone. The next assassin could be the checkout clerk at the hotel, the guard he just passed at the exhibitor's gate of the fairgrounds, the blacksmith the Derby had hired to have on the scene in case a horse lost a shoe. Everyone he ran into became someone to be wary of.

Travis shook his head, pressing his lips together as he pulled into a parking spot near the barn. The weight of dealing with the show and the threat was a lot at the same time. He felt his stomach lurch. He'd been trained, yes, but he hadn't done much with his skills for the better part of five years. He'd had the incident with Elena and helped diffuse the terror threat in New Orleans, but other than that, he was focused on his horses. He gritted his teeth for a moment. He should be more prepared.

Getting out of the truck and slamming the door behind him, Travis strode towards the barn. Voices and noise echoed off the walls, the horses walking up and down the aisles, their metal shoes making a dull metallic thud with each stride against the concrete, the laughter of kids in the background, the jingle of metal buckles as horses were being saddled. He swallowed, stopping just inside the door. If Catherine was right, then showing today would be a danger to him and the people around him, but was he ready to give someone else that kind of power over his life? The power to change what he'd built so carefully? He balled his hands into fists and swallowed, walking forward.

The answer was no.

No matter what Catherine said and what happened the night before, Travis was at the horse show to do a job. This was work. The clients were counting on him, not to mention the hit his reputation would take if he didn't finish. He was a man of his word. The commitment he had to his horses and owners was no different than when Travis was in the military or in the CIA. There were risks to everything and some risks were bigger than others. He sighed. There were people at the show who had trusted their horses to him. It was that simple.

"You got back fast!" Ellie smiled, meeting him halfway down the aisle. A grin tugged at her cheeks, her customary blonde braid dangling just beneath her shoulders, a Bishop Performance Horses baseball cap on her head.

"Yeah. Didn't take too long to get ready. I grabbed your suitcase from the hotel room. We're checked out."

She shook her head, "I totally forgot it! Thanks."

"What time is your class?"

"Ten. We're next up. Like I told you this morning, the pros ride after lunch. Somebody in the show office told me they might move it up though, so keep your ears peeled"

"All right," Travis nodded. It felt like something had tripped a switch in his mind. He stared at Ellie and Joker. "Let's get you ready. You're gonna crush this."

Travis helped Ellie get Joker saddled. He was a chestnut gelding with a wide blaze on his head that covered nearly his whole face as if someone had smeared his head with white paint. Two differently colored eyes, one blue and one brown, gave him a wild look. Travis wandered over to the exhibitor's warm-up ring and stood leaning on the fence as Ellie warmed up Joker, watching her trot him in small circles stretching his back. Two minutes before her turn, she loped him around the ring a few times, running him gently through the pattern their class had been assigned, dipping and dodging through the traffic in the ring. She stopped at the gate as she was ready to head into the ring. "You look good," Travis said, rubbing Joker's neck. "Just go in there and do what you do."

"Copy that. Be back in a flash."

8

Travis fought the urge to go and watch Ellie and Joker run their pattern. As much as he would have liked to, there was too much to do before they could leave. Leaving was the priority at the moment. Travis rubbed the back of his neck as he walked back to the barn, wondering what had happened to Catherine. He felt a sinking in his gut. He needed to talk to her but she'd disappeared. Where she was now, he had no idea. For all he knew, she could be halfway to London.

Shaking his head, he walked inside the stall they were using for storage. Grabbing the handle of the wheeled cart they'd brought with them, Travis loaded it up with the extra supplies they wouldn't need – two, still twined bales of hay, a third of a bag of sweet feed, an extra bucket of brushes and hoof picks, a plaid saddle pad and one of the schooling saddles. Wheeling it outside, he pushed the cart toward the line of trailers that were parked nearby. Luckily, the Oklahoma City Fairgrounds allowed them to keep the trailers close to the barn, at least relatively speaking. There were other shows where it felt like the trailers were left in outer Siberia, making it almost impossible to access them until it was time to head home.

The wheels of the cart ground to a halt as Travis stopped and unlocked the door to the trailer storage room. He unloaded the cart and carried the collection of things he had brought from the barn inside, putting things away as he went. Not more than a minute later, he came out, ready to walk back to the barn. Over the loudspeaker he heard the announcer call for the pro class, his voice booming over the loudspeakers. "Pro riders, get ready! Your class is on deck!" Travis checked his watch. They were ahead of schedule, just like Ellie said. He still probably had an hour or so before he had to ride, but he would need every bit of that time to get ready. Grimacing, Travis opened the trailer again, taking off his holster and gun. As much as he wanted to keep it on him, showing Gambler with a gun on his side would be a no-go.

Pushing the cart back to the barn, Travis stopped inside of the extra stall they had rented. He took off his jacket and changed into a long-sleeved, turquoise button-down shirt with a black scroll design and matching piping on the shoulders. It wasn't his taste, but Ellie said it was the newest in show fashion, so that's what he wore. He switched his baseball cap for a black felt cowboy hat with a flat brim and curled sides that he kept inside their tack locker. It was his show gear. Not as comfortable as his baseball hat, but it would do for a few minutes.

Shoving the hat down hard on his skull, Travis grabbed a lead and walked toward Gambler's stall. As a pro rider, he had his choice of which horse to ride in the finals. Unlike a lot of other equine sports, it was the rider that qualified, not the horse. Travis stopped for a second and blinked, looking at Smokey. He decided to stick with Gambler, the horse he'd qualified on. Certainly any of the other horses he'd brought could do the job, but there was something special about the black gelding with the single white star on his forehead and one white sock on his right hind leg.

Opening the stall door, Travis lifted the halter over Gambler's ears and attached the lead to it, walking him out into the aisle and securing him with the cross ties. From the bucket of grooming supplies they'd brought with them, Travis grabbed a brush, quickly cleaning up Gambler. He stood calmly as Travis ran a comb through his thick black mane and tail to get the last few knots out. Ellie had given all of the horses baths before they left. Gambler's coat was sleek and shiny, so dark it was almost mirror-like, still clean from the qualifying run the day before. He only needed a touch-up.

Travis stood back for a second, shaking his head. If he hadn't had Catherine on his mind, he might spend more time getting Gambler cleaned up, but at this point, he needed to do his job and get out of Oklahoma and back to Texas. His heart skipped a beat. He had no way to contact Catherine. It wasn't like she'd given him her cell phone number or something. She'd appeared like a blip on a radar, flying fast and low and disappearing just as quickly.

Swinging his silver inlaid show saddle onto Gambler's back, Travis secured the girth, got him bridled, and walked out of the barn. Outside, Travis stuck his left foot in the stirrup and swung his right leg over the horse's back, giving the gelding sides a little squeeze with his legs and clucking his tongue to get him moving.

The exhibitor's warm-up ring was crowded, with many of the pro riders already warming up their horses. He saw Ellie. She gave him a smile and a nod. Their run must've been good. Normally, he would've ridden over to see how she did, but he had other things on his mind.

Twenty minutes later, after getting Gambler warmed up, they called Travis's number. Travis walked the gelding up to the entrance of the arena, staring at the thousands of people that had amassed inside to watch. He felt a flutter in his stomach as he tightened up his reins. Whether it was show nerves or the threat to his life, he didn't know. Travis squared his shoulders and took a deep breath. It was time.

Cuing Gambler, the horse took off at a dead run into the arena, ears pinned, pulling into a sliding stop just seconds later at the other end of the arena to the hoots and hollers of the crowd inside. Travis rolled Gambler back the other direction and then started loping him in a slow circle, following the pattern he'd memorized. Glancing up at the stands as he passed, he spotted a woman wearing a red blouse and a beige cowboy hat. She waved. Catherine. His stomach dropped as he looked back down at Gambler. Everything in Travis wanted to stop his run and ride over to her and ask where she'd been, but he had a pattern to finish. He gritted his teeth, gave Gambler's sides another squeeze, and kept going.

Exactly a minute and a half later, Travis finished his last sliding stop, a cascade of damp clots of dirt flying into the air behind the strong Quarter Horse as he dug his hindquarters into the ground while letting his front legs run. Travis heard the yells and applause from the audience, but barely. He took off his hat, nodded at the judges, and scanned the crowd for Catherine as he rode Gambler out of the arena.

She was gone.

Georgiana and George were waiting for Travis as he rode Gambler out of the arena. "That was so good!" Georgiana cooed, rubbing Gambler's neck.

George stood by, silent, giving Travis nothing more than a single nod. Typical George, Travis thought. Nothing to say unless he had a complaint.

"Yeah, he's come a long way." Travis tried to be polite, but everything in him wanted to go find Catherine. She was still there. Why?

The announcer's voice rang out over the arena, "Ladies and gentlemen we have the score for our last rider, Travis Bishop, aboard Gambler's Latest Addiction, a 221. That gives us a new third-place rider."

"Are you happy with that? I mean, I know first place would be better, but he did good, didn't he?" The questions rattled out of Georgiana's mouth faster than Travis could answer them.

Travis nodded, "Yeah. We had a long trip here and they didn't give us very long to warm up. I'm happy with that. He's improving. That's all I can ask."

"First place would've been better," George grunted, walking away.

Georgiana rolled her eyes, still rubbing Gambler's neck, "Don't pay any attention to him. I know we're only here for the points."

"That's right." Travis glanced around him, "Listen, as much as I'd like to stay and chitchat, I need to get him cooled down. I'll talk to you after we get back to Texas, okay?" It was as nice of a blow-off as he could manage at that moment, his chest tight, knowing Catherine was still there, somewhere.

"Of course! I'm sorry. Yes, I know you have a lot to do. We aren't your only clients, after all..." she whined. It was clearly a complaint that Travis wasn't paying enough attention to them. Travis didn't have the time or the inclination to help Georgiana feel better. He gave her a nod and squeezed his legs to get Gambler moving away from the arena. He was grateful she didn't ask about his arm, especially in front of George. A score of 221 was good, one he could be happy about at some point. But at that moment, he didn't care about third-place or the 221, which should have delighted him given the stiff competition at the Derby. He had to find Catherine.

Licking his lips, Travis guided Gambler past the exhibitor's warm-up arena and back toward the barn where his stall was. Instead of stopping, Travis kept going, angling the horse in the direction that he'd walked the night before.

The crowd thinned out as they made their way past the

empty dairy barns toward the back of the fairgrounds. Things looked very different in the daytime. He heard a few birds chirping off in the distance, replacing the eerie hoot of the owl from the darkness. The low growl of a single truck or a tractor, he couldn't tell which, rumbled in the distance.

Travis turned Gambler toward the spot where the knife attack had happened the night before, a pit forming in his stomach. The same line of three green and black dumpsters was still between the two buildings, the acrid smell from the pile of rotting manure hanging in the air, waiting to be taken away from the barns.

Travis tugged at the reins, stopping Gambler, staring at the ground. The body was gone. Travis looked around him, feeling like there were eyes on the back of his neck. Was someone watching him? His gut had never been wrong. He stared at the ground, ignoring the feeling, but wishing he'd stopped to get his gun from the trailer.

He scanned the area, trying to estimate the spot where the man had died. There wasn't even a single tinge of blood on the gravel and no mention of it had been made by anyone at the show. No additional police, no crime scene tape. No nothing. Travis rested his hands on the horn of his saddle and frowned. If this had been a professional hit then it came with a professional level of cleanup. That was concerning. Not a trace had been left behind. A murder had happened at the horse show, right under everyone's noses, one Travis was responsible for, and yet no one knew...

Travis turned Gambler around and started walking back toward the barn. If there was no body, there was nothing he could learn. Travis hummed to himself, trying to take his thoughts off what had happened when all of a sudden he felt Gambler's left shoulder drop as he shied away from something. "Whoa, boy," Travis said, pulling up on the reins.

Catherine emerged around the corner of the building. "Hello, Travis."

9

Catherine took a couple of steps forward towards Travis as he got Gambler settled down. "Sorry if I scared your horse."

Travis slid down off the saddle, the gravel crunching under his boots. "Easy, boy," he said, rubbing the gelding's neck. "Yeah, you spooked him pretty good. He doesn't normally do that." Travis narrowed his eyes looking at Catherine. She was dressed like any other of the showgoers, a pair of jeans, a wide leather belt with a large silver buckle, a red blouse, and a beige cowboy hat. For all anyone knew, she could be anything from an owner to an exhibitor. She fit in well, Travis thought. "Where have you been?"

"Dealing with a few things." She stared at the ground for a second, her lips pressed together. From what Travis could tell, there was more to the story, but whatever it was, she wasn't saying. Probably classified MI6 business. "Sorry I disappeared on you last night. It's one thing for me to warn you about an attack, completely something else for an MI6 officer to get involved, especially on international soil. I had to go." A smile tugged at her cheek, "I'm glad to see you're okay, though."

Travis shook his head, frowning, "You could've at least thrown a rock at the guy with the knife or something before you took off," he grumbled. "But without the heads up, I would've been in real trouble. Thanks for that."

Catherine smiled. "Did you get hurt?"

"Just a slice on my arm. I'm all right."

"Your ride was good."

Travis narrowed his eyes. He knew Catherine didn't know anything about the sport of reining. It was primarily an American invention, although there were some riders from Europe, particularly Italy, that did well.

Travis looked off in the distance, thinking. A quiet settled between the two of them for a second, the only noise the shuffling of Gambler's metal shoes against the gravel as he rested one hip. Travis rubbed the big gelding's neck and then looked back at Catherine. "You came back. Why?" Part of him needed to know if there was some other motivation for Catherine's return. If her whole mission had been to deliver the message, she'd taken care of that last night. Why was she back?

She raised her eyebrows, "I wanted to see if you were okay, and I'm glad you are." She kicked at a chunk of gravel absentmindedly with her toe. "How's the other guy? Did you recognize him?"

Travis opened his mouth to speak and then paused. He needed to be careful. Catherine was still an agent of a foreign government. Admitting he'd killed someone else could put him in a tenuous situation. Then again, things were already a mess. How much worse could it get? As the thought passed through his mind, he felt a wave of nausea pass over him. "The guy? No. I didn't recognize him. Brown hair, brown beard. About the same height as me. I didn't really get a good look at him till he was on the ground."

"He was down?" Catherine furrowed her eyebrows.

"Yeah." Travis looked at the toe of his boot, nudging a twig with it.

By the time he looked up, Catherine was staring at him. "You killed him?"

Travis nodded. "I grabbed the knife while he still had his hands on it. Stabbed him in the gut. Must have hit the abdominal artery. The thing is…"

Catherine frowned, "What is it?"

"We're just about where it happened. He's gone. Not even a drop of blood is left."

Catherine cocked her head to the side, "Why does that surprise you, Travis Bishop? You were in the spy business for a long time. You didn't think they probably had someone watching? Either way, there was going to be a body to remove. It was either going to be yours or his…"

The matter-of-fact way that Catherine said it sent a shudder down Travis's spine. He'd been so focused on where the man's body was he didn't stop to think that whoever had sent the man had also sent a cleanup team. Travis's body could very well have been the one that they were mopping up after. He gritted his teeth and shook his head.

Catherine reached out and grabbed his arm, "Listen, Travis. I don't know you well, but I've read your background. I know you have the capacity to handle this, but I also can tell you've got questions running in your head about why you and why now."

"Of course I do. Wouldn't you? I've been out of the game for five years!"

Catherine dropped her hand back to her side, "Yes, in fact, I would. I'm not saying you shouldn't. But that doesn't change the fact that someone came after you last night and he's likely not the last one."

Travis had been thinking the same thing, but hearing Catherine say it hit him like a ton of bricks, the muscles in his chest tightening. This situation was completely different than his time with Delta Force. When he was with the military they were the hunters, not the hunted, not to mention he had a team to back him up as they eliminated targets identified by the US government as threats to the nation. And although his work with the CIA was far less violent than what he'd done with Delta Force, he was still with a team. Anyone he was working with at the time had his back.

And now no one did. He was alone.

Catherine's voice interrupted his thoughts, "Travis, you have a choice to make. You can go back to your ranch in Texas and pretend nothing happened. But trouble will come. And soon. Or, you can work with me and I will help you figure out who is coming after you and why. And maybe, just maybe, we can stop them if we work together."

Travis narrowed his eyes, "Why would you do that?"

Catherine shrugged, "I don't know. Maybe it's because I like you? Or maybe because my director told me to?"

Travis tried not to smile. He was in the middle of an assassination plot and Catherine was cracking jokes.

"Okay. I've gotta get the horses taken care of before I make any decisions. I'll think about what you said."

"Don't think too long Travis," she stared at him. "Trouble is coming to you whether you like it or not. Come to London. I have assets and resources there. We can help you if you'll let us."

10

By the time Travis swung his leg over Gambler's back and glanced up to wave at Catherine, she was gone. He shook his head. She had the uncanny ability to disappear before his eyes. She was a ghost, one with a message that had the power to end his life, or at least change it permanently, if he believed what she said.

Travis chewed his lip as he rode Gambler back to the barn. Ellie was already there. She had Joker in the cross ties, wrapping his legs with protective cotton travel bandages for the ride home. She glanced up at Travis as he walked Gambler down the aisle, "Where have you been? Your ride looked good."

"I took Gambler for a little cool-down walk after his run." It was a partial lie, not a complete one. He had used the walk to cool Gambler down, but mostly to scope out the site where the knife attack had been. Had been. As if it never happened. A tingle ran down his spine, thinking about what Catherine had said.

Ellie nodded, not seeming to think anything of Travis' disappearance. "I saw Georgiana and George grabbed you right after."

"Yeah, George wasn't happy about Gambler being third."

Ellie raised her eyebrows, "Actually second. They disqualified the rider who had second place. Went off course. They saw it in the replay. You got second."

Travis nodded. At least that was something of a win. George and Georgiana would be happy about that. A second-place finish would net him a cool thirty thousand dollars which he would split with the owners, plus the qualifying points toward the end of season show totals. He was one step closer to the Run for a Million in Las Vegas.

Ellie laughed, "I'm surprised you didn't know. Not bad for two minutes' worth of work!"

Travis grunted, "And the months of work it took to get here."

"Don't be so cynical. It was a good run. Gambler's never looked better. Now, let's get these horses home."

Travis nodded.

An hour later, Ellie and Travis had managed to load the rest of their equipment and the horses onto the truck and trailer. By the time they approached Fort Worth on their way back to the ranch, Travis was starving. He glanced at Ellie. She had nodded off for the first segment of the ride, her body curled into a ball on the leather seat next to him, her head leaning against the window. That was fine with him. Neither of them was a big talker and he needed time to think. He put his hand on her shoulder and gave her a nudge. Ellie blinked, rolling her head toward him. "You hungry?" Travis asked.

Ellie nodded.

"I'm gonna stop at the next exit for food. We can check the horses, grab a bite and use the bathroom before the last leg."

Ellie pushed herself up in the seat, brushing a stray blonde hair away from the side of her face that had escaped her braid while she'd slept. "Sounds good. I'm starved. Thanks for doing all the driving."

Travis nodded. After all of the hubbub at the horse show, he was usually grateful for the few hours they had in the truck on the way back, especially if Ellie slept. After the last twenty-four hours, he'd take any quiet he could get. Travis shifted in his seat, feeling edgy. At a normal horse show, the noise, endless conversations, voices pumping out over the PA system, the rush to get the horses there, ready for class, and shown always left him feeling drained, as if his body was a dull car battery in need of a charge.

The drive back was a reentry of sorts. In Travis's mind, he thought of it the same way a space capsule made its way back into Earth, flames licking at every inch of the hull as the friction of the surface broke through the Earth's protective atmosphere, the first view of a calm, pristine green and blue Earth below, the jolt of splashing down and the relief of opening the hatch to breathe fresh air again.

Although Travis had never experienced returning from space himself, he could imagine it in great detail, probably from the single book one of his foster moms gave him. Each mile he drove back to the ranch seemed like one closer to making reentry to a life he understood. The one that he wanted. Sure, part of him enjoyed the horse shows, but it wasn't that much different from being on an operation with the military or the CIA. Lots of prep, lots of packing, and lots of training for a very short window of action. He loved the slower, repetitive schedule of the ranch — the early mornings, hearing the birds chirp in the trees as he walked or drove down to the barn after having his first couple of sips of bitter coffee, the fresh morning air on his face, the rustling of the horses in their stalls, the smell of the hay and their warm bodies filling the barn. There was nothing like it.

Travis glanced at Ellie. She'd nodded off again. That was fine. They still had a few miles to go before getting to the exit. This trip had been particularly painful, both literally and figuratively. Travis glanced down at his arm. It'd had a dull ache since they left, the nerves objecting to being exposed to the light and the air, the raw edge of skin feeling like it was alternately burning and throbbing as he drove. Travis sighed, letting out a long breath, Catherine's warnings rattling in his head. Part of it seemed unbelievable to him. Was it really possible that there was a hit out on his life from the very people he'd been loyal to? Or was this some sort of grand deception to get him to engage in some other type of conflict? It was certainly possible that MI6 had orchestrated the knife attack to corroborate the information that Catherine had provided for him. The timing couldn't have been more perfect. She'd appeared out of the blue. The knife attack was right after she told him there was a kill order out on his life. In his mind, it was a little too perfect.

Travis narrowed his eyes, turning on the blinker for the next exit, slowing the trailer down, feeling the momentum of the horse rig, plus the nearly six tons of animals on board, pushing at the back of the truck challenging his ability to stop. Travis pumped the brakes gently, easing the trailer onto the off-ramp. He shook his head. It all seemed too convenient. Questions filled his mind. Was that even Catherine? He'd only met her one time before and at that moment she'd been heavily disguised. She did have the same eyes and the same voice, though. At least there was that.

Pulling into the truck stop, Travis headed the truck and trailer toward the gas pumps, throwing it into park and quickly setting up the pump to fill up the tank. Ellie roused from her nap as he leaned inside the truck, pulling the keys out of the ignition. She stretched overhead, wincing as if her body was achy. "We're here. Last stop before the ranch," Travis said.

"Thanks. I'll be back in a couple of minutes."

Travis heard Ellie's seatbelt unclip and the door of the truck slam behind her. He watched as she walked toward the truck stop, her strides short and clipped, her blonde braid bobbing on her back as she headed inside.

As soon as the pump clicked off, Travis got back in the truck, put the keys back in the ignition, and pulled it away from the gas station. He angled the rig into one of the spots reserved for semis and long trucks and trailers on the other side of the towering awnings that covered the bank of pumps. He walked around the trailer, opening each one of the hatches, looking inside, giving each one of the horses a little scratch on the side of their cheek, at least all of them except for Joker, who stared at him and turned his head away as if he was angry he was still stuck in the trailer. Travis shook his head. Joker was always the last one in and the first one out. He fit his name. He was a wildcard, that was for sure.

Glancing toward the door of the truck stop, he saw Ellie walking back toward the trailer, a drink in one hand and a bag of food in the other. He walked toward her, passing as she headed for the trailer. Travis paused for a second, "Horses are fine. I'll be back in a second and then we can get on the road."

Ellie nodded, "I'll be waiting."

Travis glanced behind him as he walked toward the truck stop. Ellie was standing next to the trailer, one of the hatches open, adjusting one of the feed bags next to the windows. She just couldn't resist. Travis kept walking. The horses and equipment they traveled with were valuable, valuable enough that he never left the trailer without one of the two of them standing nearby when they were on the road. He knew in a pinch, that Ellie could hold her own. If being on the road had taught him one thing, travelers could be some of the kindest people or the most brutal, depending on who you bumped into. Truck stops were an easy cover for criminals moving contraband, but they were also commonly populated by families on their way to a vacation or returning home from visiting loved ones. It all depended on who you met. But Travis wasn't willing to roll the dice, trusting that no one would mess with his equipment or animals while he was eating a burger. He was responsible for all of it, and he wasn't going to take any chances.

Stepping inside the truck stop, Travis angled for the bathroom, quickly relieving himself and stepping over to the sink to wash his hands. The ache in his arm had grown worse. He rolled up the sleeve of his jacket and looked at the bandages. The tinge of crimson blood had soaked through, staining the bright white gauze underneath the adhesive. He was bleeding again. Travis shook his head. Georgiana was probably right — he likely did need stitches, but there was no time for that. He was at a truck stop on the outskirts of Fort Worth with six horses and a truckload of equipment to get back to his ranch. His arm would have to wait.

Walking out of the bathroom, Travis tugged the sleeve of his jacket back down over his arm and ordered himself a chicken sandwich and a large fry along with a bottle of water from a fast-food stand that was near the door, the option with the shortest line. A minute later, carrying a paper bag filled with his food and a bottle of water, Travis strode toward the door, pushing it open into the early evening light.

Just outside, Travis felt his phone vibrate in his pocket. He stopped, frowning, pulling it out. He stared. It was from an unknown number. "Travis," the message read, "I'm assuming you're on your way back to Texas. I'm on a plane to London. Please take the threat I told you about as gravely serious." A phone number was listed. "This is my personal number. Reach out if you decide you want help. Don't wait. This is for real. Cath."

A tingle ran down his spine as he shoved his phone back into his pocket. Catherine and her suspicions. He still wasn't convinced that it wasn't a ploy for something else. What, he had no idea. Travis shook his head as he got into the truck, starting the engine. Ellie crumpled the paper bag that had held her food and threw it on the floor of the truck. Travis grimaced. "There's a bag for trash in the back."

"Yeah, sure. Forgot about that," she smiled weakly.

Catherine's words rang in his head as he pulled the truck and the trailer back onto the freeway. A few more miles and they would be able to get off I-35 and take the back roads to the ranch. He pushed Catherine's message to the back of his mind. There was only one thing in front of him at that moment and it was getting the horses to the ranch safely. He'd deal with Catherine and her information later.

About five miles down the road, Travis glanced in the rearview mirror. He saw a truck behind them, a tow truck, the size used for hauling semis and other large commercial equipment out of a ditch or standing them up after they jackknifed. He narrowed his eyes as the truck started to close the distance, getting larger in his rearview mirror.

Something didn't seem right, but Travis had no idea what was making the hair on the back of his neck stand up.

11

Dusk had fallen over I-35. The monstrous tow truck behind Travis's rig flipped its headlights on, the bright beams lighting the road in a blaze behind the slow-moving trailer. Travis glanced in the rearview mirror. The truck, which had been about a mile behind them, was now right on their tail, close enough he could hear the heavy engine revving over his own.

Travis veered the truck and the trailer onto the next exit, getting off the traffic-filled I-35 and angling onto a side road that would skirt Austin and lead them back into Burton, Texas, where the ranch was. He glanced at Ellie. She was awake, picking at one of her cuticles. He looked down. Her seatbelt was fastened. He licked his lips, "Something's going on. I don't have a good feeling."

Ellie furrowed her eyebrows and then stared at him, "What? With one of the horses?"

Travis shook his head, his lips parted, glancing in the rearview mirror again. The tow truck was on his back bumper, as if its massive presence could push Travis along faster. "Nope.

Something's going on with the truck that's been on our tail for the last couple of miles. Can you reach in the back and grab a couple of pistols just in case?"

Ellie didn't say anything. She just nodded. He heard the seatbelt unclip and felt the warmth of her body as she angled her way past him, lifting the bench seat in the back. "This is going to take a minute. We've got a bunch of stuff stacked on the seat."

Travis's chest tightened, "You're gonna have to move fast, Ellie. I don't have a good feeling about this."

A second later, he heard a thump as the seat dropped back down, the locked compartment that stored the guns he took everywhere with him, closing. Ellie put one of the pistols on the floor while she checked the other. She spun around in her seat. "What do you think is going on?"

Travis shook his head, "I have no idea. You got one of those ready for me?"

Travis heard a barely audible click as Ellie checked to make sure the gun was loaded and racked, ready to fire. "Yep. Here you go." Her words came out short and clipped as she handed it to him. He leaned forward, sticking it in the back of his waistband. It wasn't ideal. He would've preferred a holster, but it was what they had to work with at the moment. He glanced over at Ellie, "Fasten your seatbelt."

"What if I gotta get out fast?"

"It's going to be a lot easier to do that if your head hasn't gone through the windshield. Fasten it," he growled.

The road ahead of them twisted and twined. There was only an occasional faint glimmer of a centerline, no guardrails or edge lines to be seen. The thick Texas brush and low trees leaned over the sides of the road, casting long shadows, nearly touching the trailer as they passed. Where they were, there were no streetlights, and no houses to speak of, only an occasional farm or pasture filled with the shadows of beef cattle or dairy cows huddled together as the sun went down.

Travis turned the wheel of the truck and trailer to the right as the road arced. It was a relatively steep curve, nothing that would normally be a problem except for the fact that the tow truck was still hot on his tail, the lights bathing everything in front of him in a harsh, yellowish light.

Up ahead, Travis saw a shadow of a truck scoot off the side of the road, the smudge of a dark shadow passing into the brush. Travis furrowed his eyebrows. He glanced in the rearview mirror. The tow truck that had been practically chasing them down the road had slowed, creating distance between the two vehicles. Travis felt his stomach tighten. The truck he'd seen up ahead could be nothing, a vehicle pulling off the road and into a driveway, or it could be something entirely different…a threat.

The road continued to curl to the right, leaving Travis in a blind spot as he approached the place where the truck had disappeared off the side of the road. Ellie turned to him, glancing over her shoulder, "It looks like the tow truck is backing off. Maybe the guy's just in a hurry?"

As the words formed in Travis's mouth for him to reply, he felt the thump under the front wheels of the truck, the tires skidding on the pavement. Travis struggled to hold the wheel, trying to turn the truck and trailer but was unable to, "Hold on!" he yelled as he felt the trailer push at the truck, the rig nearly jackknifing in half, careening off the side of the road, the frantic thumping of the horses in the back trapped in their stalls. A few seconds later, the truck and trailer straightened and came to a stop in the middle of the road. Travis's heart was pounding in his chest, his breath ragged. He glanced at Ellie, noticing there was blood trickling down her forehead. "You okay?" he yelled. She touched her forehead with a single finger, "Yeah, I cut my head, but I'm all right. What happened?"

"I have no idea, but I'm gonna find out. Stay here." Travis looked back at her, "Call for help."

Travis reached for the pistol in his waistband before opening the truck door. He cracked it open, leading with the muzzle of his gun, staying low. As he pushed the truck door open, shots rang out. He looked back at Ellie, his eyes wide, "Call 9-1-1. Now! Tell them it's an active shooter situation."

"Who is shooting at us?" Ellie yelled.

"I have no idea, but make the call."

He felt a tinge of guilt at his answer, but it was easier to tell Ellie he had no idea than to try to stop and explain what he'd been through at the horse show while they were being shot at. He could trust Ellie to say calm. She'd been in the military, just like him and could handle a gun almost as well, not to mention she was like a mama bear with the horses. If anyone injured her babies, she'd come out fighting.

Travis swallowed, dropping to the ground as two shots whizzed past his baseball cap. He dodged around the body of the truck in a single smooth move, glancing around him. Behind him, curled off on the side of the road like a sleeping rattlesnake, was a tack strip. That's what he'd seen. The truck ahead of them had laid the line of tire-piercing nails across the pavement just in time for them to hit it. Luckily, he'd been able to keep the truck and trailer straight and out of the ditch, but based on the damage, he wouldn't be going anywhere soon. He glanced in front and behind him. All of the truck tires were pierced. Luckily, it hadn't hit any of the trailer tires. The momentum must have flung the tack strip off the road in time to save the horses.

Squatted next to the truck, Travis shuffled to his right, glancing toward the back of the truck, trying to determine where the shots had come from. He saw a shadow moving along the ground on the far side of the trailer. He glanced under the truck, seeing a pair of boots coming toward him, military style, black. Travis waited for a moment as the man crossed behind the trailer and walked to the other side. If he had to guess, the man probably assumed Travis had bolted off into the brush on the side of the road. That would be a logical place for him to hide. Travis hunched down and moved silently in the other direction, saying a silent prayer that Ellie would duck down in the seat and pretend she wasn't there unless she had to. Hopefully, she'd been able to call for help. He knew help wouldn't arrive in time to save them from the person in the truck unless they got lucky, not to mention whoever had laid the tack strip, though. They were on their own at least for a little bit. Travis frowned, his chest tight. Shots had only come from behind them. Where had the men who laid the tack strip in the road gone?

Travis eased his way to the other side of the trailer, watching the man approach the cab of the truck. When the man was about ten feet away, still moving slowly, Travis slid between the truck and the trailer and aimed his gun, catching the man in the chest, firing two shots. The echo of the explosion out of the gun was deafening, the man's body crumpling in a pile, the gun in his hand clattering away from him. The man's body dropped right in front of Travis, his face a mask of death.

As the shots rang out from Travis's gun, more came, this time from the front of the truck, the noise of glass shattering filling the air. Travis ran for the back of the truck, ignoring the searing pain in his arm, panting. Two sets of gunfire came from in front of him. It had to be the men who'd laid the tack strip in the first place. Travis used the cover of the truck to get close and then heard another gun fire. Ellie. She was shooting.

The gunfire stopped for a moment; their attackers apparently surprised there were two shooters. Glancing over the hood of the truck, Travis saw Ellie positioned behind the door, her face stony. She'd opened it like a shield.

The next time she fired, Travis used it as his opportunity. He charged to the front of the truck and confronted the two men who were standing about three feet apart, dropping each of them in succession, two shots to each of their chests. He stood and watched as their bodies crumpled to the ground like the first man who had assaulted them. Shaking his head, he lowered his gun. What had just happened?

12

"What was that?!" Ellie said, her mouth hanging open as she came out from behind the door of the truck.

Travis shook his head, striding over to the two bodies that were on the ground in front of the truck. He kicked the guns away from each of them. Without saying anything, he turned toward the back of the trailer and strode to the man that had driven the tow truck, double-checking that he was down. He was. Travis walked back to where Ellie was standing. He frowned, "Are you hurt? You okay?" he said, the words coming out short and clipped.

"Yeah, I'm okay," she shrugged. "But who were those guys?"

"I don't know. Did you get a call into 9-1-1?"

Ellie shook her head. "It wouldn't go through. No signal. We're out here on our own."

Travis licked his lips, his gun dangling from his right hand. He was uninjured, except for the stinging feeling in his arm where the knife had bitten through the skin the day before. He stared off into the darkness for a moment and then realized it was probably a good thing that Ellie hadn't been able to make the phone call. He tucked the gun into the back of his pants again and looked at Ellie, "Come on, give me a hand."

Ellie glanced at the trailer, her lips pressed together, "Shouldn't I check the horses? Make sure they're okay?"

Travis listened. There wasn't any noise from the trailer. "There's no time. We've gotta get out of here."

Ellie gave a single nod; as if the gunfight they'd been in finally landed in her consciousness. "Okay, what do you want me to do?"

Travis grimaced at the bodies in the road. "Help me move these guys out of the way."

Without saying anything more, Ellie walked over and joined Travis. They each grabbed an arm of a dead body and started dragging them off the side of the road. Travis pointed to the guns left in the middle of the street, "Grab those guns. We might need them."

"You think these people might be back?"

"I have no idea, but we need every advantage. He glanced down the road ahead of them. "Right before this happened, I saw a truck pull off the side of the road. Can you go up there and get it for me?"

"Sure, but why?"

"We've got to get these horses out of here. Our truck isn't going anywhere with five flat tires." The windshield and one of the side windows had been shattered in the gunfire, the two front tires completely flat, the heavy front end of the truck resting on the rims. Three of the four rear tires on the dual axle truck had been flattened as well. Travis pointed, "Let's see if we can use that other truck to hitch to the trailer."

"Should I try to call the police again?"

Travis bit his lip. He didn't have time to argue or explain. He needed her to cooperate. "Ellie, we tried that. Just go get the truck."

Ellie nodded and ran off into the darkness. Travis walked

around the back of the truck and picked up the gun from the third body, dragging it off the side of the road and rolling the man into a ditch. He climbed down as the body stopped, patting the man down for a wallet and phone. He had no ID on him. Typical, Travis thought. They were probably hired mercenaries. Those guys traveled without any ID except when they were at an airport and needed it. They usually dumped it as soon as they walked outside, assuming yet another identity. Travis grimaced, standing up. Travis would likely never know who the men were, especially without his contacts at the CIA.

As Travis emerged from around the back of the trailer, the third body disposed of in the ditch, he heard the rumble of a truck engine coming toward him. Narrowing his eyes in the darkness, he realized Ellie was behind the wheel of the black truck he'd seen right before the attack. It was nearly the same model as Travis drove, complete with the gooseneck hitch.

Travis strode back to the trailer, quickly uncoupling the truck and trailer, ignoring the pain in his arm. He got into his truck, started the engine, and pulled it forward, the truck's rims grinding against the asphalt on the road as the rubber from the flattened tires flopped around the rim. He pulled it forward, the truck shuddering a little as it moved.

Ellie pivoted the truck around, pulling the bed up underneath the gooseneck hitch, Travis standing by, dropping the coupling into place with a click. Travis fought the urge to check on the horses. They had quieted down since the gunfire stopped. They were likely in shock. The best thing for them was to get them moving, away from him and out of danger.

He ran to the driver's side window. Ellie had it rolled down, leaning out, pointing to the back seat. "Listen, they've got enough guns in the back of this truck to open a store."

Travis glanced inside. There were two shotguns, four AR-15 rifles, and three semiautomatic handguns in full view, plus a cardboard box of ammunition. He stared at Ellie, leaning his hands on the driver's side window, "Don't worry about that. Listen, can you get the horses back to the barn on your own?"

Ellie blinked, "I think so. I mean, where are you going? Are you going to stay with the truck?"

Travis set his jaw, "I have something I need to take care of. I'll probably be gone a couple of days. I need you to handle things around the ranch for me. Get the horses back. Dr. Wiley left a bottle of tranquilizers at the ranch from a couple of months back. If any of them seem to be rattled, give them a dose and call the vet. Don't ask me, don't call me. Just do it."

Travis glanced back at the trailer as he heard some thumping from one of the horse's hooves, banging against the metal sides of the trailer. "One more thing. As soon as you get in cell phone range, call Barry at the tow company in town and tell them where the truck is. Tell him to come get it and start working on it. He'll need a flatbed. Don't tell him what happened, Ellie. Don't breathe a word of this to anyone."

Ellie's eyes were wide, her lips parted. She nodded, "Okay. I can do that. You'll be back in a few days?"

"I hope so..."

"Wherever you're going, Travis, be careful."

Travis nodded and walked away.

13

Travis stood in the middle of the road surrounded by darkness as he watched the truck and trailer Ellie was driving disappear around the remainder of the bend in the road and into the night, the red glow of the trailer lights getting smaller in the distance. Travis got back in his truck, pulled it off the side of the road, and left the keys in it for the tow company, grabbing his backpack, his wallet, and cell phone from inside. From the locked compartment in the backseat, he grabbed two more full magazines for his pistol and another box of ammunition, shoving them inside of his backpack. Where he was going, he couldn't necessarily take his gun, but there was no telling what would happen in between where he was at that moment and where he needed to get to.

He glanced around him. His truck wasn't drivable, not with so many flat tires, but the tow truck should still be operational. He climbed up inside of the cab and turned the key. The engine started with a low rumble, the dashboard lighting up, the dials and gauges coming to life. The truck had nearly a full tank of diesel fuel, enough to get him where he was going. He put it into gear and pressed the accelerator feeling the rumble of the heavy-duty engine under his feet, the tow truck easing forward as he steered around what was left of his own wrecked vehicle.

Driving away, he glanced at what was left of the truck in the distance gritting his teeth. As much as he'd wanted to ignore the threat against his life, Catherine was right – it was the real deal. He needed to act, and fast.

Travis drove along in the tow truck, his hands gripping the heavy steering wheel as he headed north toward Dallas. He tapped on the phone number Catherine had sent him and penned a text message, speaking carefully into his phone as he drove, "Want to take you up on your offer. Heading to London. Can you get me a ticket out of Dallas-Fort Worth airport ASAP?"

Travis put his phone down in the cup holder next to him, picking up a Styrofoam cup the attacker had left behind as if he was having a lovely cup of tea before trying to end Travis, not to mention Ellie and the horses. Travis flung it out of the window into the darkness. He glanced at his phone, waiting for something to happen. If Catherine was already on the plane to London, it was unlikely she would get his text, but then again, MI6 was just as sophisticated as the CIA. Maybe she would.

A moment later he got his answer. His phone buzzed. He took a single hand off the wheel of the lumbering tow truck growling underneath him and glanced at it, "Ticket waiting at DFW. See you in twelve hours. Be careful."

Travis set his jaw and dropped his phone down into the cup holder again. He fumbled in his backpack for his passport, hoping it was there. It was. He might not have any answers about who was coming after him in Texas, but maybe he could get some in London.

14

By the time Travis got off of the overnight flight to London, his body felt achy, as though he'd been tightly swaddled in a giant blanket for the majority of the almost ten-hour flight over the Atlantic. Despite his dirty clothes and bandaged arm, no one seemed to give him a second look once the door to the plane closed.

The flight attendants had been masterful at their pacing while they were in the air, distracting everyone from the fact they were pinched together like sardines in a tin can, feeding them a sleep-inducing, high-carb dinner as soon as they got on board. It consisted of overcooked, gummy pasta covered with equally gooey Alfredo sauce, or at least what they said was an Alfredo sauce. Two hours later, by the time the plane was ready to leave American airspace, the majority of the people had conked out on the plane.

Despite the threat to his life, Travis was no exception.

The last day and a half had been mentally and physically exhausting between the horse show, the knife attack, and then getting run off the road and shot at by the tow truck driver and his cohorts. He needed the sleep, especially given the fact he had no idea what to expect when he got to England.

Waking up, he realized people were stirring. The flight attendants had disappeared. Travis tilted his head, staring toward the cockpit. He saw two of them, buckled into their jump seats. The captain's voice came on. "For those of you waking up, we are about to land at Heathrow. The local time is noon. Please fasten your seatbelts and prepare for landing. Enjoy your time in London."

The plane touched down without any fanfare, the enormous jet floating over the runway for a moment before the fuselage shuddered as it set down on the rubber-stained asphalt. It didn't take long for the plane to taxi to the gate and for the jetway to be extended. Along with the other passengers, Travis got up, grabbed his backpack from the overhead compartment, and shrugged it over his shoulders. He adjusted his baseball hat on his head and walked off the plane, following an elderly couple that was shuffling along. Passing them as soon as he could, Travis walked away. He was sure it was a relief to the people sitting next to him that he was off the plane. He'd showered the morning before he and Ellie left Oklahoma City but then managed to get himself covered in sweat from loading the horses, grime from the attack, and fighting off the people that had run him off the road.

As he walked down the jetway, he felt his phone buzz. It was Catherine. "I'll meet you at baggage."

It only took Travis a few minutes to wind his way through immigration and customs, scanning his passport at the immigration terminal and waiting for the gates to click open. He shook his head. It was an automated process now, as if the British government didn't much care who you were or where you came from as long as you had a passport. There were only two of Her Majesty's Border Agency Customs and Immigration officers in the entire area, two young men in uniforms leaning against the wall, chatting with each other. As Travis passed, he could hear them talking about the soccer scores from the day before. Football, not soccer, he realized as he passed, shaking his head. Soccer might be the biggest sport in the world, but there was nothing like American football, at least not in his mind.

Two rides on churning escalators descending below the gates amid a throng of other weary travelers let Travis off at the lowest level of Heathrow. The metallic clatter of the luggage turnstiles could be heard in the background delivering bags and boxes to people who had just arrived. Travis stopped and glanced around. So far, Catherine had appeared to him as an older woman and young cowgirl. Who would she be this time?

"Hello, Travis," he heard from behind him.

Travis turned to find Catherine standing in front of him. Her hair was brown and shoulder length, completely straight as though she had spent quite a bit of time with a flat iron early that morning. Given that she had only gotten back half a day before him, she looked surprisingly fresh. Catherine was wearing a pressed white blouse with a red sweater vest over it, a pair of perfectly fitting jeans, stylish brown boots with a matching messenger bag, the strap draped across her body and resting on her right hip. She had on a pair of glasses with fashionable, thick, dark frames and red lipstick that matched her vest. He blinked. This was an entirely different Catherine than he'd met before. "I almost didn't recognize you."

She smiled, "Oh this? Yeah, this is how I really look. At least most of the time..." Catherine glanced at the crowds moving around him, a faint flash of seriousness turning her face stony, "Come on, let's get out of here."

Walking out into the early afternoon sunshine, Travis blinked again, his eyes adjusting to the bright light after being sequestered on the plane overnight. It felt good to move, the aches and stiffness from his body evaporating as he and

Catherine made their way through the baggage area. The weariness of travel was nothing new to him. He'd suffered through far more uncomfortable flights during his time with the military, strapped into a jump seat for hours at a stretch. That was probably why he'd slept so well, besides the fact that he figured once he fell asleep if someone wanted to kill him, it didn't matter. It probably wasn't an opportune time to take another stab at his life anyways. Too many witnesses and nowhere to escape while flying thirty thousand feet over the Atlantic.

Catherine walked in front of him, her boots clicking on the concrete sidewalk. She stepped out near the edge of the curb and waved down a cab, getting in. As they did, she caught Travis's eye, putting her finger up to her lips. Travis nodded. The cab was unsecured and he was now on MI6 territory. Her country, her rules. Travis leaned back in the seat and stretched his neck left and right while Catherine gave the driver, an older man with a shock of gray hair sticking out from underneath a tattered plaid flat cap, an address, "320 Bucksley Southeast, please."

"Certainly." the driver replied.

While they rode in the back of the cab, Catherine started up a conversation, pretending it was Travis's first time in London, "Well, seeing that you've never been to this beautiful city of ours before, I thought for sure we should stop at Buckingham Palace and Westminster Abbey. Those are definite," she cooed. "And, since you're my cousin, I've also arranged for us to have dinner out tonight."

Travis raised his eyebrows, amused by Catherine's creative dialogue, "Really? Where are we eating?"

She slapped him on the knee playfully, "Now, if I told you, it wouldn't be a surprise, would it?" she said in a thick British accent. "You'll just have to wait. Now, I know you've heard that British food leaves something to be desired, but let me tell you, the culinary scene in London has evolved immensely over the last ten years or so..."

Travis nodded and smiled as Catherine spun the tale about his time in London for the benefit of the cab driver, droning on about young chefs and fusion food. The man had probably heard the exact same discussion twenty times just that week.

Catherine was smart and cunning. She let enough information slip that the driver wouldn't have any questions at all in his mind about who they were and what they were doing in London. If the two of them had sat in the car in silence, the driver, given human nature, would have come up with questions of his own — Were they fighting? Were they married? Had they only now come into town to attend the funeral of a close family member? Silence was dangerous. Catherine filled the time with enough boring information the cabbie would be more than happy to simply get his payment and have them leave.

Ten minutes later, after winding their way through bumper-to-bumper London traffic, the cabbie trailing the car in front of him with not more than about a two-inch buffer, they came to a screeching halt in front of an apartment building on the outskirts of downtown London. Catherine popped the door open, handed the man a few pound notes, and waited for Travis to get out, slamming the door behind him. Travis scanned the area. There was a line of tall white apartment buildings spanning the block as far as he could see. On the opposite side of the street was a wide park, thick with the bright green of early June leaves, the trees and brush dense, much like what he'd seen when he'd traveled to the Midwest, even if the temperature seemed to be a bit cooler. He cocked his head to the side. Thinking about it, the longitude of London wasn't that much different than New York, Buffalo, Columbus, or Detroit. No wonder the foliage looked so much like the Midwest. The quote, "There's nothing new under the sun," certainly applied to what he was seeing.

Catherine didn't give him much time to stop and look around. She started off at a fast clip, "This way," she waved, the messenger bag bouncing on her right hip as she took off.

Travis jogged a couple of steps to catch up, his backpack shifting over his shoulders with the sudden movement, "Where are we going?"

"Someplace you can get a shower," Catherine smiled, looking him up and down.

"I need one."

"At least that much we can agree on."

Travis walked next to Catherine for the next few minutes, as they wound their way past clusters of people strolling on the sidewalk who were either checking their phones or pointing at something, holding up the foot traffic. Across the street in the park, Travis spotted a tour group from an unnamed Asian country, all of them wearing matching blue T-shirts, the leader carrying a flag extended high in the air, a whistle around her neck. The kids followed her like she was the mother duck and they were her ducklings, the wave of them trailing her with giggles and shouts. Travis glanced back at Catherine in time to see her dodge down a narrow alley. Following, he saw she'd stopped at a single door in the side of the building. Looking left and right, she keyed in a code to the door and slipped inside. Travis followed.

"Where are we?" he frowned.

"It's a safe house we keep for visitors. A flat, really. It's up here," she pointed to a flight of steps.

As they got to the second floor, Catherine turned left down the hallway and went to the first door, keying in another code on the door panel. She pushed it open, waving Travis inside.

The apartment, or flat, that Catherine had led him to was of moderate size. The narrow entry door led to a wide living space, a bank of long, thin windows covered with gauzy white curtains that were keeping the dappled noonday sun from entering the apartment directly across from the door. The ceilings were high, at least by American standards for an apartment building. If Travis had to guess, the building was quite old, like most things in England, although it looked to have been recently redecorated. Tile covered the floor, scattered area rugs tossed about with furniture carefully laid out on top of them. The sitting room had a long wide couch with a coffee table and two chairs facing in, a flat-screen TV mounted on the wall over a fake fireplace filled with unlit candles. From where he was standing, Travis could smell the vanilla-scented wax, as though the candles were new or had been recently burned, although none of their wicks were black.

In the corner, there was a four-seat dining table next to a long counter that divided the kitchen from the sitting area, shiny stainless-steel appliances lining the walls next to a narrow hallway, which Travis expectedly led to either two or three bedrooms with probably two bathrooms. The entire apartment was appointed with the feeling of high-end luxury, certainly not something he expected to be used as a safe house. But then again, this was London. Everything was more high-end in Europe, at least fancier than what he expected to find in Texas. It wasn't his style, but then again, no one asked him.

Travis walked through the rest of the space, checking it carefully, pulling his tactical pen out of his pocket, the tip protruding out of the pinky side of his hand. It wasn't his gun, but the reinforced tip could do a lot of damage, especially given he couldn't bring a gun on the plane or into London.

As he guessed, there were three bedrooms, two on the hallway with a shared bathroom to one side and a master suite at the end of the hall, with a large bathroom complete with a clawfoot soaking tub attached.

"Oh, Travis, you don't need to do that," Catherine said,

wrinkling her nose, taking off her messenger bag and tossing it on the couch.

"What?"

"Check the space. This building is completely secure. Our agents left as we were coming into the building."

Travis narrowed his eyes. "How do you know that?"

She pointed to her ear, pulling the brown hair away from the side of her face. "Comms. I do hope you Americans use these ingenious little devices."

"Very funny," he frowned. "I bet if I looked it up, we probably invented them."

"Or the Israelis did. Lord knows they seem to come up with all of the most necessary inventions, now don't they?" Catherine said, flinging herself down on the couch.

The mention of the Israelis reminded Travis of Eli Segal, the legendary Mossad agent he'd ended up meeting a few months ago. Travis's mind wandered for a second. Had Eli heard about the threat on Travis's life? That he was now in London? It seemed like Eli had information on everyone, no matter where they were in the world. For a moment, he considered asking Catherine if she knew him but then decided not to. Espionage was a funny game. He needed to remember he was in London as Catherine's guest, which meant he was really a guest of the British government, more specifically MI6. No matter how well-intentioned they seemed to be, he was still cavorting with a foreign government.

"What now?" Travis said, tossing his backpack down on the chair across from where Catherine was sitting.

"You go take a shower. Then we go to MI6."

15

Twenty minutes later, after taking a shower, Travis felt like a new man. Catherine had told him to use the bathroom of his choice. "You'll find a few sets of fresh clothes in the first bedroom across the hallway from the bathroom, the door on the left," Catherine pointed, playing with her phone. She glanced at him, "I had to guess at your size, but I think I did all right."

"You're not putting me in one of your fancy disguises?"

"Don't tempt me," she smiled, the corners of her eyes wrinkling her grin was so wide. "Now, go get tidied up. We have an appointment to keep."

After his shower, Travis pulled on a fresh pair of jeans, a white T-shirt with a plaid long-sleeved shirt over top in a mix of aqua, black and white. He'd found a few fresh bandages in the first aid kit in the bathroom and managed to cover the wound on his arm, but the edges of it weren't looking very good, having a greenish tinge to them. He ignored it, pulling the shirtsleeve down over the bandages.

Walking out into the sitting area, Catherine popped up as

soon as she saw him. She moved toward him, reaching up and pushing a stray hair off of his forehead. His hair was still damp from the shower. She frowned, "Let me take a look at your arm. Did you get medical attention?"

Travis shook his head, "Not really. Didn't exactly have time." He tried to pull his arm away from Catherine, "It's fine. Just leave it."

Catherine pressed her lips together, taking a half step away from him, "Oh no. That's not the way we do it here. Roll up your sleeve, Agent Bishop, so I may look at your arm. That's an order."

Travis blinked. There was something forceful about Catherine that reminded him of Elena Lobranova, his former partner at the CIA. For a moment, he wondered if the CIA attracted a certain type of female personality as field agents. Maybe it was the same for MI6? There was something about them, whether it was their powerful personalities or their determination, he wasn't sure. Whatever it was, the women had it in common. It was as if they came at everything with a 'take no prisoners' attitude, as if they were storing up tokens for the moment they got into trouble, knowing they might have to spend all of their courage in order to protect their lives.

Unable to argue, or unwilling to, Travis couldn't decide which, probably because he was still so tired, he rolled up his sleeve and held his arm out for inspection. Catherine peeled back one of the fresh bandages on Travis's arm and winced, "My, that doesn't look good." She quickly resealed the bandage on his arm and took a step away from him, tapping her ear, "Could you lovelies have medical ready when we get there? Agent Bishop needs to be seen."

Travis started to protest but Catherine shook her head, "Nonsense. We have work to do. I can't have you falling apart on me in the middle of a mission."

Travis raised his eyebrows, "A mission?"

"Yes, there's more to the story than someone trying to kill you. Now, let's get moving. There's work to do and no time to waste."

16

Catherine ushered Travis out of the apartment, closing the door behind her. Travis saw her eyes dart to the ground as she touched the comm link in her ear. "On the move," she said calmly, leading Travis back down the flight of steps in the apartment building. When they got to the door they'd come in off of the alleyway, Catherine turned left, going toward the back of the building, keying another code for a doorway that led to a stairwell that went to the basement. "This way."

"You have an office in the basement of the building?"

Catherine glanced over her shoulder, smiling, "Good Lord, no. We have to get the car."

"In the basement?"

"Patience, Agent Bishop. All will be revealed," Catherine said cryptically.

Travis followed; frustration rippling through his muscles. He knew he was on Catherine's home turf. She was in charge. The problem was it had been years since he hadn't been the boss. Travis wasn't sure he liked it.

At the bottom of the steps, Catherine pushed a steel door

open, the kind that had a metal bar across it horizontally. It clicked open and closed, leaving the two of them in a dark space for a split second. As they moved, a bank of lights clicked on. There were a dozen vehicles parked on an angle, a range of sedans, SUVs, and two red convertibles. Travis frowned, "What's this?"

"Just one of our many storage garages around the city." She pointed to a blue Volvo sedan, "Come on. Get in."

As Travis walked to the right side of the car to get in the passenger seat, Catherine shook her head, "Agent Bishop, we are in England. Try the other side of the car."

Travis felt his cheeks flush. The cars in England had the driver's side on the right, not the left, as it was in the US. He knew better. He shook his head. "Sorry, I've got my mind on other things."

"Of course," Catherine said, sliding into the car. "Don't we all?"

Without saying anything else, Catherine started the car and revved the engine. Travis leaned back in the contoured leather seat. The Volvo they were driving was far nicer than nearly any of the cars he'd driven during his time with his CIA. If he had to guess, MI6 had scooped up the vehicle as part of one of their European sting operations. He knew the CIA had a similar cache of luxury vehicles, but he'd just never been lucky enough to get to drive in any of them.

As the Volvo hit the ramp leading back up to the street, a garage door parted left and right, splitting into a wide opening. Catherine stepped on the accelerator, barely checking each way before darting into traffic, eliciting a few horn blasts from behind her. Travis glanced in the side mirror, seeing the doors mysteriously close as they left. He shook his head, "I feel like I'm part of a James Bond movie right now," he said, furrowing his eyebrows.

"You should. What agency do you think inspired them?" Catherine smiled.

Travis shook his head. He appreciated the style with which Catherine did everything. He was sure that if he asked her about it she would use some fancy word like "panache" to describe her time with MI6. Maybe it was his military background or the more practical side of his personality, but he would have been happy enough in a no-name, run-of-the-mill sedan, as he was in the leather-appointed luxury vehicle they were driving.

He glanced out the window as they crisscrossed the streets of London. He'd been to Vauxhall Cross, the home of MI6, only one other time during his career, on a stop when he and Elena were coming back from one of their many trips to the Eastern Bloc, dealing with a terrorist cell in Bulgaria. They'd stopped in London and met with another agent at the MI6 building, staying for less than an hour. The memory in his mind was foggy at best. After traveling to as many countries and as many locations as he had throughout his career, all of them began to run together. Things categorized themselves in his mind under one of two headings — home, or not home. And home was where he had been for primarily the last five years.

Travis swallowed. And yet in the last twenty-four hours, someone had found what he was doing to be so threatening that they felt the need to try to kill him twice. Was it the CIA? Someone else? He chewed the inside of his lip. He knew that whatever reason people were coming for him, and whoever it was, it had nothing to do with what had gone on over the last five years. It was something beyond that. And although he'd been racking his brain to try to figure out who might have a strong enough vendetta to come after him after all of these years, he couldn't come up with anyone specifically. Or, more precisely, there were too many options for any of them to really stand out.

During his career both with the Delta Force and the CIA, Travis had come across some truly bad actors, people that shouldn't be allowed to share the same oxygen as the kind, compassionate people that lived in the majority of the world, people that simply wanted to put food on the table, raise their families and manage to do so in relative safety and security. Making sure they were able to do that had been his job. And sure, he'd managed to upset a few people while he'd kept the peace, but the people he'd upset were the ones who wanted to contaminate the world, to allow the dark underbelly of evil to take control of people's lives. That was the whole reason he'd joined Delta Force and the CIA in the first place – to bring justice.

Travis stared out the window again. The buildings had thinned out as they drove, the pedestrians not so evident in the section of London they were in. Trying to determine the direction, he realized they had wound their way directly south. Up ahead was a bridge. He could see the wide flow of the River Thames running left and right, a ferry boat traveling down the waterway, as they drove down Vauxhall Bridge Road.

The area where MI6 was housed was much like many of the other areas in London, newer architecture next to buildings that had been erected in the 1500s, tourist traps sprinkled throughout the area willy-nilly, and the major shopping area for all of London only a block or so from Downing Street, where the Prime Minister lived and did his work. It was as if the entire city was mashed together, serious business and happy-go-lucky vacationers alike all existing in the same space.

Vauxhall Cross was a massive fortress-like building, at least six stories sprawled out in a tiered design, a more modern interpretation of the castle turrets and garrisons of so many of the other buildings of the British Empire. It was right near the Vauxhall Pleasure Gardens, one of the main attractions for nature lovers who happen to need a dose of trees and birds and flowers while they were living in the concrete maze of London proper.

Catherine veered the sedan onto a driveway, driving around the back of Vauxhall Cross and putting the Volvo in a spot in the parking lot. For some reason, Travis expected that by now, with security challenges around the world, somehow the famous SIS building would be fenced and guarded much like an embassy on foreign soil, with armed shooters at every gate asking for identification. But it wasn't.

Catherine slid out of the Volvo and slammed the door. She was halfway across the parking lot before Travis could do the same. He followed, trotting behind her to catch up.

While there may not have been any security to speak of outside of the building, Travis wasn't naïve enough to think there wasn't any — it was probably more Israeli-style, covert surveillance to give the appearance the building was open and vulnerable when it actually was not, as opposed to the brute show of force American's preferred. Catherine pulled open a single glass door that led into an anteroom. A thick steel door was directly ahead of them, the space lit up by a solitary fluorescent bulb in the ceiling, a dark gray scarred concrete floor beneath their feet. Travis frowned. It was quite industrial looking for all of the lovely touches he'd experienced already while he was in London. Catherine stepped up to the keypad, pushed in a code, and then pressed her thumb to the thumbprint reader. As soon as she did, the door popped open. Travis followed her, realizing the lock they used to get into MI6 was much like the one he had in his war room back at his log cabin in Texas.

Inside, the silent industrial feel of the anteroom evaporated into a hive of activity. An armed guard stood against the wall and nodded at Catherine as she walked by. She looked at him, muttering, "He's with me," stopping long enough to snag Travis a visitor's badge attached to a lanyard. "Put this around your neck," she said, pulling a set of credentials out of her messenger bag and clipping them to the waistband of her jeans.

"Stay here for one moment, please," she said to Travis as she disappeared into the mass of moving bodies darting from desk to desk.

Travis sucked in a deep breath. In front of him was a large space, filled with cubicles, people moving quietly on the soft carpeting beneath their feet. A moment later, Catherine was back, plowing her way through a cluster of people like a missile hot on the trail of its target. She waved at Travis, beckoning him to follow, "All right, he's ready for us. This way."

17

Travis nodded, taking a few steps forward and then following Catherine through the maze of people and cubicles that made up the first floor of the MI6 building at Vauxhall Cross. There had to be nearly a hundred agents and support staff crammed in the area. Given the number of people crowded into the space, the noise level was surprisingly quiet and muffled as though someone had turned on a giant sound-dampening machine, or perhaps it was just the polite conversation the British were known for. "Excuse me," Travis said, nearly running into a woman wearing a red dress and heels, carrying a stack of files. She pressed her lips together, gave him a quick smile of forgiveness, and kept going.

The tone in MI6 was decidedly different than the last time he'd been there. If his memory served him, the last time he'd been there, there were probably a dozen or fewer agents and support staff milling around in the building. The way it looked on his trip with Catherine, it was as if the British government had taken every bit of gold in their treasury and thrown it at their espionage services. Travis paused for a second, nearly losing Catherine in the crowd of people again. It looked more like the crowded streets of Times Square than the interior of a government building, that was for sure, Travis thought. The clusters of cubicles were all occupied, sometimes by more than one person, people pointing at computer screens, reviewing documents and having conversations, their arms folded across their chest, serious looks on their faces. In the background, Travis could hear the hum of what sounded like a copier machine churning out paper. As he looked to his right, he saw a man standing over the machine, slamming the door on the side of it after loading more paper. Finally catching a glimpse of Catherine up ahead of him, Travis fought to catch up, pushing his way past a group of three people that was walking together, lanyards around their necks with their IDs swinging back and forth as they moved, talking in hushed whispers over their shoulders at each other as they move toward one of the conference rooms.

By the time Travis reached Catherine, she was on the other side of the large bay of gray felted cubicles. The traffic in the office had thinned out considerably. Catherine pushed her way through a single door at the back of the space, which opened into another office area, much smaller than the first, but with the same gray carpeting, a cluster of six or eight cubicles made of the same gray felt, off to one side. A bank of offices and conference rooms were off on the right-hand side. "We're going right over here," she pointed, walking toward an office in the corner.

Pausing outside the door, Travis glanced at the placard. Director Archie Elliott. Travis frowned for a minute. He'd heard about Archie while he was in the CIA. Tough, no-nonsense, but with all of the genteel skills the British were known for. "Is Archie your boss?"

Catherine nodded over her shoulder as she pushed his door open, "Yes. He's the only one I report to."

That single fact told Travis more than he needed to know

about the type of work Catherine was involved in, which made him even more surprised she'd take an interest in the bounty on his head. Director Elliot ran the entire MI6 global operation, not just a division. A lump formed in his throat. He realized if she directly reported Archie, and Archie knew what was going on with him, then the threat to his life might be even more serious than he realized.

"Come in, come in!" a voice boomed from behind the desk, a thick British accent weighing on every syllable. "Agent Bishop, I'm so glad you were able to join us."

As Travis stepped inside, he glanced around. Archie's office decor resembled what Travis would expect to see in the study of an English manor house somewhere out in the country. The gray carpeting that covered all of the floors outside of Archie's office had been replaced with wood, two thick area rugs covering sections of it, a wall of built-in cabinets flanking one side, their dark luster making Travis wonder if they'd been hand built out of mahogany. The same wood had been used to build Archie a wide desk, a modern, cushioned, black executive chair behind it. Near the bookcases was a well-worn, cognac-colored leather couch and two leather chairs with a low, oval-shaped coffee table in the middle, a few thick volumes stacked on top, the first title reading "The Battle of the Pacific: A Historical Perspective," by an author Travis didn't recognize. The bookshelves lining the walls were filled to the brim with enough titles to fill a library, stacked haphazardly, some of them upright, some of them on their sides, other books tucked on top of other volumes. The lighting in Archie's office was dim, except for the glow from a green glass and brass banker's light on his desk, the arching neck of it sending a glow across a stack of files and the closed lid of a laptop. Travis sniffed the air, realizing it held the faint scent of cigar smoke. He narrowed his eyes. He felt like he'd walked back in time, as if Winston Churchill might wander into Archie's office at any moment, barking orders in his gruff tone, demanding answers on their progress in defeating the Nazis.

As Travis refocused on Catherine and Archie, he noticed Catherine had her eyebrows raised as if she'd noticed him absorbing the details of Archie's office. Travis looked at Archie, "Thank you for having me, sir. I appreciate the heads-up about the bounty on my head. Not sure I would have survived the last twenty-four hours without Miss…"

At that moment, he realized he didn't know Catherine's last name. She smiled, her cheeks reddening, "Lewis," she said quietly, "Catherine Lewis."

"Well, again, thank you."

By the time Travis looked back, Archie had leaned back in his chair. He had thin brown hair, almost the same color as Catherine's, and was rather a large man by British standards, probably almost six feet tall, judging by the width of his chest and the length of his arms. His glasses were in a style that looked like he'd worn them for more than a decade. He had on khaki pants that were wrinkled from sitting, a plaid shirt and a burgundy tie strung loosely around his neck. A suit jacket was slung over the shoulders of the chair he was sitting in.

"It's my pleasure, truly. And I'm grateful we were able to get you over here. It seems we have a problem in common."

"What's that?" Travis folded his arms over his chest. Catherine had alluded to the fact that MI6 had not only wanted to warn him about the kill order on his life, but that he could help her with something she was working on. A mission, whatever that meant.

"There's been some ancillary chatter we've become interested in, in addition to the information that we received about the kill order for you."

At that moment, all Travis was interested in was the bounty on his head. "Do you know who's behind the kill order?"

"Not yet, other than it seemed to originate from the CIA.

Who in particular, we don't know. We heard about it from a few sources and are trying to lean on them to get more information." Archie picked up a pen, holding each end between his fingers, rolling it and staring at it as he spoke. His lack of eye contact made Travis wonder if there was more to the story.

As Travis sucked in a breath to ask, a knock came on the door. "Come!" Archie bellowed

The door creaked open and a man wearing a set of neat navy-blue scrubs standing in the doorway. "We're ready for Agent Bishop now, Director Elliott."

"And just as things were getting interesting!" He waved his hand, "Yes, yes. Go ahead. Take him. Return him to me as soon as you are finished."

Catherine glanced at Travis who hadn't moved from where he was standing. "They're going to take you to medical, Travis. You must get that arm looked at."

Without saying anything, Travis turned on his heel, following the man with the scrubs out of Director Elliott's office. They walked through the smaller bay of cubicles near Archie's office and then out another door, into the bright white lights of what looked like a miniature hospital, complete with the beeping of machines, the scent of disinfectant in the air, and privacy curtains dividing four medical bays. A nurse's desk was set at an angle as they walked inside, two people, a red-haired woman and a black-haired man hunched behind computers. The man in the scrubs leading Travis, said, "Right this way, Agent Bishop. The doctor is waiting for you."

The hair stood up on the back of Travis's neck. Why hadn't Catherine come with him? Was it because it was a setup? Or maybe she and Archie were talking about him while they kept him distracted in their medical department? Travis tried to shake off the thought, staring at the polished white linoleum tile on the floor. He felt like he was in the fog of war — not exactly sure who was reliable and who wasn't anymore, but he needed to trust someone if he hoped to survive. That didn't stop him from wondering why the British were so eager to help. Why hadn't his ex-partner at the CIA, Elena Lobranova, let him know about the kill order? Questions peppered the inside of his head, ricocheting through his mind like stray bullets. He shook it off. He needed to keep his wits about him. The kill order could have come from anywhere, even MI6...

18

As promised, when Travis walked into the examination room, a dark-haired woman was already sitting on a stool, thumbing through her phone, waiting for him. "Agent Bishop?"

He nodded.

"It's a pleasure to meet you. I'm Dr. Walsh. Agent Lewis said you took an injury to your arm she was concerned about?"

"I'm sure it's okay," Travis mumbled.

"Nonsense. If Agent Lewis said it needs to be looked at, then it needs to be looked at." She paused, staring at him, her eyebrows raised. "Arm, please."

As Travis sat down on the examination table and began to roll up his sleeve, he wondered why he was feeling so resistant to any help. It'd been a long time since he had to depend on anyone other than Ellie. And if there was a kill order out on his life, the last thing he wanted to do was admit he was injured. It was like when he was with Delta Force. It didn't matter what happened to him, whether he'd been injured, was sore, tired, hungry, or thirsty. He had to keep going until he got back home. When he was in the military, that was back to the base, where he could relax because he knew he was around people that were loyal to him, who'd have his back. His home had been the ranch for the last five years. He knew who to trust when he was in Texas, but now? He wasn't so sure.

Despite his resistance, Travis unbuttoned the sleeve of the new plaid shirt Catherine had gotten for him and rolled it up. Dr. Walsh stood up from her stool, pulling on a pair of blue latex gloves, the black skirt she wore underneath her white lab coat swinging around her calves as she moved toward him. As she got close to Travis, he thought he could smell the scent of lemon on her skin over the disinfectant that hung in the air in the medical bay. She gently peeled off the blood-soaked bandages on his arm, staring at it, tilting her head. She pressed on the edges; as if she was testing the doneness of a steak, which made Travis wince. It was the first time he'd really looked at the wound since it happened. The edges were torn, angry, and red, even more green than before.

"It's painful?"

"A little," Travis shrugged.

Dr. Walsh smiled, "I'd imagine you have a relatively high pain tolerance, don't you?"

"You could say that."

Dr. Walsh looked at the nurse who was standing on the other side of the examination table. "Donald, I'm gonna need a debridement kit and a suture kit. You can go ahead and fill a Cephalexin prescription for Agent Bishop. Give him two weeks of antibiotics. We're going to do an intramuscular loading dose to start so we can get ahead of this infection."

Donald nodded and disappeared for a moment, coming back with a tray of sealed equipment. Dr. Walsh looked at Travis, her face soft, but her voice firm. "Director Elliott and Agent Lewis told me they need you operational ASAP. You're lucky you came in when you did. This injury is about to go bad. I'm not sure if the knife that cut you was dirty or if you got dirt into it, but it's heavily infected." She frowned, "It was a knife, wasn't it? That's what Agent Lewis reported."

Travis nodded, "Yeah. It was."

"That's fine. Here's what we're going to do. I'm going to have you lay back on the bed and relax. Donald will make sure you're nice and comfortable. I'm going to numb up the area first. You feel a couple of pinches as I inject the anesthesia. Once that's done, I'm going to give this a good cleaning and see if I can remove some of the dead tissue. You may feel a little pulling and tugging as I do that. Once that's done, I'm going to stitch the skin up, give you a shot of antibiotics, and Donald will give you a bottle of them to take with you. How does that sound?"

Travis nodded. Dr. Walsh was the first person he'd met in the last two days who seemed to be dealing with him straight. No agenda. No intrigue. She was organized and had a plan. Those were things he could respect. Travis felt his body relax. "I'm all yours, Doc. Do what you gotta do."

"Good to hear it."

Half an hour later, Travis was sitting up on the edge of the bed again, his arm debrided, cleaned, and freshly stitched, Donald expertly injecting a dose of antibiotics into the muscle of his shoulder and then handing him a bottle of Cephalexin to take with him as he bandaged Travis's arm.

Dr. Walsh sat down on her stool again, tapping information into her phone. "All right then. I've made notes on your injury in case you come back. If I'm not here, the doctor on call will be able to see exactly what we did. From what I know about you, Agent Bishop, you are a rough-and-tumble type of fellow. That's fine except I'm asking that you keep the wound clean and take your antibiotics as prescribed. If you don't, you will be back here with a larger problem, one that will leave us fewer options. Does that sound sensible?"

Travis nodded. Doctors were not his favorite, but there was

something about Dr. Walsh, her level of precision and communication, that left him feeling more relaxed than he had in days. With the way she worked, she had to be former military. He rolled his sleeve down, taking the bag of first aid supplies and antibiotics from Donald.

As he slid off the edge of the bed, Dr. Walsh looked at him, her face firm, "Agent Bishop, and I do mean this seriously. Complete the steps I have asked you to. Clean bandages every day and take the antibiotics. I don't want to see you back here again. Understood?"

"Yes ma'am."

She glanced at Donald, "Please return him to Director Elliott and Agent Lewis."

Without saying anything, Donald glanced back at Travis, his face blank. Travis took it as his invitation to leave and followed, walking out of the medical bay and past the check-in desk. The two people were still working on their computers and never looked up, a repeat of the same scene from when he'd walked in a half hour ago. Travis trailed Donald as they made their way back to Archie's office. As he walked in, he saw Archie still positioned behind his desk, his hands folded on the surface. Catherine had settled into one of the leather chairs on the other side of the massive piece of mahogany, her legs crossed, her messenger bag on the ground next to the thick legs of the chair. They each had a china cup and a saucer in front of them. A teapot was set in the middle of the desk.

"Wonderful! You're back. Did everything go well?" Director Elliott said, his voice echoing off the walls. He talked so loudly, that Travis wondered if that was his exuberant personality or hearing loss. Which one it was, he wasn't sure.

"Yes. Thank you. Catherine was right. It was infected." Travis glanced at the ground, put the bag of gauze and bandages down and sat on the chair next to Catherine.

Catherine winced, as if the infection was in her arm. "Yes,

we already heard. Dr. Walsh called while Donald was returning you to us. Said it was a nasty cut. Those assassins, they don't play around," Archie said, pouring Travis a cup of tea. He glanced up at Travis as he set the teapot down, "Do you take cream and sugar in your tea?"

Travis would have preferred coffee, but he accepted the tea. "Neither, thank you."

"Then let's get down to business."

19

Get down to business? Archie's comment rattled him. Travis bristled, leaving the cup of tea on the edge of Archie's desk without touching it. "All right. Let's do that. Other than passing on the information about the bounty on my head, what's MI6's interest in what's happening here? I'm imagining this is more than just a good faith gesture on your part to try to save my life, although I appreciate that." The words came out sharp and careless but Travis didn't care. While he appreciated that Catherine came the whole way to Texas to find him, now it was time for some answers.

Archie raised his eyebrows, two tufts of brown hair hovering above the edge of his thick glasses, "Right to the point, are we? I can work with that." Archie picked up the pen he'd been playing with on his desk and held it once again between his fingers, his elbows touching on the thick armrests of his chair, leaning back against the upholstery. The sleeve of his suit jacket swung back and forth gently as he shifted his weight; like it had been picked up in a slight breeze.

"I wanted to tell you about the kill order, but yes, Agent

Bishop, your instinct that there is more to MI6's interest in this case is spot on," Catherine said softly.

"It's Travis. I'm not Agent Bishop anymore. I haven't been for five years, which is what makes all of this difficult to understand." Travis's voice was gruff and sharp.

"Quite perplexing indeed!" Archie said. He cleared his throat, lowering his voice for the first time. "Agent Bishop, what have you been doing for the last five years?"

Travis narrowed his eyes. There was absolutely no way that the director of MI6 would send one of his top agents to Texas to go hunt him down and not know exactly how he'd been spending his time. "I'm sure you know the answer to that question already, Director Elliott."

Archie cocked his head to the side. "I'd prefer to hear it from you, if you don't mind. Catherine said you have quite the horse business. Reining, is it? A cowboy sport?"

"You could say that."

Travis spent the next few minutes talking through how he'd formed Bishop Performance Horses after leaving the CIA, how his intent was to marry another ex-CIA agent, Kira Pozreva, until he first thought she was killed in Ecuador, then realized she'd been turned into a Russian double agent and attempted to assassinate the American president.

"Yes, I heard about that. I imagine there was a significant reorganization of security at the White House afterward, wasn't there?"

Travis shook his head, "Honestly, I have no idea."

Archie tilted his head, "Is that right?"

Travis stared at him, his face reddening, "Yes, in fact, it is. It might be hard for you guys to imagine, but I'm happy on my ranch. I don't miss the life of intrigue and drama. I just want to be left alone." The words came out impatient, but Travis didn't care.

Archie looked down at his lap for a second and then looked

back at Travis, "It appears that's not an option at the moment, Agent Bishop. But perhaps if we work together, we can get you back to your ranch without having to worry that someone is going to be coming after you on a regular basis." He took a sip of his tea, "Catherine also tells me that you have a side business. Skip tracing?"

"Yes." Travis felt his gut knot. They'd only been sitting for a few minutes, but the questions were becoming tiresome already. Every word out of Archie's mouth seemed to grate against the back of his skull. He was busy giving them answers and yet had none of his own. Travis sucked in a breath. He knew he was playing a game of chess with Archie and Catherine. They were a few moves ahead of him, taking advantage of the fact he was on their turf. A part of Travis knew he needed to answer their questions before he'd get any information of his own. It was the system. He knew how it worked. He sighed, "Yes. That's correct. I have a little skip tracing business on the side. Simple cases. Nothing complicated. Mostly domestic. Someone's missing a girlfriend, or something got stolen or a client wants to find an adopted child. I do one or two of those a month."

"No side work for the CIA or any other US agency?" Archie asked, the words coming out slowly, his eyes narrowing behind his thick glasses.

"No."

"Then how did you get dragged into the president's assassination plot and the Mardi Gras disaster? You were involved heavily with both, if I recall correctly?"

Travis felt his throat tighten, anger rising in his chest. What exactly was Archie accusing him of? "Listen," he said, standing up. "I didn't come all this way to get interrogated. And if you think I'm dumb enough to think that you haven't gone through my background with a fine-tooth comb before I got here, then you've got another think coming. Yes, I got dragged into President Mosley's assassination plot and the Mardi Gras disaster. That's correct. Did I go after those missions? No. Was I approached by any agency to take them on? No. Did I fall into them because people asked me for help? Yes. It's as simple as that. If you think there's something else happening here, you're wrong."

Silence settled over the office for a moment. Travis's hands were balled into tight fists, the adrenaline surging through his system. He stared at Archie and then Catherine. He saw them glance at each other and then Archie seemed to relax in his seat, leaning back into the upholstery of his chair again. Catherine hadn't moved a muscle and hadn't said anything, the expression on her face the same as it was when Travis started talking. It was as if they were having a conversation about something as commonplace as the weather or grain prices, not whether or not Travis had been moonlighting as an operative for the last five years.

Archie cleared his throat again and pressed his lips to the edge of the cup on his desk, slurping some of the tea into his mouth. "Thank you for that, Agent Bishop. That was quite direct. Quite to the point." He set the teacup down. "Agent Lewis, would you care to give Agent Bishop a taste of what we've heard?"

Catherine nodded as Travis sat back down. "You are completely right, Travis. As much as we did hear about the kill order on your life and wanted to warn you, we also had an ulterior purpose in inviting you here."

Travis narrowed his eyes. In his mind, whatever they wanted from him was the only purpose. He let her continue without interrupting despite the fact that he was becoming suspicious.

Catherine continued, "We've had our eye on a man named Jonah Hudson. He's a British national. Runs the largest hedge fund in the globe called Desert Indigo. They have nearly half a trillion dollars in international investments. Mr. Hudson manages them all."

Travis frowned. "I'm sorry. I feel like I'm missing something. How does a hedge fund manager with a gazillion dollars in his fund have anything to do with the kill order on me?"

"That's exactly the question we are struggling with, Agent Bishop," Archie said, folding his hands across the top of his desk, glancing at Travis over the frames of his glasses. He waved to Catherine, "Continue, please. You are doing a fine job."

"As I was saying, we have had some interest in Jonah Hudson. He keeps some curious company, businessmen around the world who seem to have other side jobs and hobbies that most people would find distasteful."

Travis shook his head. What did Catherine mean? He wished she would spit it out, "You mean like terrorists?"

Catherine nodded, "Precisely. Or at least it appears that way. In any event, last week, while you were busy on your ranch getting your horses ready to go to Oklahoma, some of the sources we've been watching sent off a few communiqués that were concerning."

"Chatter? Like chatter about the kill order?" Travis pressed his lips together. He felt like he was slogging through mud trying to get through their fancy language.

Catherine nodded, "Yes. The chatter surrounding Jonah Hudson uses some of the same sources that initiated the kill order against you."

Travis frowned. Something didn't make sense. He stared at the ground for a second, pinching the cuff of his sleeve with his fingers, thinking. "So what you're trying to figure out is how the kill order on me and the chatter around Jonah Hudson are linked?"

Recrossing her legs, Catherine said, "Exactly. There's something there. We just don't know what it is at this moment."

"And that's what you need me to help you figure out?"

Archie slurped at his tea again before setting the cup back on the saucer, "That's exactly the case, Agent Bishop. Two birds, one stone, as the saying goes. What we are offering you is assistance in determining who put the kill order out on your life and helping you figure out a way to end it. In return, you can help us understand how Jonah Hudson and the Indigo Desert Hedge fund are at the middle of all of this."

20

What Catherine and Archie were asking for was nothing short of a *quid pro quo* — you scratch my back and I'll scratch yours. Travis knew that eliminating a kill order on his own, without being linked to an agency with the resources he'd need, would be nearly impossible, the assassins continuing to come at him time and time again until someone finally succeeded.

Travis swallowed. He quickly assessed the situation in his mind. Someone had placed a kill order on his life, a bounty on his head. He was in London, a guest of the British government and now they wanted something from him, something he wasn't sure he could give. Not that he didn't want to. At this point, his allegiance to the CIA was fragile at best – especially if they had initiated the bounty on his head – like treading on a thin sheet of ice covering up a frozen lake in the early spring after temperatures had already warmed up. One false step and a thunderous crash would send the whole carefully constructed image of his life into a watery abyss, never to be found again.

In some ways, he kind of felt like he'd already fallen

through, but had somehow missed the thunderous crack that had sent him, and his life, headlong into the unknown.

Travis took a tentative sip of his tea and then put the cup back down. It was bitter and strong. If it had been coffee, he would have loved it. No wonder the Brits drank it with milk and sugar. He looked back at Archie and Catherine, "I'm not sure what I have to offer."

Archie cocked his head to the side, "You are honestly telling me you have no idea who's coming after you? No idea where the kill order could have originated from within the CIA?"

It sounded more like an accusation than a question. Travis shot up out of his seat and crossed his arms across his chest, pacing. He stopped, spinning back to face Catherine and Archie who were staring at him, neither of them moving a muscle. "Honestly? No. I can keep saying the same thing over and over again, but if you don't believe me, that's your problem. I've spent the last five years on my ranch, minding my own business. As far as who could be coming after me from before that time? That I have no idea of either. I'm sure if you've dug through my files, then you'll know as well as I do that the list is long and varied as to who I might have offended." He set his jaw. "I'm happy to help you guys as much as I can, but I'm not going to be accused of something that's not true."

As if something he said had tripped a silent alarm, Archie and Catherine got up from their seats almost simultaneously and walked out of Archie's office without saying anything, leaving Travis by himself. As they passed, Archie simply set a meaty hand on Travis's shoulder.

Travis had no idea what to think. He was so angry, he could feel the heat rise to his cheeks, the woosh of blood rushing past his ears. Travis looked over his shoulder at the door. What was going to happen next, he had no idea. For all he knew, a phalanx of MI6 officers would arrive at Archie's office door at any second, drug him, throw a black hood over his head and drag him off to a black site, never to be seen again. He closed his eyes for a second and shook his head. How had he managed to get himself in yet another scrape?

A moment later, Catherine opened the door. She was alone. She waved to him, "Let's go," she said, waving him forward.

No phalanx of officers. At least that was something.

Travis scooped up the bag of medical supplies Dr. Walsh had given him and picked up Catherine's messenger bag for her, handing it to her in the doorway. He followed her as they walked back through the cubicle outside of Archie's office and back to the main area of MI6, neither of them saying anything.

By the time they wound their way through the traffic in the busy cubicles on the main floor of MI6 and back out through the anteroom, Catherine giving a nod to the armed guard as they left, it was late afternoon, pushing towards dinnertime. As they emerged into the fresh air outside, Travis noticed it had clouded over, a solid gray blanket of low-lying stratus clouds blanketing the sky. He walked to the Volvo, following Catherine, thoughts turning in his head, his mood not much different than the weather. Now what? He glanced at her as she pulled the Volvo out of the parking spot at Vauxhall Cross, her hands gripping the wheel tightly.

Still not addressing his blowup in the office, Catherine wove the Volvo out into traffic, driving nearly on the bumper of the transport bus in front of her, which was ironically marked, "Children on Board. Give Distance," with yellow and black caution paint decorating the back. "Does everyone in England tailgate?"

Catherine frowned, "Tailgate? What does that mean?"

Travis pointed, "You all drive so close to each other, first the cab driver, now you. Is it a thing here in England? I don't remember it from the last time I was here."

"Tailgate," Catherine said as if she was trying on the word. "I haven't heard that one before. Must be an American expression." She glanced over her shoulder at Travis, "I suppose if that's the way you'd like to define it, then yes. We do all drive close together. It's more efficient, I think."

"And dangerous," Travis mumbled.

Catherine raised her eyebrows, "That coming from someone with a bounty on his head? Well, then..."

Travis could tell by Catherine's attitude that she was trying to lighten up whatever strain had happened between them in Archie's office at Vauxhall Cross. Travis wasn't ready to let go of things quite that fast, though. The muscles in his back tensed thinking about it, "What was that back there?"

"What are you talking about, Travis?" Catherine asked innocently; as if she'd not been part of the same meeting he'd been in.

Travis pressed his lips together, "You know as well as I do, Cath. You and Archie came at me pretty good. And then he disappears. I thought you Brits were supposed to have good manners. Doesn't exactly seem like the best way to treat a guest." Travis knew the words sounded like he was angry and grumpy. He was. Over the last twenty-four hours, someone tried to kill him twice, he'd been stuffed in a metal tube and shot across the Atlantic Ocean, only to then be harangued by British intelligence. They'd invited him as a guest, but were treating him more like a suspect. It wasn't sitting well.

"Are you bent out of shape about Archie's questions?" A half-smile tugged at Catherine's cheek, "Travis, he was just doing his job. He didn't become the Director of MI6 for nothing, you know."

"And why did he leave our meeting so suddenly?"

She blinked. "Got called to Downing Street by the Prime Minister." Catherine chuckled, "I know you think you're important, Travis, but when the Prime Minister calls, Archie has to go."

Travis turned and looked out the side window of the sedan

trying to bite his tongue. Catherine's sarcasm was baiting him, like a cat batting at a mouse. He didn't like the feeling, that was for sure. He sat for a second, not saying anything and then looked back at her, "All right, where are we going now?"

"Someplace we can get to work."

21

Forty minutes later, on the other side of London, well outside of what would be considered downtown, Catherine pulled down a side street, made a sharp turn onto an alley, and emerged onto another side street behind it, slipping the Volvo into the last parking spot left on the street before the corner.

Travis frowned, looking around. From what he could see, Catherine had parked the car in an area that looked like an enclave for Indian expatriates. The signs running up and down the street were half in English and half in a scrolled writing Travis couldn't understand. Probably Hindi, if he had to guess, or some other dialect. He squinted. It looked like Devanagari script. What was the national language of India? Was it Hindi? He couldn't remember. The signs boasted of spices and food, an electronics market directly across the street from where they'd parked, a dry cleaner, and a bookstore down the street on the opposite corner. Looking around, they could have easily been in a suburb of New Delhi, rather than somewhere near London.

"Where are we?"

"It's called Little Delhi, the Indian borough," Catherine said, opening her car door, not taking the time to explain anything more. "Come on."

As Travis got out of the car, he pulled his backpack from the backseat and the bag of medical supplies Dr. Walsh had sent with him. He followed as Catherine walked down the sidewalk, darted into an Indian restaurant, the smell of garlic and cumin and coriander so strong it nearly made his eyes water, and then followed her to a set of steps at the back of the restaurant. On the landing for the second floor, they met a woman, a raven-haired petite mom with a nose ring wearing a long pink and orange sari with a baby strapped to her chest. She passed them in the hallway, not paying any attention to their presence other than giving them a slight nod. The baby was crying which didn't seem to faze the woman at all. She had a blank expression on her face as if nothing was going on. She simply paced back and forth bouncing as she walked, trying to soothe the crying baby. By the time Travis looked to see where Catherine had gone, she was at the end of the hallway, disappearing into a doorway. He saw her glance in his direction. He jogged to catch up, following her.

The door shut firmly behind him and Catherine led Travis into the flat. He frowned, "What's this place?" He set his backpack and the bag of medical supplies down on an olive-green couch that had been placed against the wall, across from a single chair and a square brown coffee table.

"It's one of our safe houses. We're going to be staying here. Archie said we could use it."

Glancing around, it didn't look like much, certainly not as nice as the one Catherine had taken him to when he first arrived at Heathrow. "Why this one?"

Catherine went to a window at the other end of the flat,

pushing the curtain aside and cracking it open. A cool breeze from outside floated in, carrying more smells of food cooking — garlic and cumin and rice.

Catherine raised her eyebrows, "Believe it or not, this is one of our most secure locations. You have to have special permission from Archie to use it. There are only a handful of our flats around the country that are this well-hidden. Not to mention it gives us easy access to the freeway system and a couple of airports if we need them."

"And to think Archie didn't like me…" Travis mumbled.

Catherine smiled. "Are you referring to the grilling you got last hour?"

"You could say that."

Catherine brushed by Travis resting her hand on his arm as she passed, "Now Travis, don't take things so personally. Try not to be so sensitive. I'll bet if we get you some food and let you rest for a few minutes you will feel more like yourself."

"And what if I don't?" The one thing Catherine was right about was that he was feeling surly. Her constant pleasant tone was beginning to grate on his nerves.

"You will, dear. Just give me a few minutes to make things right. Why don't you relax and put on the telly for a few minutes while I take care of dinner?" The comment sounded more like they were an old married couple than two spies.

Travis blinked. For a second, he was confused about what she was saying and then realized she meant the television. He nodded without saying anything else, sat down on the couch, kicked off his boots, and put his feet up on the coffee table. He looked around as she disappeared out the door. Where she was going, he had no idea, although she'd left her cell phone, keys, and messenger bag nearby, so she'd be back. Or at least that was his hope.

Flipping through the channels on the television, Travis saw

the programs offered one of two choices — a nearly constant review of either what the Queen was doing or American politics or soccer games that seemed to never end. Football, he reminded himself. He left the football game on, listening to the announcers yell as one of the teams on the field scored a goal, the players all running out and hugging and jumping on each other as the referees signaled the point. Travis stared at it but couldn't get excited. Soccer was still pretty foreign to him. Football, he reminded himself again, shaking his head.

By the time he'd clicked his way through three more channels of ongoing football games, the door to the small flat opened, Catherine returning, carrying a flimsy white plastic bag. Through it, he could see Styrofoam boxes stacked up inside. "I got dinner!" she said, as though she had accomplished a major feat.

Travis cocked his head to the side. In a way, it was funny how she'd shifted to being domestic so quickly. He felt his stomach rumble. If that was how she wanted to play it for the time being, that was fine with him. He hadn't eaten anything since the night before when he'd gotten on the plane and picked at the gummy pasta covered with plasticky cheese sauce. "Thanks. What did you get?"

"Come and see," Catherine said, setting the bag down on a small, round wooden table with two matching ladder-back chairs in the corner of the room. She pulled the containers out, set them on the table, and then looked towards the kitchen, "Now, if I can just find some plates and napkins we will be all set."

A second later, Catherine returned with an armload of gear for their dinner including two bottles of water, metal cutlery, and white plates, plus a stack of paper napkins. She set everything down on the table, placing the plates in front of each chair and flanking them with the cutlery, taking a moment to fold the paper napkins and put the water bottles in their proper spot on the place setting, as if they were at a fine dining event.

Travis stood by, watching. He narrowed his eyes. "We didn't need all that, Cath. I would've been happy to eat right out of the box."

Catherine shook her head, "Nonsense. The food doesn't taste as good if it's not on a proper plate. Now, sit down. Let's eat while it's still hot. Umar sent us quite an assortment."

"Umar?"

"Yes," Catherine said, sliding into her seat across from Travis, "He owns the restaurant downstairs. He and I have become quite the fast friends. Sometimes I stop by for food even when I'm not staying here at the flat. He has the best Indian food I have ever eaten outside of India."

Over giant scoops of Tandoori chicken, Biryani rice with lamb, buttered naan, and pyramid-shaped samosas, filled with spiced potatoes, onions, and peas, Travis and Catherine spend the next few minutes eating. Their conversation turned from work to things a bit more casual. Catherine talked about when she'd been stationed in India and China for a time and how she'd grown to love the people and their food, but hated their governments and how the people were forced to live. Travis talked about the horses and the peace he'd found at the ranch.

Travis stopped and looked at his plate. The food was delicious; fragrant and spicy without being overwhelmingly so. His mouth was filled with the pungent taste of yogurt sauce on something Catherine had referred to as murgh kari, a chicken curry Omar had sent up for them to enjoy. They finished the meal with a sticky pastry that reminded him of something he might get in Greece, the outside crispy but the inside creamy. What it was exactly, he wasn't sure. He could only identify the flavors of cinnamon and honey in it. Whatever it was, it was delicious.

Wiping his face with the folded paper napkin Catherine

had set at his place, Travis leaned back in his seat and sighed. He was full and relaxed. Finally. He blinked a couple of times and then the thought hit him that while he might be off the grid temporarily, he couldn't run forever. Despite the calm he was having at the moment, the bounty was still on his head. Whether he liked it or not, he was going to have to deal with it. "This has been a nice break from the chaos, but what's next?" he asked, crumpling his napkin and tossing it on his plate. He was suddenly eager to get to work, whatever that meant.

Catherine got up from the table, took the two plates, and walked into the kitchen without answering. A moment later, Travis heard water running as if she was doing the dishes. Hearing the plates being replaced in the cabinet, she walked back and sat down in front of him. Taking a sip of her water, she looked at him. "Well, I suppose it's time for you to make a decision."

"And what decision is that?"

"If you want to help us."

Travis frowned. "I already told you I would."

"Then you need to tell me what you know."

Travis shrugged, his eyes wide. Were they having this conversation again? "I already told you, I don't know anything. I have no idea who's coming after me and I've never heard of this Jonah Hudson character you mentioned earlier. You want to clue me in as to what's going on here?"

Catherine looked away for a moment and then back at Travis, "Archie thinks the threat came from someone close to you. Someone you know well. Based on the chatter I've seen, I'd have to agree. This is somebody who knows a lot of your back story, things that other people wouldn't know. So I need you to think, really think, Travis, if there is anyone that might come after you."

Travis got up from the table and walked to the window, staring out. The fact that whoever put the bounty on him had personal details about his life was troublesome. It was the first he'd heard of that. He glanced back at Catherine, "How personal? Can you give me an example?"

"Well, they know you killed someone on your property a few months back using an antler head mounted on the wall of your front porch. Does that sound personal enough?"

Travis's mind drifted back to the moment when Uri Bazarov's men had attacked his ranch, trying to steal Elena Lobranova and the Moscow brief away from him and his protection. Elena. He chewed his lip, shaking his head. "The only other person there when that happened was Elena Lobranova. You're not saying —."

Catherine cocked her head to the side. "I'm not saying anything, Travis. You are."

The thought scratched at the back of Travis's mind like nails on a chalkboard. Was it possible Elena was behind the kill order? He knew she'd gotten a promotion with the CIA, but they were on good terms. Always had been. She'd helped him with the Mardi Gras case and had even come to his hospital room to see him afterward, before he headed back to Texas. No, it couldn't be. "I just don't see how that could be a possibility," he said. "We've worked together for years." His face flushed, "I mean not consistently, but she and I were partners when I was active with the CIA."

"But not anymore?" Catherine said, the words coming out slow and measured.

Travis narrowed his eyes. It felt like she'd led him right into a trap, he'd fallen for it, and it had sprung. "No. How many times do I have to tell you? I got sucked into the plot to kill President Mosley and the bombing in New Orleans. It was nothing more. I'm not on the payroll."

"So you aren't working on the side with the CIA or any of the other American agencies, or a foreign one, for that matter?"

Travis balled his hands into fists and turned around, facing Catherine, "No," he growled. "Now can we get off this topic?"

"Well, we only want to be sure..."

Catherine got up from her seat at the table and closed the food that was left over from dinner, not saying anything else. The dishes were done, but the food still needed to be put away. As she walked into the kitchen, Travis looked back outside. Travis was furious, furious at himself for allowing Catherine to beat him, furious at the situation, and furious that Elena's name had even come into the conversation. Elena had been loyal. Or at least he thought she had. The fact that Catherine and Archie were causing him to question every one of his relationships gave him pause. It felt like acid eating away at the edges of his soul, slowly dissolving the things he knew and morphing them into a new world where everything was unfamiliar.

After Catherine put the food away, she disappeared into the bedroom for a second, only to return wearing a pair of leggings and an oversized T-shirt. She'd pulled her hair back in a clip behind her head and washed the carefully applied makeup off her face. Where she had gotten the clothes, Travis wasn't sure. It wasn't like she had brought in any luggage with her. Another mystery. In her arms, she carried two blankets and two pillows. She set them down on the couch next to Travis, who had started watching another soccer game. "There's only one bedroom here. I thought perhaps..."

Travis nodded, "Yeah, I'm okay on the couch. No problem."

"Excellent. I have some reading to do. I'll see you in the morning. Have a good night's sleep."

Travis didn't look back as she walked away. He heard the door to the bedroom click closed behind her. He pulled his legs up onto the couch, fishing around in the bag Dr. Walsh had given him for the prescription of antibiotics. He popped one in his mouth and swallowed it dry, following it with a swig of water from the bottle Catherine had given him during dinner.

He stared at the television, the volume on low, the drone of the announcers still yelling in the background no match for the churning of the thoughts in his head.

Archie and Catherine had come at him pretty hard, but part of Travis wondered if they were right.

Did he know who was after him and just didn't realize it? Could the killer be that close?

22

"He's where?" Tom Stewart thundered.

The phone call had come in at seven minutes past four o'clock in the morning Eastern time. Tom slipped out of bed, hoping he hadn't woken Shelly, who was fast asleep on the other edge of the mattress.

"London, sir," Baker, the man Tom had charged with tracking Travis, said.

"London? What on God's green earth is Travis Bishop doing in London?"

"No idea, sir. I know you put out on the wire you were looking for his location. We tracked him coming in on a flight yesterday, noon our time, which would have been five o'clock..."

"I'm aware of the time change, you moron!" Tom yelled. In a way, he felt sorry for Agent Baker. It wasn't his fault he was on the other end of the line. After Tom had heard about the second failed attempt on Travis's life, the three mercenaries he'd hired to take out Travis on a back road on his way back to his little, podunk ranch in the middle of somewhere in no-name Texas, Tom had lost his cool. He put out a location request to all of the CIA offices over the globe. It was a clear misuse of CIA resources, but at this point, he didn't care. Someone had to know where Travis had disappeared off to and he had a desperate need to find out.

Unfortunately for Agent Baker, he'd been the one who'd found Travis.

"I'm sorry sir. It's part of our normal protocol to walk through time changes for the people we work with. As I said, Agent Bishop —"

"He's no longer an agent! Why can't anyone get that right?"

Baker stammered, "Yes, sir. Of course. After Mr. Bishop arrived at Heathrow, he cleared customs…"

Tom waited for a moment, seeing if the young man was going to finish his sentence. Tom felt the heat rise to his cheeks, "And then what? You said he cleared customs, and then…?"

"No idea, sir. He completely disappeared after that."

"I thought the British had the corner on the market in street surveillance? Are you telling me that you lost him coming out of the airport and you haven't been able to locate him since?"

"That's partially true, sir."

Tom balled his fists, his knuckles turning white. "What part is true?" he hissed. Tom was doing everything he could to hold onto his temper. He was beginning to be convinced he was surrounded by idiots. It used to be he'd ask an agent for an answer and he'd get one. Now, there was a lot of vacillating and talking around the subject. It was as if all the political correctness had filtered down into everyone's speech. No one could give a straight answer anymore.

"About their surveillance, sir. It is true, that the British government has one of the most sophisticated street surveillance systems in the world. Of course, since I'm with the CIA, as you know, I don't have access to that. We had a person stationed out front just in case Mr. Bishop arrived in London. We saw him at baggage, but somehow he got lost in the crowd.

It's a very busy tourist time of the year here in London. June is typically the peak of the..."

Tom interrupted him again. "You've got to be kidding me! Do you think I care about the peak of the tourist season? Find him," Tom said, cutting off the call. He threw his cell phone, the plastic thudding against the wall before hitting the floor. If he'd hoped not to wake Shelly, it might be too late. He was sure the clatter would have accomplished exactly what he was trying to avoid.

Exactly thirty seconds later, Shelley came shuffling into the kitchen, her eyes puffy and her skin blotchy, a soft green robe wrapped tightly around her body. She limped over to where Tom's phone had fallen on the ground, picked it up, and set it next to him. "A lot of drama for four o'clock in the morning, don't you think?"

"You have no idea," Tom said, leaning his face into his hands as he rested his elbows on top of the cold marble of the kitchen island.

Shelley put her hand on his back, "Whatever it is, why don't you come back to bed and try to get some more sleep? The problem will solve itself in the morning." The way she said it made Tom remember the Shelley he'd married, the sweet young woman who'd do anything for him.

He shot up to a standing position, "In the morning? It is morning, Shelley."

Shelley's eyes widened, "Don't you start my day like this, Tom. I don't know what your problem is, but —"

"It's Travis Bishop."

Her eyes narrowed, "What about him?"

"The second attempt failed."

"You didn't tell me that."

Tom started to pace, his arms folded across his chest, his chin jutting out and his eyes bulging, "I didn't tell you because I didn't want to hear about it. You've been pestering me about this constantly. I have a job to do, one that's a lot bigger than Travis Bishop." As the words came out of his mouth, Tom glanced at her. He saw her swallow, as though she was ignoring his jab at her, pushing the torrent of caustic words that were forming back down into her stomach. For that, he was grateful. He was on edge in a way he'd never been before.

"Where is he now?" Shelley asked quietly.

"London."

"What's he doing in London?"

"I have no idea."

23

Sleep didn't come back to Tom, even though his body desperately wanted it. After hearing the news that Travis Bishop had escaped to London and nearly having a blowup with Shelley in the middle of the night, Tom went back to the bedroom, gathered his running clothes, and went back downstairs, using the guest bathroom to change. Shelley would be angry that he'd messed up a perfectly clean bathroom to get ready, but, in his defense, it was better than getting into a long, drawn-out argument with her before the sun ever came up.

He shrugged, if they had argued before the day ever started, it wouldn't be the first time. Their marriage had been pockmarked like the surface of the moon with arguments and disagreements, most of them having nothing to do with their relationship itself, nearly all of them having to do when their career interests competed and didn't align.

Outside, the early morning air was nearly still. Tom slipped in a pair of earbuds and started his running playlist as he did a few stretches at the end of the driveway, the electric guitar from a Van Halen riff thrumming in his ears. He glanced back at their house, a white-sided colonial with black shutters barely visible in the night, except for a few lights that were placed in the landscaping around the outside of the house, casting a golden glow on the landscaping. He waved to the car that was positioned at the top of his driveway. With his position in the CIA and Shelley's as a Senator, they had a security detail that sat on the house nearly constantly. They weren't the only ones in their development who did, Tom thought, starting up a slow jog. Their neighbors were a range of corporate executives and high-level government workers, all of whom were well-versed in private security, especially the Supreme Court Justice that lived down the street, who had recently had their address broadcasted on the internet, doxed, it was called. That house now hosted a nearly constant contingent of protestors on the other side of the street. Tom gave the agent in the car another wave as he trotted by.

Tom's body was far more cranky and sore than he expected it to be that early in the morning. Whether it was the lack of a full night's sleep, waking up to bad news, or perhaps even the whole Travis Bishop business hanging over his head, he didn't know. All he knew at that moment was it felt like every muscle, tendon, and ligament in his body had been ratcheted down against the bones, unwilling, or unable to function in the way it should have. Not that he was expecting to be as flexible as Gumby, especially not at his age, but the level of tension in his body wasn't something he was used to.

After the first mile or so, his body started to loosen up, his breath was still heavy, but only at predictable intervals. Tom felt the thunder clouds in his head dissipate. His mood was still gloomy, that was for sure, but gloom was much more tolerable than fury.

Turning the corner and heading down Station Street into the center of town, Tom glanced around. The majority of the businesses he passed on the main drag through the suburban neighborhood of Conklin, Virginia where he and Shelley lived, just outside of Washington, DC, were mostly closed. That was normal, given his early morning runs. They just weren't usually this early.

There were long shadows still being cast by the overhead streetlights in the darkness, the sky only beginning to lighten slightly as though someone had turned the dimmer switch up only enough to move the sky from pitch black to charcoal gray. Every now and again, the wash of headlights hit the sidewalk in front of Tom, someone headed to a destination earlier than most people ever dreamed of getting up, or going for a run, for that matter. For a moment, he wondered where they were going. Home after an overnight shift at the local hospital? Heading into the local police department for an early morning shift? Returning from vacation, just off a red-eye flight? The answers were endless. Normally, Tom enjoyed playing head games with himself while he ran, but not today. Tom glanced over his shoulder, crossing the street, heading into the park on the other side of Station Street, feeling the cool damp air pass over his calves and ankles, gently touching the sweat on his face and cooling him as he ran.

As his stride smoothed out, his thoughts did too. He began to realize he was glad he hadn't immediately called London. He could have. Four o'clock in the morning in Washington was nine o'clock in the morning in London. Certainly by then, his counterpart at MI6, Archie Elliott, would be in the office, or at least reachable. And nine a.m. was certainly not an ungodly hour to be making a phone call, unlike four o'clock in the morning.

Tom passed the park entrance, making his way through the parking lot. He lengthened his strides, picking up his pace. He was supposed to be training for his next half marathon, but no part of him was interested in his mile time that morning. He needed the run like he needed air. He needed space to breathe, to clear his head, to decide what to do next.

The park was even more abandoned than Station Street. Ahead of him, he saw a dark shadow scuttle off into the trees. He narrowed his eyes as he ran past. Probably a raccoon. He slowed slightly, waiting for his eyes to adjust to the darkness. The arching branches made it even more difficult to see. Tom realized he probably should have grabbed his headlamp before he left, but he was so preoccupied thinking about Travis Bishop he didn't. He chastised himself, making a mental note to get the lamp charged and stowed with his running gear.

Tom picked his way carefully along the trail finally emerging at the back of the loop, returning to the parking lot. He nearly tripped on a curb as he jumped over it and caught himself before he fell, the jostling sending pain through his body. He grimaced and grunted, pushing his body forward again, ignoring the shrieking of his nerves. "No excuses, Tom," he hissed to himself as he straightened out and picked up his pace. "No excuses."

And that included dealing with Travis Bishop.

By the time Tom got back to Station Street, darting between two cars that still had their headlights on, the glow in the sky had brightened enough that Tom knew if he took out his earbuds he would hear the call of birds chirping from the park across the street. He didn't take them out though, content to hear the thrum of the music in his earbuds urging him on. He felt the fabric of his shirt stick to his back. It was drenched with sweat as he swung his arms more forcefully. He was a strong finisher, whether it was on his run or in his life. Whatever problem he had, he'd finish it.

Exactly a half mile from his house, Tom broke down to a walk. The last mile had been brutal. He'd finished at nearly a sprint for the last eight minutes, the air catching in his throat, burning and tightening it to the point when every breath sounded more like a wheeze than anything else. He walked with his hands interlaced on the top of his head, allowing his rib cage to expand and suck in all the oxygen it could handle. His soaked shirt was stuck to his back even in the cold summer morning air. He felt the heat rise to his cheeks as the blood from the run redistributed itself over his skin.

Instead of walking right up his driveway, Tom walked past, dropping his arms to his sides, and swinging them loosely. He needed another second to cool down, both physically and mentally. That two attempts on Travis's life had failed was unacceptable. The fact that he'd arranged the attacks and they hadn't worked out the way he wanted was even worse. He would have fired one of his agents for less. But he couldn't exactly fire himself, now could he?

But that didn't eliminate the problem of Travis. He needed to be dealt with. And soon.

24

By the time Tom walked back into the house, Shelley was up, working in the first-floor office they sometimes shared when they got along well enough. Whether it was because she had pressing Senate business or she was like him, and simply couldn't get back to sleep again, he had no idea. He only glanced at her as he walked by, taking the steps upstairs into his long, thin legs still warm from his run. He said nothing.

Twenty minutes later, Tom was back downstairs in the kitchen. It was still early. Even with his run, his shower, and the early morning dustup with Shelley, it was only six thirty in the morning. But he was dressed and ready for work, wearing a pair of pressed gray slacks, brown-toed oxfords, a matching brown belt, starched white shirt, and maroon tie. The matching suit coat to his pants was carefully shouldered over one of the chairs at the kitchen island. He packed his briefcase, grabbing a protein bar from the cabinet nearby and taking a couple of bites of it before tossing the rest of it in the trash, frowning. Why couldn't they make bars that didn't taste like chalk? He shook his head and was walking out the back door when he heard Shelley call behind him, "Leaving already?"

He spun around, surprised by her voice. He expected to walk out the door that morning without any other interaction with her, ignoring the spat they'd had a couple of hours earlier. He nodded, "Yes. I have some things I need to take care of."

Shelley glared at him. She was still wearing the same robe she'd been in before he'd gone for his run. "Yes, you do. See that things get taken care of, Tom. We can't afford any problems."

Her words felt like a punch in the gut. She wasn't telling him anything he didn't know already. It was just like her to pour salt in the wound. He licked his lips, pushing the urge to fight back away, but it was his turn to swallow and swallow hard. He turned back towards the door and disappeared outside without saying anything else.

Stopping in the driveway for a second, he considered whether to ask the officer sitting in front of the house to give him a ride to the office, but he changed his mind, slipping into the sleek black BMW sedan he'd purchased two months before. As he started up, he settled himself on the tan, custom leather seats. Part of him wanted to smile. There weren't many of his colleagues who could afford a luxury vehicle like the one he had or the vacation he and Shelley were planning for early that coming fall — an anniversary trip that would take them to Greece, Italy, and Spain on a private tour, just the two of them to see the most romantic spots the Mediterranean had to offer, if their marriage lasted that long…

But then again, he wasn't a typical CIA director.

He pressed his lips together. As much as he liked his toys and vacations, he wouldn't be able to enjoy them much if he didn't deal with Travis. Thumbing through his phone at the next stoplight, Tom found the contact information for MI6 Director Archie Elliott and pressed connect, hearing the overseas dial tone in short bursts pumped through the custom stereo system in the BMW. He could have waited until he got into the office to make the call, using one of the SCIFs, a sensitive, compartmented information facility, to make sure that his call was private, but then again, nothing was private in the CIA. Spies had a bad habit of spying on each other. His car was probably the most private space he owned at that moment.

"Is that you, Tom?" A booming voice with a thick British accent came over the line.

"Archie? Yes. Thanks for taking my call."

Tom had met Archie at a cybersecurity intelligence conference five years before when they were both making their way up the ranks in their respective agencies. They'd become fast friends, sharing dinner and drinks together every night of the conference, swapping war stories as only two seasoned field agents could, talking about the shortcomings and the strengths of each of their agencies, their lips loosening the more liquor they drank.

And then like a one-night stand, their friendship had quickly changed gears when they returned to their respective agencies, resuming a more professional tone the next time they'd connected, nearly eight months later when Archie had received a promotion to division lead at MI6. Tom had called to congratulate him and they'd had a quick conversation.

Their relationship had adopted a friendly, professional tone over the last five years. As each of them rose in the ranks, the other would take a moment to make a phone call, and offer well wishes on major holidays and family occasions. "I'm surprised to hear from you this morning," Archie said, sounding vaguely out of breath.

"Why's that? I can't call an old friend out of the blue?" Tom tried to sound casual, but hearing Archie's voice on the other end of the line made him feel anything but.

"Of course not! I welcome your calls at any time day or

night, Tom. What's on your mind? Did I miss a promotion and you were calling to scold me?"

"No," Tom shook his head, pressing the accelerator as he veered onto the freeway, heading into DC proper. "I'm hoping I didn't miss one of yours?"

"No, no. Of course not. Nowhere else for me to go."

Tom was getting tired of the banter. It was time to get to the point. "Listen, Archie, I'm calling today on business."

"Well, bring it on."

Tom could hear the murmur of voices in the background. "Am I calling at a bad time?"

"No, not at all. I'm in between meetings. That said, I have exactly two and a half minutes before I am due in another. Can you make it quick, or shall I call you back?"

Tom swallowed, looking at the clock on the onboard display. It was late morning in London. If his schedule was anything like Tom's, Archie was likely in the middle of a whole slew of meetings. Tom glanced up in time to slam on the brakes, avoiding ramming into a semi-truck paused in the middle of the freeway, the morning traffic already stop and go even though it wasn't even seven a.m. in Washington yet. He swore under his breath, "No, I'll make it quick." He gripped the steering wheel tightly, the shock of almost slamming into the truck in front of him settling into his bones. He sucked in a breath and relaxed his hands. "Archie, one of our former agents may be in your backyard. I'm hoping you can keep an eye out for him."

"And who's this chap you are looking for?"

"Travis Bishop."

There was a pause on the other end of the line, "Can't say the name sounds familiar. What's your interest in him?"

Tom pressed his lips together. There was danger in getting another agency involved. If Archie knew the CIA was looking for Travis, his first question would be why. It would've been

Tom's as well. If the CIA was looking for someone, especially someone who was a former agent, the individual must offer some value or, conversely, a threat. Tom knew he needed to speak carefully. Time was running out and he needed to assure Archie that it was nothing more than the CIA wanting to have a chat with Travis. "It's nothing really, some old information has come up on a past file that Agent Bishop worked on. We're trying to wrap our brain around what happened, but the reports are sketchy, to say the least."

Archie grunted, "Those dodgy reports. I'm constantly on my people for more detail. You never know when you might need it."

"Exactly," Tom felt himself relax. "Anyway, we looked for him stateside, but it looks like he might be in your neck of the woods. If you happen to bump into him, could you send him my way? It would be much appreciated." Tom drew out the words "much appreciated," to stress his feeling about it. Hopefully, Archie would interpret it that if he was helpful to Tom that someday, Tom would happily return the favor.

"Of course, old friend!" Archie boomed. Tom could hear more noise behind Archie, "Now, if you'll excuse me, my next meeting is waiting. If I hear anything about this Travis Bishop chap, I will be more than sure to send him your way with your most pleasant regards."

Overly enthusiastic, but at least it was a positive response. "Thanks, Archie."

Tom hung up the phone just in time to hear a loud honk behind him. The semi he'd almost hit had eased forward and the drivers behind him were getting impatient.

They weren't the only ones feeling impatient. Now, if he could just find and stop Travis Bishop before it was too late...

25

Travis and Catherine were on their way back to MI6 headquarters when the call from Archie came in. "You will never guess in a million years who phoned me," Archie said.

Even over the speaker in the car, Archie's voice echoed. Travis watched as Catherine turned the volume down, a sly smile on her face as she glanced at him.

"Who would that be?"

"My old friend Tom Stewart from the CIA."

Travis stared into the distance a wave of confusion crashing over him. He gripped his hands into fists. Tom Stewart? Why was he calling? And why now?

26

Just as Tom Stewart was pulling his BMW past the guard shack at Langley, his phone rang. "Good morning," he said absentmindedly.

"And good morning to you, Director Stewart," the voice from the other end of the line said.

Tom bristled. The man on the other end of the line didn't need to identify himself. It was Ercan Onan. "What do you want?" Tom hissed.

"Now don't be surly so early in the morning, Tom." There was a pause. "We need to meet."

"When?"

Tom tried not to groan. His day, which looked like it was beginning to turn around, took another abrupt U-turn. "Now."

"But I'm about to..."

"Now, Tom. Do I need to be more specific? Our normal spot, please. I'm pulling in as we speak. What's your ETA?"

Tom shook his head. He hesitated to answer the question. Everything he knew about Ercan Onan told him that the man and his network had an exact idea of Tom's location every single moment of every single day. It was preposterous that

Ercan even asked. Tom grunted, "Twenty minutes, give or take a few with traffic."

"I'll be waiting."

Spinning the black BMW around in a circle and heading back out of the gate, Tom gritted his teeth. The morning, which had started off badly, had now taken another downward turn. Reaching into the glove box, he pulled out a bottle of antacids and popped four in his mouth, chewing the pastel-colored chalky fruit-flavored tablets and washing them down with a half-consumed bottle of water he'd left in his car from the day before. He hated that he had to keep something so cheap and pedestrian as antacids in the glovebox of his custom-made BMW, but with the way his stomach had been feeling, he didn't have much of a choice.

Tom had seen Ercan at an investors conference for the Desert Indigo hedge fund three years before. He was a small man, short and thin with dark hair and an even darker beard. No matter the weather, Ercan always had on a sweater vest. It made him look more like a college professor than an investor.

At the time, Tom thought his introduction to Ercan, a Turkish national, was coincidental and the first time they'd met. Now, he knew better.

Over cocktails on the first night of the event, Tom had shown up alone, unsure of what to expect. He had gotten a surprise invitation to the hedge fund's conference only a couple of days before, the manager, a man named Jonah Hudson, calling him personally. "I've heard wonderful things about you, Tom. We are looking for additional investors for the Desert Indigo hedge fund. I was wondering if we might send the jet and have you and your wife join us for a quick twenty-four-hour getaway so you can learn a little bit more about us and so we can learn a little bit more about you. How does that sound?"

At first, Tom was suspicious. The call had come out of the blue with no information as to how Jonah Hudson had heard about Tom. He had muttered on the phone, "I'd be happy to look at the details. Can you email them to me?"

"My assistant just did. I'm looking forward to meeting you in person," Jonah said and then hung up.

Checking his email, Tom found the message from the hedge fund with a personal invitation, travel arrangements, and a note from Jonah saying how much he was looking forward to meeting Tom.

Like any good CIA agent, Tom immediately went to the database and started gathering information about the hedge fund itself. He remembered his eyes widening when he realized that Jonah Hudson managed the largest hedge fund in the world with over five hundred billion in assets, nearly half a trillion dollars. Most remarkably, the hedge fund itself, like all hedge funds, was invitation only. No average investor could express an interest in buying into Desert Indigo and be accepted. The hedge fund was much more like an exclusive, invitation-only country club than anything else. Tom had checked their website, seeing a picture of Jonah Hudson in what Tom's father would have called his, "sincere suit" — a well-tailored charcoal gray jacket, muted light blue shirt with a matching tie and pocket square. Jonah's face looked calm with the suggestion of a smile, but not one, not actually. His thin blond hair was combed off to the side and he had a small frame from what Tom could tell by the picture.

At the time, Tom's interest, not to mention his ego, had been piqued. He read through the information from Jonah's assistant and quickly penned an email back, accepting for himself and regrettably declining for Shelley, without asking her. His gut told him he should go alone.

That was on a Tuesday. The private jet from Desert Indigo picked Tom up that Friday afternoon at a private airfield field between Washington and Virginia. Tom had told Shelley that he was going to a conference. She'd been so busy with work that she merely nodded and asked when he would be back. "Saturday evening. Not sure what time. I'll keep you posted."

She nodded again without looking up from her computer, a stack of documents piled next to her. It was probably pending legislation that needed to be reviewed, Tom realized as he headed out the door.

As promised, on board the private jet from Desert Indigo he was greeted with a crystal flute of champagne and told to relax until they landed. He'd traveled on the private jet with the CIA, but it was nothing like the treatment he'd gotten from the hedge fund. Three hours later, his belly full of a lobster and steak dinner, the plane touched down in Aspen, Colorado and a long, sleek black limousine pulled alongside with a fully liveried driver dressed in a black suit, white shirt, and black tie graciously opening the door for Tom. "Good evening, Mr. Stewart. I'll have you at the conference in no time at all. Feel free to relax and enjoy the ride."

Whisked to a luxurious mountain resort, the ride in the private plane and the limo was nothing compared to the next twenty-four hours. Tom was wined and dined with only the finest foods and drinks, the professional wait staff attentive to his every need. The entire conference only included about fifty people, with plenty of time to take breaks in between Jonah's presentations on what the hedge fund was investing in and their current goals for the market. He was even presented with the Mont Blanc pen to take notes with as he listened to Jonah's finely honed talking points.

That's when he had met Ercan. The diminutive man seemed to take an extra interest in Tom, asking him questions, but not being overly nosy, at least not in a way that would have sent Tom's CIA hackles into overdrive.

By Saturday afternoon, as Tom was getting ready to check out of the resort and meet his limo for the ride to the jet which would take him back to DC, Jonah met him in the lobby. "I do hope you enjoyed yourself," Jonah said in his thick British accent.

"I certainly did. I can't thank you enough. I learned an awful lot."

Jonah grabbed Tom's arm and tugged him away from the cluster of people who were visiting in the lobby as they waited for their limos to take them back to their destinations. "I do hope you understand, Tom — may I call you Tom?"

Tom nodded.

"...That an invitation into a hedge fund like Desert Indigo doesn't come regularly. In fact, it's a once-in-a-lifetime offer, if I may be so bold. This past year, we only extended invitations to three new investors. Only two this year. You are one of them, which makes you part of a very select crowd."

Tom narrowed his eyes. Was this a sales job?

"Now listen," Jonah continued, glancing at the floor and then looking back at Tom with watery blue eyes, "you may be thinking that this isn't the type of opportunity for you, that the buy-in would be too large, but we know that you have the funds to get yourself started."

Tom cocked his head to the side, "You do?"

Jonah chuckled, "Of course we do. You're in the spy business, Tom. You know how easy it is to get information on people. We need to do our due diligence before we even introduce ourselves to one of our investors. Now, normally, the buy-in for our fund is one million dollars."

Tom swallowed. He and Shelley didn't have a million to invest, not even close.

Jonah continued, "But, the other investor that we are bringing in this year is considerable. That has given us a unique opportunity to lower that for you, as long as you can keep it quiet."

"How much lower?" Tom felt perspiration bead on his upper lip.

"Two hundred thousand."

Tom stared off in the distance and then swallowed. He didn't say anything.

"Now, I know that it might sound like a lot of money, but based on our research, you have over three hundred thousand set aside in your 401(k). And I can promise you, taking two hundred out and giving it to me to let me manage as part of the hedge fund will give you millions and millions of dollars of income that you normally wouldn't be able to enjoy."

Tom shook his head. He had to give it to Jonah. The man had done his research. It was true, Tom did have three hundred thousand in investments. He'd gotten two hundred of it when his parents had passed away after selling their house and splitting it with his brother. The investments Jonah was talking about included not only that money, but money that he and Shelley had put together. Tom scratched his chin. If he moved it without telling her... He shook his head, pushing Shelley and her concerns out of his head. "Okay. I'll do it."

"Excellent," Jonah beamed. He guided Tom back to a private office where a young woman, appropriately dressed in a navy-blue pantsuit waited, her hair tied in a neat ponytail. She looked up at Tom with wide emerald green eyes and then at Jonah. "Cynthia, Tom has decided to join our merry band of fools. You have his paperwork, don't you?"

"Certainly, Mr. Hudson." She thumbed through a stack of papers, turning them toward Tom and Jonah with a flourish. "They're right here."

Jonah pointed at the paperwork. "You can certainly sit and read every jot and tittle on the paperwork if you would like to, Tom, but the sum of it is that you are committing the money to the hedge fund for six months. At that point, we'll report back to you about how your money has grown." Jonah smiled, "And let me tell you, we have yet to have a six-month reporting period when it didn't grow..." He paused for a dramatic moment, "...significantly."

The word significantly hung in the air like a passing eagle riding the winds aloft. "All you need to do is sign right here and we will get you started. Six months from now, we'll be having a very pleasant conversation about how much money you've made. If things go as they have been," Jonah held up his hand, "and no promises, but you could be seeing double what you've invested today."

Part of Tom wanted to take a step back, read all of the information thoroughly, and talk to Shelley about it, but his body, as though it was on some sort of autopilot, stepped forward, took the silver pen Jonah had offered him from the inside of his suit coat and scrawled his name at the bottom of the documents.

"Excellent!" Jonah smiled, extending Tom his hand and pumping it vigorously, "I know you are going to be happy a few years down the line as we build the portfolio together. Congratulations, Tom, you are now part of the Desert Indigo family!"

And that's when the trouble with Ercan had started.

27

The relationship with Ercan had started slowly, Tom remembered as he gave the guard at the shack a brief wave and a half salute as he jetted out of the parking lot. The guard looked confused at Tom's quick U-turn. Tom ignored him and headed toward the freeway.

About six months into his relationship with Desert Indigo, Ercan called Tom asking for advice about the geopolitical situation in another part of the world. India, in particular. Tom remembered being surprised by the phone call, "Ercan, I'm glad you felt comfortable reaching out to me, but I have to be honest, that's not my area of expertise. I have a background with the Eastern bloc in Russia, specifically the Baltic countries, not really India."

The next request came a few months later, when Ercan wanted to meet for coffee while he was in Washington, DC, saying he wanted to get to know Tom better. "Since we are all part of Desert Indigo," Ercan said, his voice barely above a whisper on the phone, "I like to try to sit down with the other investors when I can. It's always good to share information when it's possible." He paused for a moment, "Of course, I understand that in your business, you have to be quite careful with what information you share…"

Since Ercan had admitted that Tom couldn't talk much, Tom agreed to the conversation, figuring he'd show up and listen. What could be bad about that?

From there, his connection with Ercan grew, the two men sending texts on a regular basis, Ercan sharing where he was — frequently somewhere between his family's home in Turkey, or somewhere else, like Paris, London, Toronto, Sydney, or Rio de Janeiro. Tom had no reason to question Ercan's motives for the first year, until one of the meetings where things changed, and changed dramatically.

Ercan had come into the meeting, wearing his customary sweater vest, looking pale and drawn, even with his dark skin. Tom was immediately concerned. This wasn't the Ercan he knew. "Are you all right, Ercan?"

"We've been struggling with some business issues that I cannot seem to get in front of," Ercan said, his head hanging. He spent the next few minutes describing an import-export issue one of his companies was having. Their entire shipment was stopped in New York Harbor, unable to proceed because of bad paperwork. "What's in the shipment?"

Ercan shrugged, "Just household goods. That's the thing that's so confusing about it. We've used this shipping company and this route for years. My father was the one that found it. And now, for some reason, they have stymied us."

Tom straightened in his seat, "Let me see if I can do something about that for you."

Ercan looked visibly relieved, "Oh, that would be wonderful. I would much appreciate it."

Ten minutes later, after a call to the CIA office in New York City, he had two agents down at the port, who quickly approved the paperwork as a matter of national security.

The next request Ercan made was more detailed and came

only a few weeks later, "Tom, I'm sorry to bother you, but I feel like I need your help again and you're the only person I know who has the power to assist me."

Part of Tom was flattered. Ercan and the other Desert Indigo investors played in a different league than Tom did, one that he'd never even known about until he'd met Jonah Hudson. The other part of him was concerned. Was this becoming a pattern with Ercan? He tried to play it off. "As you can imagine, I'm very busy."

"I know, I know. I wouldn't ask except that it's very important. My family is being harassed by a local tribal leader back in Turkey. I was wondering if you know anything about this? Is there anything we can do?"

Tom frowned. Turkey wasn't an area of the world where he had extensive experience. He'd only been there on a single mission early in his career. "Let me see what I can find out."

Feeling the pressure of the Desert Indigo family, Tom called his counterpart that ran the Turkish desk. "Yeah, there's a lot going on there now. We're in the middle of a major operation with the Navy SEALs, coordinating the end of a drug running and arms campaign. We just had a huge influx of drugs and weapons come into the New York Harbor. Can't figure out how it got through...."

The words rang in Tom's ears. He felt a cold sweat bead on his forehead. Stammering, he looked at his colleague and blinked, "Okay, thanks. I gotta go."

"But..."

Tom ran outside and called Ercan back away from prying ears. "You didn't tell me the truth about that shipment, did you?"

Ercan chuckled, "The one with the consumer goods in it?"

"That one? Yes. That's not all that was in that shipment, was it?"

Ercan's tone changed, his voice low, "Nope. Not by a long shot, as you Americans say."

Tom started to pace back and forth, "What have you done to me?" he muttered.

Ercan sighed, "Looks like we're in business together, now brother. And it's not the first time…"

28

The way Ercan had called him "brother" two years before rang in Tom's ears as he pulled up outside the abandoned warehouse in an industrial park on the border between Virginia and Washington, DC. Another black sedan was parked in front, a Bentley. Ercan sat on the trunk of it, his feet resting on the polished silver bumper. Tom shook his head, closing his eyes for a moment as he shifted the BMW into park. No one sat on a Bentley that way. No one.

Tom got out of the car and walked towards Ercan. "What do you want?"

"Now that's not the way you should greet a friend, do you think?" Ercan said, picking at a cuticle.

"I wouldn't exactly call us friends."

Ercan raised his eyebrows, a half-smile creeping across his face. "What would you call us then?"

"I have no idea."

"Well, given the number of state secrets you've handed over to me to keep a lid on your involvement in Desert Indigo, I'd say we're brothers." The words dangled in the air like bait. Tom swallowed, trying to ignore Ercan's comment. The last thing he wanted to do was get into an argument with him.

Tom surveyed the situation. Ercan sat on the trunk of the Bentley, the only muted spot on the otherwise gleaming vehicle. Wearing his sweater vest with a short sleeve shirt underneath, a pair of jeans and worn, stained tennis shoes, Ercan looked more like a little kid perched on the back of his dad's car than a powerful terrorist. Correction: Ercan didn't view himself as a terrorist. He viewed himself as a businessman. Only government types like Tom would define him as someone who brought terror to the United States and other countries.

Near the front bumper of the vehicle, two of his men stood nearby. They had the same dark hair, dark eyes, and black beard that Ercan did. They stood silently, watching. Men like Ercan Onan had enemies. Lots of them.

A sour smell from somewhere behind the warehouse carried on the light breeze toward Tom. It smelled like rotting trash, or something worse, maybe a dead animal. The smell reminded him of how he felt inside every time he talked to Ercan. Dead. A traitor.

"Earth to Tom? Come in Tom," Ercan said sarcastically, breaking Tom's train of thought.

Tom shook his head, narrowing his eyes. "There's no need for that, Ercan. I'm here. What do you want?"

"Just a little bit of information."

All of Ercan's requests started exactly the same. He needed a little bit of information in order to move one of his projects forward. Nothing too complicated. Nothing too demanding. Only a little nudge in the right direction. All of those nudges had turned into a big problem for Tom. "Information about what?" Tom crossed his arms in front of his chest. As he did, he noticed Ercan's eyes settle on him. His face was stony. Tom dropped his arms back to his sides, shoving his hands in his pockets. By the time he looked up again, Ercan's face had relaxed. "This request is very simple. I'm going to be moving a load of very important items out of Russia and into Mongolia tonight. I need to make sure that my people are not intercepted at the border."

Tom narrowed his eyes. "What exactly are you moving across the border?"

"You don't want to know," Ercan smiled.

Tom pressed his lips together. Ercan was probably right. He didn't want to know. He did a quick calculation. If Ercan was moving something into Mongolia, it was probably weapons. Straddling the mountainous territory between Russia and China, Mongolia was an easy passage for terrorists and other black marketeers with a limited government and lots of infighting. It wouldn't be a big deal to get arms into China or even to skirt the border and move shipments through Kyrgyzstan or Tajikistan, on their way to Afghanistan and into the hands of ISIS terrorists.

"We've chosen a southern route that will take the truck quietly over the border into Mongolia. From our own reconnaissance, we've seen the road is only patrolled infrequently. I need to make sure it stays that way. The ideal situation would be that no one was there."

"You know I can't change the patrol schedules. I don't have any control over what other countries do at their borders." It was a partial truth. Bribes could change many things, even border security.

Ercan narrowed his eyes. "But perhaps you can find out the patrol schedule for me? That way my shipment can make a smooth transition out of Russia. I know my clients would be very appreciative. And if they are appreciative of me, then I can be appreciative of you."

Tom frowned, "Meaning what?"

A smile tugged at Ercan's cheek, pushing the frames of his

silver glasses up a little higher on his face as he smiled, "Meaning I can keep your secret quiet for another day."

The words landed like a ton of bricks on Tom. It was the same thing Ercan had held over his head for the last couple of years. There was always the threat that Ercan would tell someone that Tom had gotten involved in the Desert Indigo hedge fund and that he'd passed on sensitive CIA information to unknown terrorists as a way to curry favor. Worse yet, Tom had become a multimillionaire in the process. Jonah's investment strategy had worked. Tom's original two hundred-thousand-dollar investment had grown to ten million. How, he wasn't exactly sure. All he knew was that was the balance that showed in his account.

Part of Tom wanted to kick himself. Why he hadn't done his due diligence on Ercan before they'd met the first time, Tom didn't know. Or rather, he did. Pride. What was that saying his mother used to repeat to him from the Bible? "Pride goes before a fall."

If his secret got out, it would be a big fall. His only hope was if he got to Travis Bishop before Travis realized what he knew. Time was running out.

"I'll have your information in a few hours, Ercan," Tom said, walking away.

29

"Say that again? Tom Stewart called you?"

As Archie grunted a yes, a knot formed in Travis's stomach, along with about a hundred questions. He narrowed his eyes. Why was Tom calling Archie? Naturally, the two men were work colleagues. The spy business was a small industry that got even smaller at the top. Very few individuals could claim they had access and information that people like Archie Elliott and Tom Stewart did at this stage of their careers. It was an elite club of men and women that had the power to turn and twist the tides of history across the globe at their fingertips, a club Travis had no interest in being a part of.

Catherine's voice interrupted Travis's thoughts, "He did, now did he? And I'm assuming there's a reason you're telling us this?"

"Indeed, indeed. Turns out he's looking for you, Travis. Said you have information on an old case they need help with."

Travis's stomach settled a bit. He'd gotten calls periodically over the last five years from agents asking him to walk them through a part of a past case he'd been assigned for more detail. Elena had even called a few times asking him to refresh her memory about something they'd done together. The call wasn't exactly surprising, except for the fact that it came from Tom and that it went to Archie. Why hadn't Tom reached out to Travis directly? Travis checked his cell phone. There were no calls from unknown numbers, blocked numbers, or anything else that would've indicated Tom had tried to reach out directly to Travis. The knot formed again in his stomach. "Did he happen to tell you what case he was interested in?"

"Unfortunately, no."

Travis glanced at Catherine who had a frown on her face. "We are on our way to MI6 now, Archie."

"Good, good. Come straight away to my office when you get here."

"Will do."

As Catherine ended the call, she glanced over at Travis. "What do you suppose that's about?"

Travis looked at her as she drove. Her brown hair, which had been in a perfectly straight bob the day before was now pulled back in a single clip at the back of her head. She was wearing the same glasses but had changed her outfit, wearing a flowered wrap dress over a pair of leggings, ballet slippers on her feet. As she turned the wheel of the Volvo around the corner, a stack of silver and gold bracelets jingled on her left wrist. Travis shook his head. The day before, Travis would have sworn Catherine was a young woman in law school, learning how to be a barrister, or a lawyer, in American lingo. Today, she looked like a woman who spent her time going to art and yoga retreats, more comfortable outdoors or in front of a canvas discussing the value of a line or the deep issues of the soul than anything else. Catherine was a master of disguise, even within her own wardrobe. He only hoped she wasn't disguising her own motives from him.

He shook his head, glancing at her out of the corner of his eye, "I have no idea…"

30

"Mr. Hudson, I have Darden Peco on the line for you."

Jonah glanced away from the trinity of three monitors he had perched in the center of his desk. He'd been sitting in his office watching the movements of the global markets, making notes on an old-fashioned yellow legal pad with a pen he'd gotten at the drugstore on his walk to work. A pack of six cost him just under two dollars. Glancing between the screens, he sometimes felt like the conductor of an orchestra. Each section was doing different things — oil was going down, bonds were stagnant, stocks, particularly in the mining sector, were seeing a slight rise. It was organizing and understanding all of that information that brought his investment strategy together. And with nearly half a trillion dollars to play with, it wasn't hard to win.

The offices of Desert Indigo, given that it was the largest operating hedge fund in the world, were surprisingly modest. When the fund had hit the one hundred-million-dollar mark, Jonah had asked his team to find a single floor in an office building in downtown Manhattan. It seemed like the right place to be for a hedge fund. They found an older building, one that needed a good deal of rehab in order to make it presentable, but could be rented for pennies on the dollar. After walking through it, Jonah looked at his assistant and the architect and said, "I don't want anything fancy. When you size the offices, make sure each one of them is exactly the same size, including mine."

The architect frowned, "Including yours?"

Jonah nodded, "Desert Indigo hasn't succeeded because of me. It has succeeded because of all of us working together. My office shouldn't be any bigger or more opulent than anyone else's. See to that, please."

The office that Jonah Hudson ended up with was exactly as he requested, the same size as every other office on the floor. He didn't keep a large staff. At that moment, it ranged between eighteen and twenty-two people, depending on the project he had going at the moment. He had a personal assistant, Cynthia, who helped him keep his schedule organized, managed paperwork, fielded phone calls and helped arrange events, but that was really the only staff that was dedicated to him. The remainder of the staff worked on investor relations, communication, and event planning, with the bulk of the personnel working in research.

And although Jonah relied heavily on his research team, he ultimately made all of the decisions himself. Desert Indigo either soared or sunk on his say-so.

Blinking, Jonah pulled off his glasses and wiped his eyes before responding to his assistant, "You said Darden?"

"Yes sir," came the voice through the speaker.

"Put him through. Thank you."

In addition to Jonah's sensibilities about office size, he also was a stickler for manners. "Manners matter," his mother used to say, God rest her soul, he thought.

"Jonah?"

"Mr. Peco! How nice to hear from you today." Jonah quickly opened up Darden's investment account on his computer and scanned it. With so few investors in Desert Indigo, it gave Jonah the benefit of knowing each of his investors personally. He felt like they were family — cousins and aunts and uncles, and even a few grandparents – that he was responsible for. "Are you in Albania? I've heard it's lovely this time of the year."

Jonah didn't spend much time researching his clients, but what he knew about Darden Peco was that he was high up in the Albanian mob. They were shrewd business people, ones who excelled at moving arms from country to country. Jonah frowned. He wasn't sure if Darden was involved in the drug trade as well. Drugs were not something that Jonah was interested in, but like any other industry, it had its place. After all, Jonah reasoned, taking drugs was someone's choice. It was never forced upon them. For better or worse, he believed fully in the free market economy.

"It is. I will be heading there shortly," Darden said, his voice a low growl on the other end of the line. He didn't reveal where he was presently and Jonah knew better than to ask.

Jonah blinked, focusing again on Darden's portfolio. Darden currently had nearly a hundred million in assets with Desert Indigo. He was one of the people that Jonah referred to as a "shuffler," someone who put money in and then took it out on a regular basis.

"I have some money I need to move," Darden grunted.

"Of course, of course. What did you have in mind?" Jonah narrowed his eyes. The one thing all of his investors had in common was their need to move their money from their underground business into the market to clean it, to make it legitimate. Every one of the Desert Indigo investors had significant off-the-books activities. Jonah tried quite hard not to think about exactly what those activities were. In reality, it didn't matter to him how they got the money, only that they had money to invest.

And invest they did.

His investors, with their illicit activities, frequently had trouble using regular banks throughout the world. Large cash deposits were questioned, and large cash withdrawals even more so. Jonah, with the structure of the Desert Indigo hedge fund, had been able to circumvent that issue for his investors.

It was a simple process. Jonah had negotiated a contract with the Century Nation Bank in the Cayman Islands. All cash deposits were presented there and deposited into a shell corporation owned by Jonah. From there, they were instantly transferred to the Desert Indigo account, only spending a microsecond in Jonah's shell account. That was the first step to legitimacy. Once in the Desert Indigo account, the cash was transferred to several different investment houses where Jonah did his trading. Within moments, cash that had been dirtied by drugs, sex trafficking, arms deals, and a hundred other crimes was clean as a whistle.

Once the money was in the system, newly cleaned and untainted from his client's business dealings, Jonah was able to invest it. Hedge funds operating in the United States weren't required to register with the SEC. Desert Indigo had a simple limited liability company structure with Jonah at the helm.

The best part of Desert Indigo was that like every other hedge fund, people had to be invited to participate. No average Jack or Jill off the street could join. After Jonah had stumbled upon his first two investors, Venezuelan oil investor, Gonzalo Laguna, and import-exporter Ercan Onan, those two men had recommended others who had the same cash needs that Gonzalo and Ercan's companies did.

Jonah had been able to invest Desert Indigo heavily in strong American companies like FedEx, Walmart, Alcoa, Caterpillar, AMEX, Goldman Sachs, Johnson & Johnson, and Walt Disney – all icons of American ingenuity in industry. His clients were industry leaders too, just not in industries that were well recognized or respected throughout the globe. Their structure allowed them to bring in cash that people like Ercan Onan and Gonzalo Laguna had acquired from real estate transfers, drug manufacturing, weapons, sex trafficking, and even illegal shipments of consumer goods, like oil and natural gas. As far as Jonah could tell, the black market was alive and well, perhaps even more so than the legal market. And no one seemed to care as long as Desert Indigo had plenty of money to invest in the stock market.

And they did.

Darden cleared his throat, "I have ten million to add to my portfolio and I need to withdraw five."

Jonah squinted at the screen, taking a moment to wipe his glasses off on the hem of his pressed white shirt. He wasn't wearing a tie that day, only a pair of pressed khaki pants and a shirt to the office with a pair of scuffed brown loafers he'd had since college. Though he wasn't dressed up, he always kept a clean suit in his office in case he needed to meet with the client at the last moment. Or more correctly, his assistant, Cynthia, made sure it was always available to him. Luckily, Darden was only a phone call and nothing more. "We can certainly arrange for that. When did you want to make the deposit?"

"We'll have the cash at the docks at two a.m."

"That's fine. I'll alert the bank and they will have a team ready to receive your deposit. And the five million you need moved, will that be going to your account in Switzerland?"

"Yes. Can you get it there today?"

Jonah stared at his screen, quickly adding a transfer request out of Darden's portion of the hedge fund and moving it to his Swiss account.

"While I have you on the phone, Darden, I see that you

have about twenty-five million that we need to get invested. You have any cash needs over the next six months? The transfer window is about to close and then you'll be locked in until the end of the year."

"Keep ten million in cash. We're flush other than that."

"Business is good then, I suspect?"

"Yes, very good," Darden responded in a thick accent

Confirming the transfer, Jonah said, "All right, Darden. You are all set. I'll have Cynthia send along the confirmation and the bank will see you at two o'clock this coming morning for the drop-off of your deposit. Please do feel free to call if you need anything else. Cynthia and I are always here to help."

The call ended with Darden's silence.

31

Senator Shelley Stewart had a pit in her stomach she simply couldn't get rid of.

She'd spent the last few hours sitting in a Senate intelligence hearing. She'd tried antacids, ginger ale, and mint tea, all of which kept her assistant running. None of it was working.

Being on the Senate Intelligence Committee was one of the many intersections between her work as a Senator and Tom's work for the CIA. More than once, they'd spent half the day together without saying a word to each other besides answering a few basic questions. Normally in the closed-door hearings, Shelley stayed quiet, letting the other senators ask their questions if Tom was testifying, trying not to get defensive of Tom when one of the opposition party members went after him. It was all bluster anyways. Most of the people that she served with on the intelligence committee had been to their house for multiple barbecues, cocktail parties, and weekend dinners. They all made it look good for their constituents, acting irritated and hitting on all the necessary talking points, especially when the TV cameras were in their faces, but behind closed doors, things were usually congenial. Usually.

The meetings that morning had been particularly dry and boring. Tom wasn't there. They'd received a briefing from liaisons with the FBI, NSA, and the Army on the status of North Korea. In her mind, North Korea was so far away from a legitimate threat that she wasn't exactly sure why they paid any attention to the country at all. Let them blow off a few missiles. No one really cared anyway.

Shelley stabbed at the legal pad in front of her with the pencil in her hand, making little dots on the paper. Then the tip broke. She set the pencil down, hoping that no one noticed her agitation at sitting still for so long. As she looked up, she caught the eye of Senator Jeff Akers directly across from her on the other side of the room. He smiled, raising his eyebrows. She gave a slight shrug. He looked down and then refocused on the Army general who was finishing his presentation.

Two minutes later, the noise of the gavel clapped against the wooden pad where it rested. Senator Linette Riggs closed the meeting. "This hearing is adjourned, everyone. Thank you for your time."

Shelley stood up, smoothing the black skirt down over her legs. She took a few halting steps forward, feeling like her body had stiffened while she sat. Having one leg shorter than the other didn't make moving any easier. She gathered up her paper, the broken pencil, the files she brought with her, and her bottle of water and shoved everything into her bag, along with her cell phone. She was just turning to leave when she heard a voice behind her.

"Shelley?"

Senator Riggs was calling behind her. Shelley stopped and waited for her colleague. Senator Linette Riggs was a veteran. She'd served in the Air Force, although in what capacity, Shelley couldn't remember. Linette had scratched and clawed her way to becoming Chair of the Senate Intelligence Committee. It was a high honor, one that Shelley was sure Linette wouldn't have even been considered for if she wasn't a veteran. Being former military did have perks when it came to working in Washington, DC. That hadn't been an option for Shelley with her leg, but she was happy another woman was getting to run the intelligence committee. It was a rare feat.

When she'd first met Linette, they'd spent the first few months figuring each other out, dodging each other like boxers in a ring, taking sporadic jabs at each other. Then after a working dinner one night that Shelley had been more than hesitant to attend, the two women had finally found their footing over containers of cold Thai food, sharing their career goals and their struggles with maintaining family and relationships and work at the same time.

"I wanted to check in with you. I've been hearing something strange," Linette said, speaking quietly, as she set her overflowing briefcase onto the chair next to where Shelley was standing.

Shelley frowned, shifting her weight to her longer leg, "About what?"

Linette looked over her shoulder in both directions as if she was checking to see who was nearby. Everyone except for the Capitol Hill police officer posted in the room had left. The officer wouldn't leave the room until she and Linette did. "It's about Tom, Shelley. I have quite a few friends on the banking committee and one of them pulled me aside. He knows we're friends. I guess they requested the CIA do a deep dive into some banking irregularities they found having to do with hedge funds that are operating out of New York. They've made the request a bunch of times and Tom has yet to provide them with data. Treasury already responded. People are getting nervous, Shelley. I thought you should know…"

Linette didn't wait for Shelley to provide a defense or an

answer. She picked up her briefcase, shrugged it over her shoulder and glanced back at Shelley as she walked away, raising her eyebrows. Shelley stared at the floor. Tom. She'd told him months ago to deal with Desert Indigo, to get them out, to legitimize what he'd done in some way. Once people were suspicious it was nearly impossible to stop the speculation. Tom hadn't taken care of the problem and now questions were being asked.

Gritting her teeth, Shelley picked up her briefcase, pushed her chair in, and walked out of the briefing room. She pulled her cell phone out of her pocket and typed a quick text to Tom, "Linette grabbed me. People are starting to ask questions."

Shelley was intentionally vague. Tom would know exactly what she was talking about. And if anyone ever asked what the problem they were referring to, Shelley would make up some lie. That's what politicians did, after all.

32

Tom raced back to Langley after his impromptu meeting with Ercan, stopping by the desk of the agent in charge of the Eastern Bloc, Elena Lobranova. He bent over her desk and whispered in her ear, "Elena, can you please pull the border patrol routes for the next week between Russia and Mongolia? I need whatever you can get for me in the next hour. Keep it off the books."

The faintest glimmer of concern crossed Elena's face as he made the request, but she didn't say anything, giving him a quick nod, "Of course, sir. I'll have it for you shortly. Should I email it?"

"No. Put it in a file."

In the digital age, it had become more and more common for there to be issues with digital transactions. Many crime organizations had gone back to doing things on paper, the old-fashioned way, using ledgers and notebooks like generations past. The CIA and other spy agencies had begun to do the same, keeping their most sensitive information on paper, where it could be quickly burned, shredded, or otherwise destroyed, unlike digital copies. Storing something on a computer, even something as simple as sending an email, was like writing it on a stone tablet. It could never be destroyed. There always seemed to be a copy of it somewhere on some server where it could be leveraged.

Tom strode away, looking at his cell phone. He'd gotten a curt message from Shelley telling him to take care of his problem because people on the hill were starting to ask. Another message from an anonymous number that he knew was Ercan telling him to bring the information back to a park at lunchtime that day. Tom shook his head. How had he gotten in the position of being Ercan's gopher?

Tom knew the answer to that and so did Travis Bishop, and it wasn't just Desert Indigo...

The next three hours went by quickly. Tom settled into his office, dealt with some emails, and attended a meeting of department and division heads who brought him up to date on a few ongoing operations that were happening that week. Luckily, there was nothing pressing. By the time he got back to his office, and settled in front of his computer, Elena was in his doorway. She knocked on the frame of the door, which was open, getting Tom's attention.

Elena had become one of his best agents, leading the analysis of Russia and the Eastern Bloc states. She was also a good friend of Travis Bishop's, and the irony of that wasn't lost on Tom.

She approached his desk, setting a file down on his desk, her expression neutral, although Tom guessed she had questions. They weren't asked. "I prepared the information you asked me for, sir. I had it a couple of hours ago, but you were tied up and I didn't want to leave it on your desk." She handed him a file.

Tom flipped through it quickly, seeing surveillance photos marked with times and troop movements, the prediction of how the border between Russia and Mongolia would be protected over the next week.

Elena cocked her head to the side, "These types of predictive analyses can be fraught with issues, as you know, sir. I did my best to detail where the border would be protected versus empty over the next few days, but it's not a perfect science."

Tom nodded. The information was good enough. It didn't have to be perfect. If Ercan couldn't get whatever it was he wanted across the border, that was his problem. Just thinking about Ercan's demands tightened his stomach. "Thanks, Elena. I appreciate it."

As Elena turned to walk away, Tom stopped her, "Hey, Elena?"

She turned around, her slight frame, ruby red lips, and blonde pixie haircut no indicator of how talented she was as an agent. "Have you heard from Travis recently? I know you guys are close. I was wondering how he's been doing."

It was a fishing expedition. Tom knew that. He watched Elena's face carefully for any flicker of concern. There wasn't any. That was good. He'd have to be careful not to push too hard. She was a savvy agent, one that could pick up on body language faster than most. Tom took a deep breath, keeping his face relaxed and friendly.

"Can't say I have, sir. It's been a few months. Last I heard, he was working on rebuilding the barn that got burned down. That's all I know. Did you need me to reach out to him?"

Tom shook his head slowly, "No, no," he said, trying to sound casual. "I was just thinking about him. Wondered how he was doing. You know, we do miss him around here." Tom tried to shift the conversation away from any specific request.

"That we do, sir." Elena glanced at the door, "If that's all…"

"Of course, Agent Lobranova. I know you've got a lot to do."

"Yes, sir. That I do."

33

As soon as Elena left his office, Tom gathered up the file Elena had given to him, plus a few more for good measure, his cell phone, a notepad, and his car keys. He stopped at his assistant's desk on the way out, "I've a few things to attend to. I'll be back."

"Yes, sir," the young man nodded without asking any questions.

He was a good assistant, Tom thought as he strode out of the building. One of the few people that didn't give Tom a hard time.

Ercan at least had the courtesy to choose a meeting place that was close to Langley rather than making Tom drive the entire way back out to the abandoned warehouse again. Tom grimaced as he put pressure on the accelerator of the BMW. The day had gotten off to a bad start and hadn't really righted itself yet. Hopefully, after he passed along the information to Ercan, he would be able to get back on track. He swallowed, remembering the text he'd gotten from Shelley. Vague, but pointed. There was a reason he'd been hesitant to pass along CIA research regarding hedge funds to the Senate Intelligence

Committee. It would put a target on his back. How would he ever begin to explain his involvement in Desert Indigo? He'd gone through it in his head a million times. Part of him knew he was going to get caught, but part of him was still optimistic that he might be able to give a plausible enough explanation, tell his colleagues he was running his own undercover, covert operation and then somehow escape with the money Jonah had made from him in the process. It was a tall order with a lot of moving parts.

Then he'd have to disappear…

Time was running out. He'd have to go, with or without Shelley. The question was, would she want to leave, scarring her legacy as a Senator? He didn't have the answer for that. He wasn't sure he wanted to think about it.

Pulling into Highlands Park, a quick three-mile drive from the Langley campus, Tom saw Ercan's Bentley parked nearby. Ercan was perched on the back of the trunk again, his phone pressed to his ear. As Tom got out of the car, Ercan waved him over and then quickly hung up. Tom looked over his shoulder both ways. They were in the middle of an open parking lot. Anyone with even a reasonable telephoto lens on a camera, or even the camera app on their phone, for that matter, could have been snapping pictures of him as they met. His stomach knotted, acid churning up the back of his throat.

Ercan smiled, "It's nice to see you twice in one day. Did you get what I need?"

Tom didn't say anything, simply handing over the manila file Elena had prepared for him.

Ercan flipped through the sheaf of papers inside. "This seems fairly comprehensive. Glad to see that the taxpayers are getting their money's worth here in the United States."

Tom grimaced, "You don't pay taxes here, Ercan. This isn't on your dime."

Ercan narrowed his eyes and then grinned, "Correct. Actually, I don't pay taxes anywhere." He tilted his head to the side, "I guess you could look at it as an investment in your future, then." As he thumbed through the file, he pointed to the last page, which listed the CIA asset that was located nearby, the one who had been doing the reconnaissance. "What about this person? This CIA asset? Who is this?"

Tom reached forward, lunging, trying to get the last sheet of paper out of the file, but Ercan was too quick. He snatched the file away from Tom, just as Ercan's bodyguards blocked Tom from getting any closer. "Now, now. No reason to get aggressive, Tom. The file is mine."

Tom's face flushed. It was a rookie mistake. He should have pulled the last page out of the file and shredded it before he ever left the office. Now Ercan had the name of one of their local assets. "Don't do anything to him. He feeds us information, that's all."

Ercan raised his eyebrows, "Well, good for him. Maybe he'd like to provide information to me too. I bet I pay better than you do."

"Just don't kill him, okay?" The last thing Tom needed was an asset murdered because of the information he gave to Ercan.

"We'll see about that..." Ercan smirked as he slid off the back of the Bentley and walked to the side of the car, one of his guards opening the door. "Thanks for this, Tom. I'll be in touch," he said, disappearing inside.

A moment later, the black Bentley slid out of the parking spot and rolled away, Ercan giving Tom a little wave and a smile as he left.

Tom stared at the ground and then strode back to the BMW and got in, dialing Shelley. "Where have you been? I've been waiting for you to call me all morning. It's nearly lunchtime."

Tom chewed the inside of his lip. The last thing he needed was the third degree from his wife. "It's been a busy morning."

"Mine's been busy too. I had to deal with the embarrassment of Linette Riggs coming at me about you hedging on the banking information. Tom, people are starting to talk. You need to do something."

Tom lost his cool, "What exactly do you want me to do, Shelley? The proverbial horse has left the barn. We've been involved in Desert Indigo for the last three years. At this point, there's a paper trail, not to mention all the money."

"You have been involved in Desert Indigo for the last three years. Not me! That wasn't my money."

Tom gripped the steering wheel harder, his knuckles turning white, yelling into the speaker, "It came from the same account! Any good investigator is going to say it's contaminated. You're in this as well as I am. You may not have turned over secrets like I did, but what if they claim you did?" Part of him didn't want to be on the run alone. Butterflies flooded his stomach. He grabbed the antacids from the glove compartment again, tossing a handful into his mouth.

There was silence on the other end of the line for a moment. Tom knew Shelley was collecting her thoughts, ready to attack, "I'm not the one that passed the secrets on, Tom. And I didn't sign the original paperwork. You did. This is all on you. Not on me. I keep telling you it's gotta get fixed, but you aren't listening to me. You know what you need to do."

Back to the same refrain about Travis Bishop. "Yes, I know. I need to take care of Travis."

"Yes. If you do, that eliminates one line of evidence from the story. If you get rid of him and what he saw, then maybe the rest of it will go away. Maybe there's a way we can position it like it was all intentional and it was an undercover op, one that was so secret nobody knew anything about it."

Shelley's thinking was overly simplistic, not to mention optimistic. "You've got to be kidding me, Shelley. Who on God's green earth is going to believe that this is an undercover op with all the money we've made? Your hands are just as dirty as mine. You've gotten stuff out of this, too. You know that fancy vacation we're planning in the fall? Desert Indigo money is paying for that."

"The way we're going Tom, you're going to be taking that vacation on your own. And if you don't get things straightened out, that won't be the only thing you're doing alone..."

Shelley hung up on him.

For the rest of the drive back to Langley, Tom kept his eyes on the road. He felt like he was suffocating, the breath in his chest compressed by the crush of fear. He rolled down the windows, allowing fresh air to circulate through the BMW's tan leather compartment. Everything in him wanted to ram the custom car into the nearest guardrail to work some of his aggression out, but he drove calmly back to the office, waved at the guard at the entrance, strode into his office, and shut the door. The pressure was mounting. He had to figure out what to do next.

He had only one move left. Tom picked up the phone. It was time.

34

By the time Travis and Catherine arrived at the MI6 office, Archie was buried in paperwork behind his desk. They sat down in the two chairs in front of him, waiting.

A moment later, Archie pulled the thick glasses off of his nose and set them on the pile of files in front of him, using his hand to pinch the bridge of his nose with his thick fingers. He closed his eyes for a moment. When he looked up, he stared at each of them, settling his gaze on Travis. "Agent Bishop, I'm sorry, but I have news."

Travis frowned. "You already told me that Tom Stewart called. Is that it?"

Archie shook his head, "I wish it was. I just received a call from one of our agents who monitors chatter. We intercepted a post that was put on a site on the dark web that we know is one used for hiring contract killers. They've spent the last hour tracking the communications."

Catherine frowned, uncrossing her legs, the fabric from the floral dress shifted and settled around her calves as she leaned forward, "Archie? What's going on?"

Archie glanced at Catherine for a moment, replaced his glasses on his nose, and looked back at Travis. "There's no easy way to say this, Travis, but it looks like another assassin has been hired to come after you."

Travis shook his head and shrugged. What was so earth-shattering about that? "Tell me something I didn't know. You told me they're going to keep coming at me until we get this bounty off, right?"

Archie nodded his head slowly, leaning back in his chair, knitting his fingers in front of his chest, leaning his elbows on the armrests, "The problem is, this time, whoever is hiring them has upped the ante."

Travis frowned, "In what way?"

"They've hired Agnes."

"Agnes?" Travis leaned back in his seat for a moment, thinking. The name sounded familiar, but he couldn't quite place it. "She's an assassin from Nigeria?"

Archie nodded, "Yes, you've got a good memory, Travis. In the last five years, since you've been out of the Agency, she's become the most highly sought-after assassin in the world. Has a one hundred percent success rate. Guarantees her kills, no matter what it takes or how long. She charges a bloody fortune to do what needs to get done, but she's in and out, quiet and stealthy. In most of her kills, the people had no idea she was even there. She's an expert with weapons of all varieties. I saw a report that three months ago she killed the Vice President of Paraguay with a small piece of cord."

"Like a garrote?"

"No. Not wire. Just a piece of cord. That's what makes her so dangerous."

Travis stopped to think about what Archie was saying. An assassin who was gifted enough to take a common piece of cord and manage to murder someone was likely to have been trained heavily in the martial arts or at least had significant on-the-job training, if you could call it that. It was someone who was creative and well organized, someone adaptable, who was quick to change their tactics depending on the situation. Agnes was a legend in the espionage field. No one was actually sure who she was or how old she could be. Travis licked his lips and then looked up at Archie and Catherine. They were both staring at him as the news settled in, "And she's been hired to take me out?"

Archie nodded, "Best we can tell." He sighed and then shuffled a few papers on his desk, drawing a file out, unearthing it from one of the many stacks he had close to him. He flipped it open and looked down at it, peering at it half through and half over his thick glasses. "When I say we think she's Nigerian, pretty much everything we know is anecdotal. When everyone she's ever targeted dies, it's hard to get a read on the person, let alone solid data." He slid a photo out of the file across the desk to Travis. It showed a woman with dark skin and a set of dark braids coursing over the top of her head and down the sides like a pair of snakes. She was only half visible in the darkness. It was a meager profile view of her, and saying that was generous. Archie pointed, "We think this is her."

"Think?" Travis swallowed. If an assassin of this caliber had been hired to take him out, then things are more serious than he thought. He pressed his lips together and shook his head. He'd been out of the CIA for five years. What could he possibly know or have witnessed that would put this level of a target on his head? Hiring someone like Agnes cost a fair bit of money, not to mention she would be hard to find. He realized his hands were sweating. He wiped them on the legs of his jeans. As he did, he saw Cath glance his way. She'd noticed. He shook his head. She'd be sweating too if she was Agnes's newest target.

"What we don't know, Travis, is if Agnes is a codename, or if it is this woman's true identity. What I mean is that there have been cases where different people have assumed the identity of a single codename over time. Now, we haven't seen that with her, but then again we don't have much information on her to speak of, unfortunately."

Travis balled his hands into fists. "What do you mean you don't have information on her? You have a whole file sitting right in front of you." The words came out sharp and direct. At this point, Travis didn't care if they were disrespectful. It was his life that was on the line, not Archie's and not Catherine's. Neither of them had any answers for him.

Archie cleared his throat, closed the file, and passed it across the desk without saying anything. As he handed it to Travis, he said, "Point well taken. Feel free to have a look. You'll see what I mean. We have only a few pieces of information on her."

"Such as?" Travis said, flipping open the file.

"Such as we believe she was born in Nigeria. From what we can tell, she was from one of the areas that was badly scarred by war. Biafra. It looks as though at one point she lost her whole family and was orphaned. Our profilers believe she was captured by the Nigerian Army, forced into serving, and then went AWOL. There is no record of her for several years and then all of a sudden she pops up as a mercenary. Even then, we've had to use aging software and a lot of assumptions to get this far. Any of our data points could be wrong. Or all of them."

"For someone that doesn't know much, that's a pretty good background," Travis mumbled.

Travis stared at the file, trying to focus. He'd chased after similar or worse characters in his time with Delta Force. He felt a shift inside of him, a hardening. Sure, Agnes was going to be formidable, but she breathed and moved just like he did. She might be well-trained, but so was he. He wasn't willing to give up, not until he figured out who put the bounty on his head and why.

Archie cradled his teacup in his hands, "The other thing to

know about her is that anyone who is nearby and attempts to help you instantly becomes a target." Archie directed his gaze at Catherine, "That means you, young lady. Watch your back."

Catherine nodded, "Yes, sir. I will."

A tingle ran down Travis's spine. It was one thing to put himself in harm's way, but knowing he was responsible for Catherine was something else entirely. He glanced at the side of her face. A few hairs had escaped the clip, hovering near the line of her jaw. To anyone else, she looked pleasant and lovely, completely harmless. But Travis knew under that friendly exterior, she had skills. He only hoped they would be enough for the two of them to figure out what was going on and stay alive while doing it.

Archie checked the watch on his wrist. It had a broad gold bezel with a thick brown leather strap. Travis was surprised Archie didn't carry a pocket watch. It seemed more his style. "Well, ladies and gentlemen, as much as I have enjoyed your company, duty calls. I'm off to another set of bloody useless meetings for the remainder of the afternoon. Your job is to figure out who is coming after you, Travis. You and Catherine need to spend the afternoon doing a deep dive into your background. And Catherine, you need to figure out the link between the chatter we've heard and your current case."

"What about the call from Director Stewart?" Catherine asked, shifting in her seat.

Archie nodded, "Yes, I found that timing to be a bit suspect myself. Although, I do have to admit Tom sounded perfectly pleasant on the phone and not all that concerned that I didn't know where you were, Travis." Archie stood up, walking over to a heavy cabinet in the corner of the office. From where Travis was sitting, he couldn't see what Archie was doing, the big man's frame covering the interior of the cabinet as he rummaged around.

As Archie turned around, Travis realized Archie had a gun

in his hand, more specifically a full-sized Glock 17. "Given the situation, it seems you might need a few tools of the trade," Archie said calmly, setting the Glock down on the desk in front of Travis. He returned to the cabinet, scrounged around inside, and came back with another pistol, a Walther for Catherine, plus extra magazines, holsters, and ammunition. Out of his pocket, he produced a knife. He nodded at Travis, "Sharpened this one myself a few days ago. She cuts perfectly."

Travis blinked at Archie. He would have never thought Archie would have produced an arsenal for them, not to mention tending to his own knives. Archie was full of surprises. Travis checked the Glock. It was empty. He inserted a magazine, added the holster to his hip, and slid the gun in. It was ready to fire if he needed it.

Carrying a gun was strictly prohibited in England, especially for a foreign national. Travis sat back down again, picking up the knife. He rolled it over in his hand, opening the blade. The light from the banker's lamp that was on top of Archie's desk caught the blade, the metal glinting back at him, the fine edge carefully honed. Travis knitted his eyebrows together, "Don't you need this, Director Elliott?"

"That's my backup." He pulled another knife out of his other pocket and flipped the blade open, whipping it around a couple of times as if it was a set of nun chucks.

Travis raised his eyebrows. Clearly, Archie was comfortable with a knife. Living in a country where guns were frowned upon, it suddenly occurred to Travis that more people probably carried knives than he ever realized. He nodded, "Thank you."

"Of course. Just don't tell anyone. You know how the British are around weapons. Bunch of old fuddy-duddies." He chuckled to himself, picking up a stack of files and lumbering out the door. It was a clear signal their meeting was over.

As Travis stood up, he collected the file Archie handed him

and nodded to Catherine, "Stick this in your bag. We might need it later."

"Will do."

Catherine looked at him, "Where are we off to now?"

"Back to the safe house. I've got some thinking to do."

35

Neither Travis nor Catherine said much of anything on the way back to the safe house, Catherine silently piloting the blue Volvo sedan through a tangle of traffic and curving back roads before sliding into a spot on the street nearby. Travis got out of the vehicle gingerly, scanning the area. If another assassin had been hired, whoever it was could strike at any time. That didn't even begin to deal with the issue of Agnes. He felt the muscles tighten across his back and shoulders. It felt good to have the Glock holstered on his side and the knife in his pocket. At least that was something.

He strode behind Catherine as they made their way through the restaurant and up the rickety set of steps to get to the safe house. Travis watched the hallway while Catherine unlocked the door. He pushed his way in front of her, lifting the hem of his shirt and grabbing the butt of his gun as he walked in. He wasn't taking any chances of the two of them getting ambushed. He'd be on high alert until this was over.

Once he was convinced the apartment was clear, he waved Catherine forward. "We're good. No one here, at least not yet," he grimaced.

"Well, that's a relief," Catherine said sarcastically. She dropped her bag down on the couch. "Since Archie has issued us weapons, I need to change. It's hard to wear a holster with a dress, if you know what I mean. If you'll excuse me for a few minutes…"

Travis nodded but didn't say anything. Catherine walked into the bedroom, closing the door. Whether she needed to change her clothes or just take a minute for herself, he wasn't sure. It didn't matter. He pulled his cell phone out of his back pocket, searching through his contacts. He dialed Ellie.

"Hey you!" she said cheerfully after two rings.

"Hey, yourself. Calling to see how things are going."

Travis checked the time on his watch. It was nearly dinnertime in London, which made it closer to lunch in Texas.

"Everything's fine. Joker had a bit of a meltdown today. He's out in the corral working off his anxiety as we speak."

Travis nodded. Joker was known for his high energy. He'd be an amazing reiner if he could just settle down. He was young. Maybe he'd calm down in another year or two, Travis thought. "Did the contractors show up today?" It had taken months to get the fire claim on the old barn settled. The check had finally come in three weeks before. The contractors had just begun work when he and Ellie had headed off to the reining competition in Oklahoma City. Travis shook his head. It seemed like a lifetime ago, and yet it had only been a couple of days.

"Yeah. They were looking for you. Demolition is done. It looks a lot better, all that charred stuff finally got hauled away. The truck is in the shop, too." There was a pause, "Where are you, Travis? Are you okay?"

"On the East Coast. I'm looking at prospects." Part of Travis felt bad about lying to Ellie, but he couldn't take any chances and the last thing he wanted to do was to talk about the shooting over the phone. It was entirely possible someone was listening to his phone calls, and although saying he was on the East Coast wasn't much of a red herring, it was at least something, something that would force whoever was coming at him to work a little harder to find him.

"Did you find anything good? When are you coming home?"

"Nothing yet. Should be able to come back in the next couple of days. Hold down the fort for me, okay?"

"Copy that."

As Travis hung up the phone, he suddenly started to feel claustrophobic, trapped in the small flat with a woman he hardly knew in a country far from home. He strode over to the closed bedroom door where Catherine had cordoned herself off and yelled through it, "I'm going for a walk. I'll be back in a little bit."

Travis didn't bother waiting for an answer. He walked to the safe house door and closed it quietly behind him, running down the steps and through the air that was laced with pungent spices from the restaurant, the clink of knives and dishes clattering in the background as they began to prepare for dinner service. As Travis darted through the restaurant, he saw a few early diners had already straggled in for dinner. Travis's stomach turned. The idea of eating anything at that moment sounded repulsive.

He sucked in a deep breath as he stepped outside into the fresh air and turned to his right, starting to walk. He needed to think. The best way for him to do it was alone.

36

The neighborhood where the safe house was located was basically a replica of New Delhi, India. To anyone who dropped onto the street not knowing what country they were in, they would expect they'd found their way into south Asia, not the middle of England. The signs for the shops and stores were in both Hindi and English, the curled writing highlighted on every single sign. From the apartments above the stores that lined the street, clothes could be seen waving in the wind, drying after being freshly washed, and the sound of children alternately crying and laughing carried on the breeze.

Travis walked down the block, dodging in and out of foot traffic. There was a wide range of saris, sarongs, and other traditional Indian clothing, Sherwani jackets, and narrow-legged pants, nearly everyone had black hair and dark skin.

Travis stuck to the edge of the sidewalk that was closest to the road. Doorways were the perfect place to conceal a killer. And if Agnes or some other assassin was really on to him, then he needed to be doubly careful. Someone else might think he was taking an unnecessary chance by walking outside in the late afternoon, but he needed to clear his head. Being stuck inside between the MI6 headquarters at Vauxhall Cross and the safe house wasn't doing it. He was used to being outside in the fresh air. He thought for a moment about what Ellie had said about Joker and his meltdown. He would have much preferred to be at home to watch Joker work off his extra energy and anxiety in the corral than walking on the streets of Little Delhi, that was for sure.

But that was the hand he'd been dealt, at least for the moment.

Travis wasn't one to worry about what should've been. He had a problem. It was that simple. He'd get it solved and then go home.

Hopefully...

He chewed the inside of his lip as he walked. The problem he was having was that he wasn't sure who exactly was behind the threat.

The whole situation would be much easier if he'd still been an active agent. It would be simple to think through which cases had been particularly problematic in the last year or two, figure out who had a vendetta and then deal with it from there. And, he'd have the backup of his own agency. Where was the CIA in all of this? Did they really want him dead? He shook his head. After all of his loyalty, it was hard to imagine they would betray him.

The most troublesome part was the fact that he had no idea who his enemy was. That was one thing that was always clear in his work with both Delta Force and the CIA. They had named their enemy. In Delta Force, it had been completely obvious. Each mission had a target with a name, a photo, and a long list of atrocities attached to them. With his CIA projects, the outcomes weren't always so obvious, but he rarely felt like he was operating in a vacuum, at least not one as big as this one.

Travis crossed the street when he got to the end of the business district of Little Delhi and walked back in the other direction, keeping an eye on the shadows. As he passed the Surya Bookstore, he felt eyes on his back, as if someone was watching him. He glanced over his shoulder to see a black-haired man in the window, alternately looking at him and looking at the book in his hands.

Travis shrugged it off. It shouldn't come as any surprise that people were staring at him. At just over six feet tall with a lean, muscular build, Travis stuck out like a sore thumb amid the residents of the Indian enclave. He had at least five inches on the tallest man he'd passed on the street, even more on the diminutive women in their fuchsia, yellow and orange saris as they passed him. A wave of tension passed over his body. Travis stuck his hand in the pocket of his jeans, feeling for the knife that Archie had given him, resting it in his grip, concealed by the thick denim. The old adage, "You should never bring a knife to a gunfight," rattled through his head. It was only partially true. Knives were an effective weapon, as evidenced by the slice on his arm and what he'd been able to do to his attacker.

Would he be as lucky with Agnes? He wasn't sure. Only time would tell.

Turning back toward the safe house, a plan started to formulate in Travis's head. If Archie had been able to find out who was coming after him next, then maybe there was a way to figure out who had hired Agnes. Maybe.

That was the key question, wasn't it?

The other question that rattled in his mind was why all the sudden CIA Director Tom Stewart had such an interest in him. Had he heard the chatter? If so, why hadn't he reached out? Sure, Tom was busy, but they'd worked together, been on multiple operations when they were both field agents, having each other's backs until Tom got promoted. Then Elena became his partner. The group of them — Tom, Elena, Kira, Gus —had all been close at one time. Now, two of the five of them were dead. If he didn't figure out who hired the assassins, he'd be the third of the group to die.

Which brought him to Elena. Did she know anything? Travis had a sudden urge to call her but fought it off. At the moment, he had no idea who was responsible for the bounty on his head. The fewer people that knew about it the better.

No, at that moment, the only people that could be trusted were Archie and Catherine. They were the only ones that had come clean and offered to help him.

And if he hoped to survive, that's exactly what he would need — their help.

37

Once he got back to the safe house, Travis knocked on the door quietly. Catherine answered immediately. Maybe she was watching the street for his approach. The smell of food filled the apartment. As she closed the door behind her, she looked at him, as if he had just come home from a long journey, her eyes narrowed. "Feeling better?"

"A little, I guess."

"Yes, you did seem a bit preoccupied on the drive back here."

Travis raised his eyebrows, "Wouldn't you be?"

"Of course, silly. Anyone would." Catherine bustled past him, "I thought that by the time you got back you might be hungry, so I made us a little dinner. Figured we could work while we eat."

Travis stared at the small kitchen table. Catherine had set it with plates, placemats, and dishes, a steaming bowl of pasta in the middle of the table, the tendrils of heat still curling up over the top of it, the haze of melted cheese on top. There was a platter of chicken breast and another bowl, filled with a colorful salad.

"Where did you get all this?" Travis said, sitting down at the table. He stopped himself, "I mean, thank you."

Catherine smiled, "I ran downstairs and raided the restaurant refrigerators for ingredients. Umar doesn't mind. I figured another night of Indian food might kill you."

Travis nodded. "Again, thank you. This looks good." In fact, it looked better than good to him, probably the nicest meal anyone had made for him in a long time and far superior to the gummy pasta he'd eaten on the airplane ride over or the Indian food he'd eaten the day before.

Catherine slipped into her seat, "Let's not wait. It'll get cold. Dig in."

The two of them ate in silence, Travis putting two chicken breasts, a large pile of pasta, and a heap of salad on his plate. He got about halfway through his meal when he set his knife and fork down, and took a drink of water from the glass Catherine had left at his place setting. He looked at her. "I may be stating the obvious here, but the news that another assassin has been hired to get at me isn't good."

Catherine put her knife and fork down on an angle at the edge of her plate and folded her hands in her lap as if she was at a finishing school dinner before speaking, "No, it isn't. I'm glad you brought it up. Any thoughts as to what could possibly be going on?"

He was tired of the questions. Travis shook his head, "Nothing concrete, not really. Just fragments. I do think it's strange that Director Stewart called Archie today."

"As did I," Catherine said, picking up her knife and fork again, sticking a piece of chicken in her mouth and chewing slowly.

"I was thinking about it while I was walking. Tom and a few of the other agents, we were close at one time. Things kinda drifted apart after Tom got promoted. Then a guy named Gus took over the unit I was in. Once I left the CIA, Gus stayed in his position. Tom kept getting promoted, and then after Gus died, Elena was the next in line to run the unit. But what doesn't make sense is that all the cases are old, at least the ones I was involved in. Why come after me now?"

"I agree," Catherine said. Finishing the bite she was chewing, she took a sip of water and then looked at Travis, "Like I said, the thing I find to be strange is that there is a direct link between the chatter on your bounty and some of the sources we're using to look into this Jonah Hudson character."

Just as Catherine finished her sentence, her phone rang. She glanced at it and answered, "Archie?" There was a pause, "Certainly. I can put him on speaker. No problem."

Catherine nodded at Travis, her eyes wide, "It's Archie. He wants to talk to both of us."

"Sorry to interrupt your relaxing evening, but I come bearing news."

Travis shook his head. He wasn't sure he was in the mood for any more of Archie's news. "What's going on? Did you hear something about Agnes?"

"In a roundabout way, yes. I only now received word that an asset we cultivated in Mongolia has been found dead. Murdered to be more specific."

Travis furrowed his eyebrows, confusion washing over him. "Mongolia? What does that have to do with me?" It sounded like Archie was grasping at straws. He still couldn't quite understand why Archie had offered to help him. Was this another diversion? Were the British the ones behind the bounty? A tingle ran up his spine, pushing the thought away. He looked at Catherine, but she was staring at the phone, her face relaxed. If this was part of some plot, then clearly she didn't know about it.

"What's the connection, Archie?" Catherine asked.

"Yes, yes. I'd imagine on the face of it you're wondering this same question, aren't you Travis?"

"Yep." Travis held his breath. The answer to the question would tell him a lot.

"The asset we had in Mongolia was feeding us information on weapons shipments that were going over the northern border between Mongolia and Russia, and on the southern border between Mongolia and China. Mongolia's government is generally a mess," Archie grunted, "and so it makes it ripe for terrorists and other businessmen that should live in a black hole to do business there. Mongolia is a perfect place for people who don't want to be found or, likewise, people who want to move illicit merchandise into larger countries, like Russia or China. This asset we had was being co-used by us and the CIA. Tolun Bat was a Code Black asset."

"What does that mean?" Travis asked.

Catherine glanced at him, "That means that only the highest level of operators would have access to the asset. I'm not sure what the Americans call it, though."

"Level I," Travis nodded. "That means the Director of the CIA would know about the person as well as the unit chief. That would be it. No one else would have access to the person's identity." Travis scratched his head, running his fingers through his hair. "What happened?"

"I got a call a few minutes ago from one of our agents on the ground. He'd gone to check on Tolun. It's customary for us. We look in on our people about once a week. He arrived at Tolun's house, a hut really, and found his three children outside, their throats slashed. Inside, he'd found the man's wife, her skirt pulled up over her waist, unfortunately. She'd been raped and then had her throat cut, or vice versa, I'm not sure which. Mr. Bat was strapped to a chair. He'd been beaten and tortured. From the looks of it, our operator assumes that the wife was raped and killed in front of him. The man probably heard the cries of his children as they were being killed too. Horrifying."

Travis shuddered. The level of brutality was unbelievable.

He swallowed and then frowned. "I don't get it. What's the link to my case?"

Archie cleared his throat again, as if telling the story about Tolun had taken the life out of him, "Two connections of concern, Travis. The source of the chatter on the Agnes hit popped up at the same time with a message saying that an asset in Mongolia had been compromised. There was no detail other than that except for a name that was linked to the case, Ercan Onan."

Travis shook his head. "Ercan Onan? Who's that?"

Catherine got up and started pacing, "Wait! I know that name. He's one of the investors that Jonah Hudson brought in for his hedge fund." She stared at Travis, "Remember? I told you I needed help exposing a British national who we think is working at cross purposes with the government?"

Travis nodded. He remembered the conversation, but only vaguely. "Yeah, tell me again?"

"Jonah Hudson is the manager of the largest hedge fund in the world. Nearly half a trillion in assets. He's a British national, but the fund is located in New York. Normally, we keep an eye on our people to see what they're up to. Anyone with access to that amount of money should be watched. When I went to pull a list of his investors, I couldn't get them. I was only able to find two names — Ercan Onan and Gonzalo Laguna. Neither of them is on the up and up. Onan considers himself a businessman, but his form of business involves black-market weapons. Laguna is a real beauty. He's a Venezuelan national, who manages to sell oil right out from underneath the nose of the government to whoever the highest bidder is. And that's only a small portion of his business. He and Onan are involved in all sorts of black-market dealings."

"Somehow the source you used to get that information on Jonah Hudson also knew about the hit on me?"

"Exactly. We have someone in the Desert Indigo organization who is feeding us bits of information. She's very hesitant. But what she has given us has been reliable. There has to be an intersection between Desert Indigo and the bounty on your life. Neither of those names mean anything to you? Think, Travis. Ercan Onan or Gonzalo Laguna?"

Travis leaned back in his chair. "Laguna, no. Venezuela wasn't my area of expertise. We had a completely different division that dealt with everything in Central and South America. The only tie I have to that at all is my fiancée, Kira was sent on a mission to Ecuador, but she didn't come back." Travis skipped the part about how Kira had faked her death, betrayed him and their country, and became a double agent for Russia. He glanced at Catherine, who gave him a nod as if she already knew the rest of the story. Travis chewed his lip for a second, "Ercan Onan? The name sounds faintly familiar, but I can't place it."

"Turkish national, Travis," Archie said. "Did you have any dealings in Turkey?"

"No, but I did spend a fair amount of time in Afghanistan. There were a lot of Turks there. I could've run across him on an operation, but nothing sticks out, nothing I remember from my Delta Force days or my time with the CIA."

Catherine shook her head, "Archie, there has to be something there. If nothing else, there's a leak, somewhere between MI6 and CIA. There were only a handful of people that knew about Tolun. He was one of our most reliable assets."

"Agreed, Catherine. I'm looking into it as we speak. But as for the MI6 side, there were only three of us that knew anything about Mr. Bat. Myself, you, and the head of the desk."

"And I can't imagine that poor Roger would have said anything, can you?"

Archie grunted, "I just concluded a rather unpleasant conversation with him, and no, he hasn't. He's as devastated as we are about the loss and the way it was handled."

Travis shook his head. He couldn't imagine the last hours of Tolun Bat's life, his children slaughtered, and his wife violated right in front of him. Travis's stomach tumbled. "So what do we do now?"

"Get yourself to the office," Archie ordered. "Right now."

38

It didn't take long for Catherine and Travis to leave the safe house. Catherine quickly wrapped up the rest of the food while Travis did the dishes. He checked to make sure he had Archie's knife and the gun loaded and ready at his side. As they stood at the doorway ready to go, he looked at Catherine, "You have your pistol?"

Catherine nodded, tapping her left side. She'd hidden it underneath the flowing shirt she'd put on over a pair of jeans. By looking at the two of them, anyone else would think they were a couple, heading out for a late dinner or possibly a show.

And yet they weren't. Far from it.

They ran out to the Volvo and slipped inside, Catherine immediately started the engine as Travis locked the doors and scanned the mirrors. They pulled away from the curb into a stream of traffic and got about a mile down the road when Travis picked up a set of tail lights in the mirror four cars back. A black sedan with tinted windows. He turned around in the passenger seat, watching. The sun had set, so it was nearly impossible for the drivers behind them to see inside the cabin of the Volvo. He turned back in his seat, looking forward, pulling the gun out of his holster and setting it on his right thigh, his hand wrapped around the grip, his index finger extended along the rail. "We've got company."

Catherine didn't look at him, "Do we?" she said pleasantly. "How many cars back?"

Travis looked in the side view mirror again. The black sedan he'd seen was still there. "Three cars back."

Catherine glanced at him, noticing the gun out on his thigh. "Seems you're ready for a fight."

"'Better to be prepared and not need it, than need it and not be prepared.' That's what my dad used to say."

"Sounds like a sensible strategy," Catherine said, gripping the wheel and glancing in the rearview mirror. "Let's see if we can dodge the tail before you have to spend any of Archie's expensive ammunition. Hold on."

Without saying anything else, Catherine darted across the lanes of traffic and down an alleyway, making a last-second turn, heading past a woman walking three dogs and nearly clipping them as she sped by. The woman grunted and frowned as Catherine called to her, "Excuse me!"; as if saying the words would make the near collision okay.

When she got to the end of the alleyway, Catherine turned the opposite direction, aiming the Volvo toward Little Delhi, back toward the direction they'd come. Zigzagging a couple more blocks over, Catherine resumed their route to MI6. Travis checked the side mirror. "Sedan is still there. You didn't lose them."

Catherine huffed, "Are you kidding me?"

"Wish I was," Travis grunted.

"This may require an alternative strategy." Catherine drummed her fingers on the steering wheel. "I have an idea."

From what Travis could tell, Catherine drove the car directly into downtown London proper. The black sedan stayed on their tail several cars back the entire time, never wavering.

How they hadn't lost the car on Catherine's first diversionary route, Travis wasn't sure, unless there was more than one car following them. A lump formed in Travis's throat. If there was more than one vehicle, it was likely they were communicating and simply waiting for a moment in which they could all converge on the Volvo at the same time. Travis unclipped his seatbelt, ready to take action, the muscles across his back were tight. He could feel the adrenaline surging in his system.

Catherine glanced at him and then back at the road. "Hold on there, Tex," she quipped. "Give me a couple of minutes. I think I have an idea."

"It'd better be good. They're getting closer."

"They?"

"Yep," he nodded. "Now we've got two of them. Two cars back and four cars back. Looks like two targets in each vehicle."

Catherine hit the call button on her phone, "This is Royal Ascot. I need an emergency landing. I've got two bogeys on my tail. ETA two minutes."

Travis looked at Catherine, frowning, "Royal Ascot?"

"Don't ask," she smiled. "You know how Brits are. We are all about our Royals."

Travis grunted, "At least you didn't call yourself James Bond."

"Now, Travis. I couldn't possibly use that name. James is a man!"

As soon as the words came out of her mouth, her face hardened, her hands tightened on the steering wheel. She pressed the accelerator on the Volvo, pushing it even faster as they wove their way through the streets of London. Travis squinted in the darkness, trying to make out exactly where they were. They weren't far from Downing Street, by his best estimation, in the area of London that held most of the government buildings and the foreign embassies. Up ahead, he could see a line of foreign flags flying proudly in the distance — Italy, Canada, Austria,

Switzerland, Bulgaria, and the United States. Catherine glanced at him, "Be ready for a sharp right turn in about fifteen seconds. Don't want to have you end up in my lap."

Travis had spent enough time in the car with Catherine to know her driving was nearly as unpredictable as her clothing. "I'm ready when you are."

The engine on the Volvo revved as the car streaked down the road passing the embassies. At the last second, as they approached the American Embassy, Travis saw the gate was open, the concrete barriers sunk into the ground. Catherine jerked the wheel hard to the right, the tires squealing as they hit the curb and ended up on American soil inside of the fence. Ten armed Marines filled the space as the gate was closed, their M14 rifles at the ready.

Gliding down the side of the embassy building, the Volvo came to stop. Travis had unconsciously grabbed the dashboard, bracing himself as they hit the curb. He relaxed and looked at her, his eyebrows raised, "You brought me home?"

Catherine giggled, "At least as much of home as I can manage from this side of the pond. Now, let's go."

Standing outside of the car door, a Marine approached Catherine. She handed him the keys. "MI6 sends their thanks and their love."

Travis couldn't see well in the dark, but it looked to him like the young Marine practically blushed at the attention he was getting from Catherine. He straightened up, "You are most welcome, ma'am. Your ride is ready and waiting at the back gate."

Catherine glanced at Travis and waved at him, taking off at a jog, "Come on. We gotta go. Archie's waiting for us."

39

Sitting at the back gate of the American Embassy was a white utility van. The artwork on the side read, "Sweets by Alana for Every Occasion" in red lettering with a picture of a festively decorated cake next to it, plus a phone number. Travis glanced at the side of it, taking in the fresh paint job. He was just about to ask if the cake van was for real or a dummy vehicle MI6 used for these kinds of moments until he slid inside. The faint hint of sugar hung in the air, as though a fresh tray of cookies had just been delivered to the embassy. Travis turned around, looking in the rear of the van. It was empty except for a rolling cart that had sheet pans on it. They clattered as soon as Catherine put the van into gear.

"Do you do this quick switch on a regular basis?"

"Getting chased down by multiple vehicles through the London streets?" Catherine cracked a smile, "No, not really, but then again that's why we have arrangements such as these."

Travis narrowed his eyes, as they pulled out onto the street, Catherine driving slowly like they had a wedding cake that was about to topple braced in the back, ready for delivery. "That Marine back there seemed quite taken with you," Travis teased.

Catherine's face reddened, "Oh, that poor young boy. Yes, I see him regularly when I stop by the embassy. His name is Jeffrey. He's from Idaho. I like to bake. A girl's gotta watch her figure, you know? I drop cookies and such off at people I would prefer to stay friends with."

"The Marines at the US Embassy are one of such groups?"

"Indeed."

Travis had about twenty more sarcastic comments he wanted to use to poke fun at Catherine, but he held back. The dark memory of the black sedans herding them through the London streets caused a tingle to run up his spine. He wondered who had been behind the wheel, not to mention the coordination. Was it Agnes already? Someone else? At least he was away from the ranch. As much as he wanted to be there, if he was he knew trouble would follow him.

Travis stared out of the van's side window as it lumbered along on the London streets. The majority of the traffic had thinned out, and most workers were home with their families or out for a late supper after work. A few straggling shoppers littered the sidewalks on Oxford Street, darting in and out of the brightly lit stores with their beautifully curated windows of merchandise for sale — everything from high fashion to collectible sneakers to the finest cookware. Travis gawked as they passed a furniture store that featured a living room set up, a man and a woman sitting watching television, the screen flickering as they drove by.

Catherine's voice interrupted his thoughts, "Did you see that furniture display?"

Travis nodded.

"They pay people to sit there and watch television every night," Catherine said, conspiratorially, as if she'd revealed one of London's major secrets.

Travis's lips parted, "You mean those weren't mannequins?"

Catherine chuckled, "Not in the least. Not a job I'd want.

Sitting still that long would make me batty. You have to give them credit for creativity, though."

"I suppose." Travis sucked in a breath and then looked back at Catherine. Talking about the display was mildly amusing, but it didn't solve the problem of the black sedans. "Any thoughts on who was tailing us? My understanding is that Agnes works alone. There were clearly two chase cars."

Catherine shook her head, chewing her lip, "Your guess is as good as mine, Travis. I don't know." She glanced in the rearview mirror, "I thought she worked solo too."

A chill ran down Travis's spine. "Then who do you think was following us?"

Catherine pressed her lips together, her hands tightening on the steering wheel. "I have no idea, but we better find out before things get out of hand."

40

By the time Travis and Catherine arrived at MI6, another thirty minutes had gone by, Catherine carefully navigating the van past some of the most well-known spots in London — Buckingham Palace, the Big Ben clock tower, and Westminster Abbey. Halfway through the drive, Travis had started to get impatient, wondering if there was a more direct route. If Archie wanted them in the office, what was taking so long? He was about to say something to Catherine when he saw the sign for Vauxhall Cross Bridge. They were close now.

After darting across the bridge in the darkness, Catherine pulled into the rear lot of the MI6 building. The two of them jumped out and quickly walked across the open parking lot, Travis's head on a swivel, fingering Archie's blade. "Sorry about all of that twisting and twining through the London streets," Catherine whispered as they strode inside and got to the steel door. She inputted her code and pressed her thumb on the fingerprint reader. "I was checking for tails."

Travis shook his head, followed her, and sighed, "I was too, but I didn't see any. Score one for the good guys, I guess."

Inside of MI6, for a building that should have been largely empty in the late evening, there was a significant amount of commotion. The cubicle area was nearly as full as the last time Travis had been there. Clusters of people were talking, some of them with their arms folded across their chests, some of them waving their hands wildly as they spoke, but everyone, without exception, used a hushed tone. Parked in the corner of the room was a large man talking to two other people, his glasses dangling dangerously on the tip of his nose, his suit looking rumpled after a long day. Archie.

Travis followed Catherine as they angled directly for the portly, yet powerful, Director of MI6, dodging past the stares of other agents. Archie greeted them with a nod, "Glad you made it. Heard you had a little diversion along the way."

Catherine nodded, "Yes, our lovely friends at the American Embassy gave us quite the assist." She pulled the keys from the van out of her pocket and deposited them into Archie's thick hand, "Please pass on my thanks to the ambassador."

Archie gave a single nod, "Of course," handing her the set for the Volvo. "The Marines just returned your vehicle. I'll see to it they come and get the van."

Travis stared at the ground, nudging the carpet with the toe of his boot. He was becoming impatient at how long it was taking to get anything accomplished. He felt like he had spent the entire day asking questions and not getting answers. Not a single one. Nothing actionable. Nothing solid. Acid ate at the back of his throat. He swallowed. In twenty-four hours, all he'd managed to learn was that another assassin was coming at him, there was some vague link to a hedge fund investor Catherine was worried about, a Mongolian asset had been murdered, and as much as he liked garlic, he still wasn't sure about Indian food. It was time to get a move on, or he'd be on the next plane and head back to Texas and take his chances there. At least at home he knew the lay of the land and would be more in control, not wasting his time running around London for no reason. He gripped his hands into fists, "All right, why are we here?" He pointed at all the people milling around, "What's with all the people here this late at night? Is that normal?"

Archie narrowed his eyes, probably sensing Travis's impatience. "Right to the point again, I see, Agent Bishop. All right, I'll play along. We are in a state of high alert since our dear friend in Mongolia was murdered. Catherine was right. There is a leak and we must find it before more of our assets are in danger. All of these people," he pointed to the cadre of MI6 agents moving about the building, "Are here because of that. They are putting out the word to our agents and informants around the globe to watch their back." Archie looked to the ground for a second, stuffing his hands in his pockets. As he looked up, he cleared his throat, a cue Travis had learned meant he was feeling frustrated. "As for why you are here," Archie looked over his shoulder, pointed at an agent on the other side of the room, and beckoned them forward, grabbing a file from them, "You need to go to a meet."

"With who?" Travis asked.

"Rose Powell," he said, handing Travis the file. "She's a dear old friend. Has worked at Barclays Investment Bank for longer than God himself. She knows everyone and everything. I got a message from her a few hours ago. Said she needs to meet. Has information about a major transfer to a hedge fund."

Catherine's eyes widened, "You don't suppose?"

Archie's pink tongue flicked at his lip as he nodded, "I do suppose. She's on her way to Vauxhall Pleasure Gardens. Head over there now. See what you can find out, all right?"

Travis nodded, handing the file back to Archie. At least it was something solid for once. He followed Catherine back out exactly the way they'd come in. The park wasn't far – he'd seen it in the darkness on the way to MI6, or at least the entrance of it.

Catherine took off across the street at a quick clip, her bag swinging on her hip. Travis matched her speed, looking over his shoulder. They walked in silence down the sidewalk for two blocks and then turned into the park's entrance, at which point Catherine gave him the brief history of the park.

The Vauxhall Pleasure Gardens, as they were properly called, were built sometime in the 1600s, although no one, despite the excellent historical record keeping of the British, seemed to know exactly when. Several acres of land were set aside for decorative plantings and gracious walkways as a new attraction for Londoners as the city grew. Originally only accessible by boat, once the Vauxhall Bridge was built in the 1800s, more and more people began to use the Pleasure Gardens as a place for a romantic getaway. The gardens were well-maintained until the mid-1900s, at which point they fell into disrepair, much of the land being taken over by the overgrowth of the London slums as a result of the industrial revolution and World War II. By the late 1970s, the gardens had been reclaimed, or at least as much of it could be restored from the surrounding slums, replanted and rejuvenated with new beds and plants that were botanically important to England. It was just one of them many projects the Queen herself had insisted on, as part of the image restoration of the city of London proper, which seemed to swing wildly back and forth between still grieving the damage done to the city during World War II and their need to move forward, being a beacon for modern, well-mannered Western society.

The entrance to the park was stately. Two stone columns, one on each side of a double-lane road, with beautiful, lit signage proclaiming Vauxhall Pleasure Gardens as a historical site. Catherine glanced back at Travis after checking her phone, "Archie texted. Said we can meet Rose over by the observation tower."

Travis nodded, feeling the darkness wrap him in relative

obscurity. His stomach knotted. The night provided some cover, but they were still out in the open. He glanced around. If Agnes had gotten a bead on them going to the garden, it wouldn't be difficult to conceal herself in some of the shadows, behind some of the more elaborate plantings and hedgerows maintained by the Vauxhall Pleasure Garden staff, and quickly dart out of the inky blackness and stage an attack. He shook his head, his eyes scanning around him. Rose better have something incredibly important to say, he thought to himself, still thinking about the level of exposure.

"How far," he hissed.

Catherine pointed. Up ahead, there was a stone building, only the outline discernible in the darkness. "It's the old observation tower," she whispered, picking up the pace.

Travis's heart started to beat faster as they got close. If they could make it to the observation tower, he'd at least have a position to defend. But defend from what? His mind reeled. If Agnes was coming after him, he had no idea what to expect. A sniper rifle could take him out before he had any idea what was going on. And for what? He still didn't know.

A half a minute later, they approached the tower, only to see a single shadowed figure standing nearby. Catherine lifted her chin, "That's Rose."

"You know her?"

Catherine nodded, moving closer to Travis. "Yes. She goes back and forth between Archie and me, depending on the day. I haven't been able to figure out a pattern to it, to be honest. She works for Barclay's investment division. As Archie said, she's been there practically longer than the bank itself. Knows everyone."

"What's her position with the bank?"

Catherine shook her head, "You name it, she's done it. She tends to float around as an administrative assistant, but she's worked for the research division, the trading floor, and even their records group. But now, I think she works directly for some of their top advisors or portfolio managers. I don't know which. We'll have to ask her."

As they approached Rose, Travis took in the scene. Rose Powell looked minuscule against the leaning stone observation tower, or what was left of it, the remainder stretching a good two stories into the sky. She stood halfway in a shadow, her arms crossed in front of her chest. She was dressed as he would expect a British woman to be — a solid colored blouse with a bow at the neck, dark colored skirt, the exact tone of which he couldn't detect because of the lack of light, and what looked to be sensible, block-heeled shoes. A light sweater covered her shoulders. She held a pocketbook pinched between her elbow and her rib cage, as if it held the world's secrets in it. From the scanty light in the park, Travis saw a nest of gray hair, teased and combed carefully framing a pout of pale pink lipstick. If Travis had to guess, Rose Powell had probably worn the same color of lipstick since she was a young girl. By his estimation, she was at least seventy, but based on the looks of her, he'd bet there were many forty-year-olds she could outpace.

"Rose?" Catherine said softly.

The woman spun around, her eyes wide, "Catherine! You gave me a jolt," she said, dropping her hands to her sides.

"So sorry. Archie said you had some information for us?"

Rose narrowed her eyes, staring at Travis. "Who are you?"

"A friend," he said. Travis didn't feel the need to explain who he was. The fewer people that knew his name, the better. With any luck, the darkness would obscure enough of his face that Rose Powell would quickly forget his presence and focus on the people she knew — Catherine and Archie.

Catherine glanced from Travis to Rose, "Rose? We don't have a lot of time. Can you tell me what you've heard?"

Her mouth hung slightly open and she paused for a second, as if searching for the words, "Yes, yes. A couple of the portfolio managers came back from a luncheon this afternoon. They were quite distressed, waving their hands in the air to the point where Mr. Sutherland told them to take their issues into a conference room because they were being so disruptive. Terribly rude."

"Paul Sutherland is the CEO of Barclays investment division," Catherine said to Travis.

He nodded.

"And did you hear what the men were arguing about, Rose?"

"I just happened to walk by, as I heard two of them. It was hard to miss, to be honest. They were being quite loud. They were talking about a huge investment that was getting ready to be moved into one of the hedge funds. They seem to be quite riled up about it."

Travis shook his head, "I don't understand, Rose. Why would anyone be concerned about that kind of a transfer?"

Rose wrinkled her nose, "These portfolio managers, they're quite insecure and competitive, I fear. It's every man for himself. Whoever can land the biggest fish is the king of the hill if you'll pardon the euphemism," she said. "To be plain, the Barclays portfolio managers were quite angry that someone else had access to the number of funds that were going to another investor. It's sizable. I suppose they'd gone after the account themselves, though I don't know that for a fact."

Catherine shook her head, "I don't understand, Rose."

Rose cleared her throat, "Yes, let me stop beating around the bush. I stood outside the room, making a few unnecessary copies while taking even a few more unnecessary notes while I listened. Of course, I didn't write any of this down. No need to leave a paper trail, if you know what I mean." She glanced at Travis, "I've become quite good at ferreting out information over the last few decades in order to help my country."

Travis gave her a nod, encouraging her to continue speaking.

"Anyway, one of the younger portfolio managers was particularly unhinged. He said it was a schoolmate of his who had landed this large asset, a man named Jonah. He was clearly jealous"

Catherine's eyes widened, her mouth dropping open. She glanced at Travis, "Jonah Hudson?" she said, leaning toward Rose.

Rose straightened, her lips thin. "I expect so, Catherine. As I said, I couldn't hear everything through the walls of the conference room even with all of their bellowing like a bunch of wildebeests in heat. Quite embarrassing, if you ask me. Such a commotion. There should be a bit more decorum in business, but that's a discussion for another time."

"Any idea who this investor is or how much money he's bringing in?" Travis shifted his weight, watching the shadows. Nothing yet, but the longer they spent in the open, the more nervous he was getting.

"I heard them say it's oil money. And a lot of it, to the tune of a billion dollars."

"A billion dollars?" Travis stammered. "Are you kidding?"

Rose started, "I most certainly am not. I don't joke about these things. The portfolio managers were incensed because the deposit will increase the control that Jonah has on the market. He could pool the money and take a controlling share of basically any company represented on the trading floor."

Catherine furrowed her eyebrows, "Any idea of where the money is coming from?"

Rose glanced up at the sky for a moment as if she was trying to remember, "Yes, yes. I've got it. A man named Gonzalo Laguna, I believe. Something like that. They said he's South American, or from that portion of the world, at least."

Travis frowned. Catherine had told him they'd been unable

to get the names of the investors in the hedge fund she was looking at. It seemed that Rose had been able to find one, even if it had been one of the same names they already had. "Rose, do you have access to the investors for that hedge fund? Do you know how we could get them?"

Rose shook her head, "Oh no. Hedge fund investors are kept anonymous for the most part. Usually, only the manager knows who has put money in the fund. They're like small, elite country clubs with too many secrets hidden in their closets." She glanced at Catherine, "Much like our Royals, I'm afraid." She glanced over her shoulder, suddenly clutching her purse tighter, "That's all I have for tonight. Now, I must go."

Rose turned away without saying goodbye, only the clicking of the square heels of her shoes echoing in the darkness.

Without saying anything else, Catherine turned back in the direction they'd come. Travis followed, watching the shadows for movement, feeling exposed. Rose's information was yet another flimsy thread added to the fabric of the questions he had running through his head. His gut told him that Catherine was right — somehow, the fund Jonah Hudson was running was tied to the attempts on his life, but it felt like he was searching through the fog to find a needle in a haystack; as if finding the needle in a haystack on its own in the light of day wasn't difficult enough. Frustration knotted his gut. Part of him wanted to take a baseball bat to the leaning observation tower and spend the next two days whacking it into a pile of rubble. He was getting angry, angry about the interruption to his life, angry about the lack of information. He'd left the Agency five years ago. How was he back in this situation again?

As they walked, he shook his head. Catherine didn't say anything; lost in her own thoughts. A few minutes later, back in the MI6 building, they headed to Archie's office. Catherine had been silent the entire walk back. Archie looked up at them over the top rim of his glasses, "Well?" he said, slurping at yet another cup of tea. "Did Rose provide anything valuable?"

"A little something," Catherine said, throwing her bag down on the floor and flopping into a chair. "She said Gonzalo Laguna is about to make a billion-dollar investment into the hedge fund owned by someone named Jonah."

Archie raised a single bushy eyebrow. It looked like a caterpillar with spiked hair perched above his eye, "Curious. And we are supposing this is the same Jonah Hudson of Desert Indigo?"

"Yes, I think it's time we reach out to our source again. See if she knows anything."

Archie nodded, "Indeed. Make it happen."

"What about the other investors? We still don't know who they are." Travis hadn't said anything, not yet at least.

"I'm not sure we're going to be able to get that list, Travis," Catherine said, her face downcast.

"Then why am I here? You said you thought all of this is tied together, but I'm not seeing any evidence of that. The only thing that seems unusual is Tom's call to you, Archie, but even that isn't totally out of the realm of possibility."

Travis knew he was about to lose his cool. He was in a strange country that he didn't want to be in, with an assassin coming after him for some unknown reason. The people that had promised to help him were moving as slowly as molasses in January, as far as he could tell. "I mean, seriously! You seem far more interested in chasing down whatever's going on with the bank and your compromised asset than my end of the case. I might as well go home and fight this on my own turf." Travis got up and started to pace, his arms crossed in front of his chest.

Archie's voice came out low and calm, in a practiced tone Travis imagined he'd used for years with agents who were upset at the status of their cases, "Travis, you've been an agent for long enough to know that sometimes intelligence work is slow and plodding. We have the fibers of the connection between you, Jonah Hudson with the chatter we've heard. Now, we just added the death of our dear Mongolian asset to the pile. My gut tells me things are linked. We simply can't see how, but it's there. I know it."

Travis poked his finger in Archie's direction, "Don't you dare play me. I'm not an agent anymore. And I'm not willing to stand around here for weeks while you guys play poke and tickle with whoever this Jonah Hudson character is. To top it all off, he isn't even here! From what you've told me he's in New York. What are we doing?"

Catherine sighed, "Listen, Travis, I completely understand why you're frustrated. I need to reach out to our contact at Desert Indigo. I'm going to give her a good push and see if we can't for once and all figure out what the tie is to you. I agree with Archie. It has to be there; we're just not seeing it yet. We don't have enough data. Our contact can get it for us. I have to give her a bit more of a shove than a nudge. It's time." She fumbled in her bag. "Listen, why don't you take the car and go get yourself a coffee and come back in an hour or so while I take care of this? The embassy switched them out for us. The Volvo's parked out back. By then, hopefully, I'll know something. That will give my source a chance to get back to me and then the three of us can strategize."

Travis stopped pacing and stared at the two of them. He was being placated. He knew he was. It was as if they were saying, "Now, now, Travis, calm down. Everything is under control." But it wasn't. Not by a long shot. If his gut was right, they were teetering on the brink of something big and couldn't see the forest for the trees.

The one thing Catherine was right about was that he couldn't spend one more minute in that MI6 building; not without answers. He needed to cool off before he said or did something that he might regret. "All right."

Catherine tossed him the keys. "I'll tell the guard at the door to be waiting for you when you get back. He'll let you in. There's a coffee shop down the road that's open all night. If you turn right out of the driveway you'll see it in about a mile or so. Give me an hour. That's all I'm asking, Travis. One hour. If I don't have anything for you at that point, I'll drive you to Heathrow myself."

Travis swallowed. He had gotten his point across, but to what end? He still didn't know anything.

41

Travis jingled the keys in his hand as he looked for the blue Volvo in the back parking lot. Catherine had been right. The white cake decorating van they'd used to get to MI6 had been replaced by the blue Volvo sedan they'd left at the American embassy. "Must be some pretty darn good cookies Catherine makes," Travis mumbled to himself, stepping inside. If nothing else, Agent Catherine Lewis was able to work her mojo on the people around her to get what she wanted. Was she doing the same to Travis?

Travis got in and revved the engine, pulling out of the parking lot, the tires squealing as he stepped on the accelerator a little too fast. He turned right; the direction Catherine had suggested. There wasn't much traffic on the road at all. Questions pounded through his head. They were the same ones he felt like he'd asked a hundred times since the attacker had come at him with a knife in Oklahoma City. Everything broke down to a very simple question – who was after him and why? There were certainly other items linked to that single big one, like a carefully woven spider web that was heavily obscured in the darkness. No one had been able to answer his questions up until that time. He slammed his palm against the steering wheel, furious. Yes, he'd give Catherine one more hour. But after that, if she didn't have any answers...

Travis didn't have a chance to finish his thought. A set of blinding headlights came out of nowhere, careening for the side of the Volvo, aiming directly for Travis's door. Travis turned at the last second, the front bumper of a heavy truck ramming into the side of the Volvo. Travis heard the crumpling of metal as he felt his body get thrown toward the truck and then away from it, the airbags of the safety-conscious Volvo quickly deploying with a loud bang. He heard glass shatter, his eyes automatically closing as his body was thrown across the front seat. The Volvo skidded across the other lane, the force of the truck hitting it so hard, that the rear wheels ended up on the sidewalk across the road.

Travis sat up, dazed. He felt like someone had stuffed his head full of cotton. The truck that had rammed into him had backed away, the much heavier vehicle not sustaining any significant damage. Both doors opened, dark figures getting out, walking slowly toward the Volvo. Travis scrambled to the far side of the car, getting out on the opposite side and dropping to the ground, positioning the Volvo between him and the attackers. He slid down onto the street, trying to catch his breath, adrenaline pouring into his system. He ignored the pain that was running through his body, surging from his ankle to the slice on his arm. Drawing the pistol out of his holster, he held it in front of him, looking left and right for signs of movement. He was a sitting duck where he was, but the searing pain in his left ankle almost stopped him from moving. Almost.

If the attackers came around each side of the car, he'd be a dead man. Two on one. He'd be dead in no time. Travis flattened his body and rolled underneath the crumpled car, looking for the men who were coming after him. If it was a man. Was this Agnes?

Travis watched the attackers circle around the wrecked Volvo from underneath the car. He rolled to the side, dousing himself in something that smelled like oil and gas dripping from the bottom side of the vehicle. On the other side of the car, near the truck, he pushed himself up into a squat and stared as the attackers searched for him. He could see the shadow of guns in their hands. No, this was no accident. His mind flashed back to the tack strips that were used to stop his truck and trailer. This was no different. This was intentional. Travis had been targeted. Again.

"Over here!" Travis yelled, standing up as he lifted his gun and centered himself behind the sights.

The two men turned almost simultaneously. The slight delay gave Travis enough time to take out the man on his left first and then the man on his right with two shots each. Travis ducked back down around the side of the car avoiding return fire. It didn't come. He'd managed to surprise them.

Travis moved slowly, circling around to get a better look at who had attacked him. Over his shoulder he could hear the Volvo engine cut out, the sound of the truck still humming in the background, the blazing beams from the headlights casting long sharp golden shadows on the ground. Travis moved quickly around the back bumper, low to the ground, ignoring the pain in his ankle. He approached the first man. The blank stare on the man's face told him that the man was already dead. Travis kicked the gun away from him and patted down his pockets. No wallet, no ID. Travis went to the second man who was taking a few labored breaths, the bubbling wound in his chest telling Travis that the projectile had punctured a lung. If Travis had been charitable, he would've made some sort of a bandage for it and called for help. "Today is not your lucky day, pal. Who do you work for? Tell me!" Travis shouted, grabbing the man's shirt in his free hand.

"Wouldn't you like to know, Agent Bishop," the man hissed,

a trickle of blood coming out of the corner of his mouth. Before Travis could respond, the man's body went limp. Travis patted down the second man. No cell phone, no ID. That could mean only one thing. Mercenaries.

Looking around, Travis knew he needed to get away from the scene. If he was picked up by the British police, it could be hours before he'd be able to get a call to either Archie or Catherine and likely even longer before he'd be able to explain his way out of how he was in possession of a gun on British soil when he was an American citizen. He heard the whine of sirens in the background. He had to go. Now.

His heart thumping in his chest, Travis limped away from the scene as quickly as he could, staying in the shadows, darting down the first dark alley he came upon. He stopped for a second, leaning his back against the solid brick building that flanked the far side of the alley, listening, his breath ragged. He took stock of his injuries. The area Dr. Walsh had stitched the day before felt sore, as though he'd popped a stitch or two, and his left ankle was pulsing with pain. He bet if he took his boot off, he'd see it was already swollen, probably twisted on something during the crash. It all happened so fast he couldn't remember exactly what. He caught his breath for a second, the anger rising in his chest. He needed to know who was coming after him and he needed to know now. It was the only chance he had.

He pulled the cell phone out of his back pocket, dialing Catherine.

"Travis?" she answered after the first ring. "Is everything okay?"

"There's been an accident. I need you to come get me."

"On my way. Where can I find you?" Catherine didn't ask any questions. For that, he was grateful.

"When you leave the building, go right. You'll see the accident. It's hard to miss," he grunted. "I'm in the next alleyway on the right. Blink your headlights twice when you get here so I know it's you. Otherwise, I'm a ghost."

As Travis hung up his phone, he opened up the back of it, pulled out the battery and the SIM card, and stuffed them in his pocket. Someone was tracking him. That was the only explanation for how they knew where he'd be. It was time to get serious. His phone disabled, the only person on the planet that knew exactly where he was at that moment was Catherine.

Now he'd have to see if she could be trusted.

42

What felt like an eternity passed before Travis heard the hum of an engine drawing close to him. In reality, it was probably no longer than four minutes since his call to Catherine.

Sirens, what sounded to be a whole army of them, had passed his location, but Travis hadn't moved from his position in the darkness. He'd managed to take cover between two dumpsters that had been left on the side of the alley. The stench was nearly intolerable, but it was far better than exposing himself.

Hearing the engine approach, Travis watched as the headlights glimmered on the road in front of him, quickly flashing on and off twice. He emerged from between the dumpsters, the gun in his hand, checking to see that it was Catherine behind the wheel. He walked to the driver's side and tapped on the glass with the butt of his gun, "Open the trunk," he growled as Catherine rolled down the window.

"Why?" she asked, leaning forward toward him.

"Do it." Travis walked around the back of the vehicle and lifted the lid, checking it. There was no one inside. He opened the back door of the vehicle and checked that as well before sliding into the passenger side.

As he got in the car, he noticed Catherine's eyes were wide. "Are you all right? What happened? That was quite the wreck."

"Drive," he said without answering. He checked the status of his Glock, dropping the magazine out. Of the seventeen-round magazine Archie had given him, he'd used four. That left him thirteen rounds, plus the extra, but that was at the safe house.

The car Catherine was driving, a black Ford sedan, pulled forward, easing its way out of the alleyway. Catherine pointed it back towards MI6. "Seriously, Travis, what happened?"

Travis glared at her, "You're a smart girl, you can figure it out. I left MI6 in the car you told me to take, drove a half mile down the road, and got T-boned. As if that's not bad enough, the driver and his passenger got out and were ready to finish me. Luckily, I got to them first." Travis narrowed his eyes, "The funny thing is the only person that knew when I was leaving or where I was going was you."

A flash of anger crossed Catherine's face as she pulled into the parking lot of MI6, "Are you suggesting that I had something to do with this? You can't be serious."

"Give me another explanation."

"Your phone, possibly?"

"Yes. Possible. I took the battery and the SIM card out of it. Don't try to call me. I won't answer," Travis said, staring out the window.

Ignoring his comments, Catherine said, "Let's go in, Travis. Archie actually might have something for us by now."

"That would be a first," Travis said sarcastically.

Inside MI6 the building was bustling as much as it had before he'd left for the coffee shop not more than a half hour before, if not more. It seemed like each person was wrestling with their part of the puzzle in a hushed silence, either whispering among themselves or staring at the dim screens of the MI6 computers, or both. Unlike the other times Travis had walked into the building when he'd been largely ignored, this time, he felt eyes on him — not directly staring, of course. That would be rude and the British were far too well-mannered to do that. But he could feel eyes on him as he passed the desks and cubicles, cradling his re-injured arm, a pronounced limp on his left side.

Standing outside of Archie's office door was a white-coated Dr. Walsh. She narrowed her eyes as soon as she saw Travis. "Young man, what kind of trouble have you gotten yourself into this time?"

Travis shook his head. "Nothing good, Doc."

"I trust whoever did this to you looks worse than you do?"

Travis felt a wash of surprise rush over him. "I thought doctors were all about 'do no harm'?"

Dr. Walsh shook her head, "Not this one. I like the idea of 'do no harm' for the good guys. The bad ones? Everyone has their own comeuppance. Behave badly, reap the consequences. It's that simple."

She stepped towards Travis, gently rolling up the sleeve of his shirt and lifting the bandages. "Looks like you popped a stitch. You're not walking all that great either. Think you can make it to sick bay or do you want me to have Donald bring the wheelchair around?"

By the time Travis looked up, Archie was standing in the doorway, a grave look on his face, his meaty hands stuck in his pockets. Travis didn't say anything to him. He looked back at Dr. Walsh, "I can make it. Let's go."

Travis took a few steps forward, still limping, but trying not to. The pain in his ankle was like someone was stabbing him with white-hot poker with every step. Glancing behind him, he saw that Archie and Catherine were following him and Dr. Walsh to sick bay. His curiosity was piqued. He half expected Catherine to follow, but Archie? What was going on?

Inside the sick bay wing of the building, things were quiet, much more so than they'd been the first time he was in there. Donald was sitting alone behind one of the computers, playing with his phone. Dr. Walsh looked at him as they passed, "Come on, Donald. We have a patient to attend to."

He jumped out of his seat, as if she'd punched an invisible eject button. "Yes, ma'am."

Dr. Walsh pointed to the first bay. "Travis, have a seat." She looked at Donald. "Get the portable x-ray for me? I need to take a look at his arm and then we'll need an image of that ankle."

Donald nodded but didn't say anything, disappearing from Travis's view. While they waited for Donald to return with the equipment, Dr. Walsh pulled on a pair of gloves and rolled up Travis's sleeve, unrolling the bandages. "Looks like you've been keeping it clean," she nodded. "But you did pop a stitch." She cocked her head to the side, "It doesn't look too bad, though. I'm going to butterfly it for you." She looked up at Travis, blinking and then smiled, "Actually, I think I'm going to butterfly the whole thing."

Travis cocked his head to the side. "I guess you don't trust the stitches will hold."

"On an operator like you? No," she said curtly.

A moment later, Travis heard the rattle of wheels coming down the hallway. Donald pushed the curtain aside and handed Dr. Walsh a heavy, lead vest which she put on over top of her white lab coat. Donald knelt down and carefully removed Travis's boot. Travis winced. As Donald peeled the sock off of his foot, Travis could see there was a lump over where the ankle bone was, already swollen, purple and hard.

"Travis, I need you to lay back while we get a picture of your ankle. I want to see if you managed to break anything."

Travis grudgingly cooperated. At that point, it didn't matter if he'd broken his ankle or not. His body could scream all it wanted to, but he was going to keep moving.

Thirty seconds later, the x-ray was over. Dr. Walsh handed her lead vest to Donald and stared at the screen, licking her lower lip. She cocked her head to the side, blinked twice, and then looked back at Travis, "Lucky for you, there's no break. Did your ankle get twisted in the crash?"

Archie must have told Dr. Walsh. News traveled fast in MI6, that was for sure. Travis shook his head, sitting up on the table, "I have no idea. It all happened so fast. It could have. I got thrown across the front seat."

"You had your seatbelt on?"

Travis nodded, "But I got broadsided."

"That was quite an impact. You're lucky you don't have any other injuries." She whipped her head around staring at him, "You don't, do you? Nothing you're hiding from me?"

Travis shook his head. "No."

Dr. Walsh sighed, "That's good. I'm going to get some butterfly bandages and a wrap for your ankle. Ideally, I'd like to put you in an immobilization boot and have you see a colleague of mine who is a foot and ankle specialist, but given what I see in front of me, you would wear it as far as Archie's office and then chuck it in the trash. No need to go through that. We'll settle for a wrap. Give me a few moments and I'll have you on your way."

The flurry of the exam over, it was Travis, Archie and Catherine left in the medical bay. Dr. Walsh and Donald had disappeared to get supplies and return equipment from where it was stowed. Travis tried to roll his ankle. He winced and then looked at Archie and Catherine. "Now what?"

Archie crossed his arms across his doughy chest and stared at the ground for a second before looking up at Travis through his thick glasses. He grimaced, "We need to go on the offensive here, Travis."

Travis rolled his eyes, "I thought that's what we've been trying to do."

"No, I mean really. I thought we could wait to gather more data, but it's clear that's not a solid plan."

Travis raised his eyebrows. That was quite the admission from the Director of MI6. "What do you have in mind?"

"I want you to call Tom."

Travis narrowed his eyes. It hadn't occurred to him to call Tom Stewart directly. "You think he's involved?" A wave of nausea passed over Travis. Whether it was from his injuries or from the idea that someone who had been his colleague and someone he considered a friend for many years could be involved, he wasn't sure.

"Honestly, I have no idea. I'd be shattered to think that he was the one behind all of this, but we have to look at the facts. And the fact is, he is the only one that has contacted any of us directly about you."

"You're saying he's the only lead we have." It was hard for Travis to believe that with the sophisticated technology of MI6 that the Director of the CIA was the only plausible target they had. How was that even possible?

Travis pressed his lips together and stared at the ground, waiting for the nausea to dissipate. Before he could answer, Dr. Walsh and Donald came back into the room, Donald carrying an armload of supplies which he set down on a rolling stainless-steel cart he pulled up next to Travis's bedside. Without saying anything, Dr. Walsh quickly cleaned the wound on Travis's arm again, dried it using a square of white, sterile gauze, and then carefully applied butterfly bandages to the entire incision, replacing the bandages she'd taken off with fresh ones.

Once that was done, she unrolled an Ace bandage, wrapping it around Travis's ankle and then handing him an ice pack. "Keep going with the antibiotics." She pulled a bottle of pills out of her pocket, "This is for the pain. Just know they will make you groggy if you take them."

Travis shook his head, "No thanks, Doc. I can't afford it."

Dr. Walsh narrowed her eyes and then shook her head, but walked away without saying anything else, Donald in her wake.

With the room restored to just Travis, Archie, and Catherine, Travis stared at the floor for a second as he rolled the sleeve of his shirt down back over the fresh bandages Dr. Walsh had put on his arm. His mind rattled with thoughts. The one thing Archie was right about was that they didn't have any other suspects. No other leads. All they had was a good deal of chatter from a source that seemed to be close to Jonah Hudson about the bounty on his head, and the single call to Archie from Tom Stewart asking about Travis's location. Travis licked his lips. They needed to do something to shake things loose. Maybe a call to Tom would do it. Although he hadn't had strong feelings about Tom before, he would if Tom was behind the kill order. "Okay, I'll make the call."

From out of his pocket, Archie pulled a burner phone. "I was hoping you'd say that."

43

Travis held the burner phone in his hand. As he looked at the screen, he realized Tom's number had already been programmed into it, as if Archie had assumed he'd agree to make the call. He waited for the call to connect. As he listened to the ringing, he looked at Catherine and Archie. Archie was still standing with his arms folded across his chest, his eyes boring holes in the shiny, white tile floor of sick bay. Catherine had begun pacing back and forth, not out of earshot, but almost as if she couldn't bear to stand in one position while she waited to see what was going to happen.

One ring, two rings, three rings. No Tom.

Travis glanced at the two of them and then looked away, his stomach knotting. Their stares made him uncomfortable. Travis checked the time. It was late in London, even more so on the East Coast. Would Tom even pick up?

A moment later, Travis got his answer. "Travis? Is that you?"

Travis glanced at Archie and Catherine. Catherine had stopped moving, her lips parted, her eyes wide. She gave a slow nod. Travis pulled the phone away from his ear and tapped the button to put it on speaker, "I heard you were looking for me."

Tom cleared his throat, "Yeah, I have been," he stammered. "Had some questions about one of the old cases we worked on together. Where are you?"

To anyone else, it would have sounded like a perfectly reasonable question. Not to Travis, though. Travis glanced at Archie and Catherine. Archie swung his head slowly from side to side, though he didn't need to. There was no way Travis would tell Tom where he was. He didn't bother answering the question. "Which case?"

"You know, I don't have my notes in front of me right now," he chuckled as if he didn't know. "Didn't bring them to bed with me. Didn't expect you to be calling this late." There was a pause. "It seems your number is blocked. Why don't you give it to me, and I'll give you a call back when I'm in the office in the morning. You know, with the time change and all that..." Tom's voice drifted off, though Travis could hear a hint of tension in it.

"That's okay, Tom. I'll call you back when I'm freed up. You know, the horse business is busy. Working all hours of the day and night."

"Yeah, I heard you were in Oklahoma. Are you headed to another show?" The words came out slow, calculated.

Another stab at getting Travis's location. "No, I had some other stuff to take care of. I'll call you later."

Travis was just about to hang up when he heard Tom say, "No, Travis. Wait!"

"What is it?"

Tom lowered his voice, "Listen, I have to level with you. Shelley's got herself involved in some stuff. I might need somebody like you to help me out. Off-the-books, if you know what I mean. Can you tell me where you are in case I need you?"

Travis glanced up at Archie and Catherine. This time they were both shaking their heads, "Like I said, Tom, I'll call you when I get a chance." Travis hung up and handed the phone back to Archie.

"Keep it," Archie growled. He ran his hand through his hair, shaking his head. "What was that?"

Travis slid off of the examination table and did his best to force his swollen ankle back into the pair of boots he'd been wearing. He licked his lips, "I have no idea."

Catherine narrowed her eyes, "He couldn't even tell you what case he needed help on. Pretty flimsy, if you ask me."

Travis shook his head. "He didn't sound right. Not like the same Tom I knew. The guy I knew was pretty upfront. Crossed a few lines, but always had good in mind. And whatever he said about Shelley, it wasn't the truth. He was lying."

Catherine narrowed her eyes at him, crossing her arms in front of her chest, "So what are you thinking?"

"That we should get back to the safe house and try to get some rest. I need a little time to figure things out. My gut tells me we are in for a rough ride."

44

By the time Travis and Catherine made it back to the safe house, it was nearly one o'clock in the morning. The dinner Catherine had made seemed a few hours earlier seemed like a lifetime had passed. Catherine grabbed a bottle of water and started for the bedroom. "Do you need anything before I go to bed?"

Travis shook his head, "No. I'm good."

"In that case, I'll see you in the morning."

Travis didn't say anything, only nodding. He watched as Catherine closed the door behind her, the door clicking into place. He was glad to be alone. Honestly, it wasn't much. His brain was working overtime, trying to decipher the few strands of information they had into something of a case, something more than a call from Tom Stewart. He shut off the single lamp Catherine had left on and slumped down onto the soft couch, yanking his boots off and pulling a thin blanket across his legs. He used an extra pillow to prop up his ankle. The throbbing was still there but seemed to slow down a little with his boot off and his leg up in the air.

Travis started to think about his conversation with Tom,

weighing each word. It was no surprise that Tom answered his phone. Anyone who worked for the CIA for any period of time knew that although you were hired based on a forty-hour-a-week position, the job required dedication twenty-four-seven. The fact that Tom picked up the phone was no big surprise.

The surprise had been how ineffective Tom was at figuring out where Travis was calling from and how obvious he'd been at wanting to know. Not that Tom could force the information out of Travis, but it was clear that Tom's only concern was Travis's location, not case information. If there even was a case Tom was worried about, or Shelley, for that matter.

Travis's mind flickered over to his memories of Shelley. He'd only met her a couple of times, at a barbecue or some dinner held at Tom's house for an occasion he couldn't remember. Travis pictured her as being short with dark hair and a pronounced limp, the result of getting hit by a car when she was a child. From the story the way Tom told it, her leg ended up shorter than it should have been because the doctors didn't set the bone correctly. In the darkness of the safe house, Travis narrowed his eyes as he stared at the ceiling. What could Shelley possibly have gotten herself involved in that Tom would contact an ex-agent for help?

Maybe it was a diversion.

Maybe there was absolutely nothing that Shelley was involved in. Maybe Tom had brought up her name in a ploy to elicit sympathy from Travis, as though that would release the switch that would tell Tom where Travis was.

His tactic didn't work.

Travis rolled on his side, pulling the blanket up a little higher over his shoulder, wedging the pillow under his ankle to keep it elevated. Every inch of his body ached in sympathy for what had happened to his arm and his ankle. Dr. Walsh had asked if he had any other injuries. He didn't. He knew that. But he knew the achiness he felt in his body at that moment would be nothing like what he felt in a few hours after lying still.

Travis's gut told him that Tom had something to do with what was going on. Was Tom connected somehow to Desert Indigo? What the connection was, Travis wasn't sure. He'd need to be if he was planning on hunting the Director of the CIA.

Travis closed his eyes, pushing off the question until he could get some sleep. Maybe then, things would begin to make sense.

Or maybe they wouldn't...

45

When Travis heard the first rustling, a slight metallic scraping near the door, he had no idea how much time had passed since he'd fallen asleep. The only thing he knew was that it was still dark and that it sounded like someone was making an attempt to pick the lock. Travis sucked in a breath, the adrenaline surging in his body from a dead sleep. It felt like electricity had shocked him.

He rolled toward the coffee table, hearing the door pop open, grabbing the gun Archie had given to him, feeling the first shot whiz past the side of his face as he threw himself on the floor. He returned fire as he landed on his right arm, searing pain from the knife wound surging through his body. In the darkness, it was impossible to see. The safe house was a pit of blackness. Travis's heart was pounding in his chest. Part of him wanted to yell for Catherine, but he knew the minute he did, whoever was in the apartment would know his location. Hopefully, the shots ringing out from his gun would be enough to roust Catherine out of her sleep. "Please don't be wearing earphones to bed," Travis whispered.

Travis crawled on the floor behind the couch, waiting for his eyes to adjust. He couldn't have knelt there for more than two seconds when Catherine's bedroom door opened. Travis pivoted on his knees to warn Catherine about the intruder, but no one was there. More shots fired through the doorway from somewhere near the kitchen. From inside the room, Travis saw a shadow of something launched through the door. Squinting, he realized Catherine had thrown a chair. Whoever was in the apartment took the bait and shot at it, as Catherine darted to Travis's side, her small hands wrapped around the grip of her pistol.

Travis waited for a moment for the next round of shots to ring out. They didn't come. He was just about to stand up when he felt one of the kitchen chairs whiz over his head. The intruder was taking a cue from them. Furniture throwing was a good distraction. Travis ducked and returned fire in time to see a shadow moving in the kitchen. Whoever was in the apartment had turned one of the burners on. The apartment began to fill with the sweet, acrid smell of gas. Travis glanced at Catherine. They were running out of time. As the gas filled the small apartment, all anyone would have to do was fire a single round or throw a match and the entire building could go up.

"We gotta get outta here," Travis hissed.

"The only way out is the way we came in."

Travis shook his head. "Can't go that way. They're waiting for us. They're using the gas to get us out of the apartment."

Holstering his gun, Travis stood up, dragging Catherine with him. He grabbed the leg of a chair that had fallen near where he stood and ran to the window, breaking out the glass as Catherine ducked. Over his shoulder, he saw the light of a match, a heavily accented woman's voice calling out, "Time's up,"

Travis grabbed Catherine and pulled her out of the second-floor window as he saw a blinding flash, feeling the heat of the explosion behind him.

Travis's body hit the ground hard, as the explosion took out the majority of the second floor of the building above the Indian restaurant Umar owned. A rain of debris and glass hit the ground just after Travis. He covered his head with his arms as he landed. He laid there for a second, the wind knocked out of him from the fall, his heart pounding. He opened his eyes to see Catherine a few feet from him, lying on her side. Travis struggled to his feet, "Catherine, we've gotta go. Can you move?" The words came out as fast as gunfire from an automatic weapon. Agnes would be coming. They only had a little time to get away.

"I think so," she said, struggling to her feet. Travis saw a trickle of blood running down her face in the glow of the fire above. The smell was acrid. They both started to cough as the smoke collected near the building. Travis grabbed her hand and half dragged her away from the building into the darkness, heading for the parking area behind the building.

"Where are we going?" Catherine asked as they stopped in an alleyway on the other side of the building. She was leaning against the brick building, her chest heaving, the words coming out between breaths. Travis bent over, putting his hands on his knees, trying to regroup. His head was pounding. "Do you think we can get to the car?"

Catherine nodded. "Yeah. Probably. Will they be watching it? I don't have the fob. It was in the flat."

Travis glanced around him. Catherine was right. The car was parked in front of the building, near the corner. Sure, whoever was after them was probably waiting for them to come back, but it wouldn't do them any good anyway if Catherine didn't have a fob. Travis glanced around him and then looked at Catherine. "Your head," he pointed. "It's bleeding." He saw her dab at it under the streetlight. She shook her head, her eyes unfocused, "It's nothing. Just a scratch."

"Good," he said. He knew they couldn't stay where they were. There was no telling if the person who had come after them figured they died in the blast or assumed they'd gotten away. But at some point, the assassin would confirm whether they'd gotten killed or not. They had to move and move now.

Travis stood up, staring. In the back parking lot, left under a flickering streetlamp was a boxy yellow Peugeot that had seen better days. Travis grabbed Catherine's hand, "Let's go."

Running towards the yellow car, Travis tugged at the door handle on the driver's side. Luckily, it was unlocked, the owner probably figuring the car wasn't worth stealing. Travis knelt down on the ground next to the car and pulled the wiring harness out from under the steering column. Using Archie's knife that somehow had managed to stay in his pocket after the jump from the apartment, Travis stripped a couple of the wires, twisting them together. The little car sputtered and then started up, the engine whirring to life.

Travis stood up, glancing at Catherine, "Get in!"

As Catherine slipped inside the car, Travis put it into gear. He'd let Catherine do the driving when he'd first gotten to London, not used to cruising on the opposite side of the road, but they didn't have time to argue about who had driving privileges and who didn't at that moment. Someone was coming after them and they needed to get away from the safe house and the onslaught of emergency vehicles Travis could hear whining in the distance. He said a silent prayer that no one else had gotten injured in the blast, except maybe, the assassin. Blinking, he remembered the woman with her infant he'd seen walking in the hallway the day before. His stomach flipped, imagining their torn, burned bodies left behind.

As Catherine slammed the door to the tiny car, Travis eased away from the parking lot quickly, without squealing the tires.

He drove in the opposite direction of Main Street in Little Delhi, winding his way through a few empty roads before glancing at Catherine. She was using the sleeve of her shirt to dab at her head. "You okay?"

Catherine nodded. "Yeah. I'm just rattled. What happened there? I was having a lovely dream about a grove of oranges and then the flat blows up. How does that happen?"

Travis gritted his teeth, "I think it's pretty obvious. Agnes found the safe house."

"That sounds like a reasonable conclusion. Where are we going now?"

"I don't know. Have any ideas? We can't stay on the move like this permanently. We need to regroup."

"I know where we can go. It'll be safe. Turn left here," Catherine pointed.

46

"What in the dickens happened to the two of you?" Archie asked, his eyebrows furrowed. Travis and Catherine stood soot-stained and filthy in the doorway of his home on the outskirts of London, his bulk framed in a dim light that was on inside. Archie stepped aside, glancing down the road, as if he expected a car to come careening around the corner at any time to mow them down. "Come in, come in," he waved to Travis and Catherine.

As soon as they made their way into Archie's house, Archie closed the door behind them, the opaque etched glass in the door hiding their entry. Archie doused the hallway lights and motioned for the two of them to come toward the back of the house. Catherine followed, Travis brought up the rear.

Archie led the two of them down a long, narrow hallway littered with family pictures hung precariously in dusty frames into what could best be described as a study. The room was cluttered, even worse than Archie's office at MI6, a desk in the corner stacked with so many teetering piles of files that it looked unusable, two matching leather chairs with footstools angled toward each other, a coffee table in between, a small lamp perched on the scratched wood emitting a yellow glow. Across from the chairs was a tattered olive couch, more books, and files piled up at one end of it. Archie closed the door to the study and stared at the two of them.

"What have you two gotten yourselves into?"

Travis shook his head, sitting down on the couch, "I think the better question would be how we survived the last hour."

Archie sat quietly as Catherine described what they'd been through — the assault on the safe house, the flying furniture, and then finally the surge of gas and their escape through the broken window. "Apologies for bringing a stolen car to your home, Archie, but we couldn't exactly go get the Volvo."

Archie waved them off, "That's the least of my worries." He took off his glasses and wiped the lenses with the sleeve of his robe.

Travis looked at him. From underneath the chocolate brown robe that came to his knees, Travis could see the legs of burgundy pajama bottoms. Archie's feet were covered by scuffed brown slippers in the same color as his robe. Travis's mind drifted, wondering if the robe and slippers had been a Christmas gift from Archie's wife or one of his children. Archie's hair was sticking straight up in the back, his thick glasses still perched on his nose. His face looked like it had shriveled, likely with concern and surprise at his two uninvited houseguests. "You think this is Agnes's work?" he said, staring at each of them. He frowned before letting them answer, "Do you need medical attention, either of you? I can have Dr. Walsh attend to you right here."

Travis shook his head, "Other than feeling like I've been through a car wreck and gotten thrown out of a two-story window, I'm all right, sir," Travis said.

"I'm fine as well. The cut on my head is tiny. Probably from a flying piece of glass or debris. I'm no worse for the wear," Catherine said, curling up on the leather chair next to Archie.

Travis narrowed his eyes as he looked at Catherine. She was resilient, that was for sure. Though she might not have felt relaxed, she certainly looked at ease especially for someone who'd just been woken up out of a dead sleep, shot at, and then thrown out of a two-story window. He looked back at Archie. "As for whether it was Agnes or not, I have no idea," Travis said, chewing the inside of his lip. "I have to be honest, these assassins are all starting to look like each other."

Archie narrowed his eyes and then a smile peeled across his face, followed by the roar of a deep laugh. "Indeed, my good fellow," he boomed, "I'd expect they would." When the laughter died down, Archie looked at Travis, his eyes boring into him. "I was going to bring you in first thing in the morning, but since you're here, I may have stumbled upon another piece of the puzzle."

Travis leaned back in his seat, "Like what?"

"Does the name Meset Gul mean anything to you?"

"I'm not sure. Should it?"

Archie nodded, "It might be the key to this whole puzzle."

47

Travis furrowed his eyebrows, "Say the name again?"

Archie nodded, "Meset Gul."

"It sounds vaguely familiar, but I can't place it." Travis looked down at the floor of Archie's study, noticing the worn fringe at the end of the threadbare Oriental rug that was in the middle of the room. He nudged at what was left of the tassel with his toe. "Do you have anything else that would jog my memory?"

"Meset Gul lived in the city of Tosya in the north of Turkey. The Black Sea region."

Travis nodded slowly, "Yes, the village of Ekincik. It was one of my first operations when I started with the CIA." He ran a hand through his dark hair, shaking his head, surprised about how many mission details had been buried in his mind. Many of them were better left buried. "It's been a long time."

Silence hung over the room for a moment as the memories began to collect themselves in Travis's mind. He cupped his hand under his chin, rubbing the stubble of his beard and then looked at Archie and Catherine, "I'd only been with the CIA for a few months. Maybe three or four. Tom was a senior operative.

Still working in the field. He took me on a mission to Turkey where we met with someone by that name, Meset Gul."

"Operation Black Cobra," Archie whispered.

Travis nodded, furrowing his eyebrows. How Archie knew about Operation Black Cobra was a question for another day. "That's right. It was an operation before Tom Stewart was the director. He and I were in Turkey, looking for an arms dealer named Ercan Onan. The CIA was interested in him because he was laundering money to fund the Al Qaeda operations in the Middle East, specifically Iraq." Travis leaned back on the couch and ran his hand through his hair, the memory of his time in Turkey flooding back into his mind. He hadn't thought about it in a long time, the operations between his time with Delta Force in the CIA seemingly running together, "Meset Gul was the asset we used to find Ercan Onan. We finally tracked Onan down to a cave just outside Ekincik in the mountains of the Black Sea."

Travis paused for a second, waiting for the next batch of memories to surface in his mind. Catherine's voice interrupted his thoughts, "Then what happened, Travis?"

"Onan came outside with a couple of his men. It was me and Tom. We didn't come with a military detail or anything. Just the two of us out on the road. Tom told me to stay by the truck. I assumed that was the normal protocol. I was new. I didn't know any better. I saw Tom walk over to Onan. Tom pulled something out of his pocket and handed it to him. The two men shook hands and then Tom walked away."

"What did Tom give Onan?" Archie asked.

"When Tom got back to the car, I asked him what the meeting was about. He said that he'd given Onan some information to prime the pump. He said it wasn't a big deal – the name of a few of our assets in the area, local tribes, people low down on the food chain, informants that weren't carrying any classified information."

Catherine raised her eyebrows, "Are you kidding me? Tom gave over CIA assets to a known arms dealer?"

Travis shook his head, "I remember thinking at the time that the whole thing seemed hinky. I challenged Tom on it, but he said that it was a normal course of business. The CIA traded information all the time and I shouldn't worry about it. I was no longer with Delta Force, what did I know? Tom swore me to secrecy."

Catherine shot a look at Archie, frowning. "Ercan Onan is one of the founding members of Desert Indigo. I knew this was all tied together," she said, clapping her hands. "Travis, whatever did happen with the information Tom gave him?"

Travis shrugged, "I don't know. I never heard anything about it again. Honestly, I totally forgot about the link between Tom and this Onan character until right now. I had a lot of other operations under my belt by the time I left five years ago. Add that to the desire to just forget everything I ever saw and I put it out of my mind." He licked his lips, "But now, looking back, it's clear Onan has something on Tom, and it's probably the fact that he gave up CIA secrets while he was still in the field."

"And you're the only one who knows," Catherine said slowly.

48

"I think it's time we go to New York," Catherine said, standing up from Archie's chair.

Travis raised his eyebrows, "Are you sure?"

Archie nodded, "I concur. It seems that Desert Indigo is at the center of all of the trouble. You two will probably have better luck if you are stateside for the rest of this mission." Archie pulled his cell phone from his pocket. "I'll get the two of you on the next flight back to New York. Catherine, you and Travis should head over to MI6, get cleaned up, and grab some changes of clothes while you are there, since everything got blown up at the safe house."

If Agnes was on the prowl, and it certainly seemed she was, then the fewer stops they made between Archie's house and their flight back to the United States would be for the best. Travis sat bolt upright, his eyes wide, "My backpack. It was at the safehouse. My passport's in there."

Archie shook his head, "Not to worry. By the time the two of you get to MI6, I'll have your travel documents ready to go."

Catherine got up off of the chair where she was sitting, a

broad smile on her face, "Off to New York! I love New York," she muttered, striding out of Archie's study.

Travis followed, the memories of Operation Black Cobra circling in his mind. The mission objective had been to cut off the head of the snake and stop the flood of funds and weapons to Al Qaeda. The head of that snake was Ercan Onan. It seemed as though Tom Stewart had done nothing but given him more power, maybe even gotten into bed with him. And if Ercan Onan was at the center of this, then it needed to stop.

49

Shelley Stewart wasn't the kind of wife that spied on her husband's phone and emails, at least not until the whole mess with Travis Bishop had started.

While Tom was in the shower early that morning after his run, Shelley slipped out of bed and checked his cell phone. There was a message from an unknown number that read, "First attempt unsuccessful. Coming back to the US under the name Iyabo Ide. Will handle the issue when I arrive."

Shelley grimaced. The message in front of her could only mean one thing. Agnes, the most highly recommended assassin Tom could find, had been unsuccessful. Tom had now made three separate hires, trying to end the life of Travis Bishop. Travis had evaded each one. Either he was extremely lucky or he was a cat in disguise, living out his nine lives. By Shelley's count, he was down to six left.

That was six too many for her.

By the time Tom got out of the shower, Shelley was already dressed and ready for work. She left without saying goodbye.

In her car on the way into DC, she placed a call. "Gerald? It's Shelley Stewart."

Gerald cleared his throat, "Senator Stewart? It's nice to hear from you bright and early on this beautiful morning. How can I be of assistance?"

Gerald Chatterton was one of the contacts Shelley had cultivated at Homeland Security. She'd found out he would be testifying in front of her committee and took the time to call him and meet with him beforehand, coaching him on the finer points of what to say, what not to say, and especially what not to do. In his own words, Gerald had confessed that he owed her. Shelley hated using the IOU on something this small, especially since Tom should have handled things, but it might be the only way to get things moving in a positive direction.

"I found out that an old classmate of mine is going to be coming from Heathrow into New York sometime today. I wanted to surprise her. Do you think you could use your contacts and track her flight for me? Her name is Iyabo Ide."

"That seems like an easy request, Senator. Certainly. I'd be happy to. Can you give me twenty minutes?"

"Sure. Just make sure not to tell anyone else and call me directly. I don't want to spoil the surprise."

Exactly seventeen minutes later, Shelley's phone rang, "Gerald? Did you find out anything?"

"Yes, in fact, I did. We have a United Airlines flight coming into LaGuardia tonight at eight p.m. Flight number 7032. On it, I think you'll find your friend Iyabo Ide. I'll text you the flight information. Is there anything else I can do to brighten your day, Senator?"

Shelley shook her head. Sometimes talking to Gerald reminded her more of dealing with someone who had been trained by Disney customer service than a Homeland security agent. Then again, maybe more of the people she called should be so cooperative. "No. A text with the flight information would be sufficient. Thank you."

50

At seven forty-seven p.m., Shelley Stewart parked her car in the short-term parking at New York's LaGuardia Airport. Darting inside as quickly as she could with her limp, she carried the sign she'd printed with Iyabo Ide's name on it. Shelley had changed out of the brightly colored jacket she'd worn to work that morning and donned a black jacket to match the black pants and white blouse she already had on, trying to look the part of a chauffeur. As the stream of passengers thickened, walking toward baggage, Shelley held the sign up in front of her, waiting, scanning the crowd.

Families with young children who were delighted to be out of the confines of an airplane buzzed around their parents' ankles, businessmen getting back from their trips, murmured into their phones, their black backpacks slung over their shoulders, their phones pressed up to their ears, and a couple of packs of college kids, earphones slung around their necks as they smiled and chatted with each other passed her. The smell of stale air and jet fumes hung around the passengers as Shelley scanned the crowd.

At the back of a particularly thick group of people, Shelley saw an African woman with her hair tightly braided to the top of her head walking toward the exit. She wore a brightly colored dress in yellows and oranges with a hint of red and green in the fabric. The dress itself was loud and busy, but among the wide variety of passengers that were coming off the plane, the woman fit in perfectly. She was so outlandish in her dress that no one paid any attention to her, especially in New York, with every other person sporting green hair, piercings, and tattoos.

Shelley's eyes widened slightly as she watched the woman stop and stare at her quizzically, her head cocked to the side. Agnes wasn't expecting a ride. Would she walk past and ignore Shelley? Shelley took a half step forward, trying to catch her eye, not wanting to spook the woman but trying to connect with her, "Ms. Ide? I was told to come pick you up and take you to the location of your choice." Shelley tried to sound friendly and as non-intimidating as she could.

The woman sucked in a breath, paused for a second as if she was considering her options, and then gave a quick nod. Shelley smiled, waving her forward, "May I carry your bags for you?" Agnes had a large soft black bag slung over her shoulder and was rolling a nondescript black nylon suitcase on her right side.

"No, thank you," she replied in a thick Nigerian accent.

"If that's the case, then right this way. The car is close by."

Shelley led Agnes out to the short-term parking lot where Shelley had left the car with its hazards blinking in the spots reserved for chauffeurs and limo drivers. She walked around the side and opened the door for Agnes and waited while she got in. "I was told you have a hotel booked in Manhattan? Is that where you'd like to go?"

Agnes shook her head, speaking in a thick African accent,

"No. I won't be going there." She handed Shelley a slip of paper. "Please take me to this address."

After keying the address into her phone, Shelley started the engine, and drove slowly out of the airport parking lot, quickly jumping on the freeway and heading to the outskirts of New York City. Agnes had given her an address in Floral City off of Route 25, halfway between the city and Long Island.

Once they were clear of the heavy airport traffic around LaGuardia and got on the freeway, the traffic lightened up considerably. Shelley kept checking the rearview mirror, watching to see what Agnes was doing. For a world-renowned assassin, she seemed quite calm. A shiver ran down Shelley's spine. She'd seen the files of what Agnes could do to people when provoked. It was like having a caged lion in the back seat.

Shelly glanced in the rearview mirror again at Agnes. She seemed to be staring out of the window, watching the sights go by as if she'd never been to New York before, or perhaps Agnes was just distracted by her failed attempt to kill Travis Bishop. Shelley had to press her lips together in order to avoid mentioning anything about it as they drove.

About twenty minutes later, Shelley pulled the sedan off of the freeway and drove down a tangle of side streets, finding the address Agnes had given her. It was for the Starlight Motel, a two-floor ramshackle building that looked like it had been built in the 1960s and probably hadn't been updated since then except for the electronic locks on the doors. "You can pull up right here," Agnes said, pointing directly ahead of the vehicle.

The motel was configured so that the occupants could park directly outside of the door. "I already have my key code, so I don't need anything else," she said, getting out of the car and carrying her bag with her. She didn't offer payment or a tip. Shelley sat in the car for a second, watching Agnes open the door to the room, blinking, her mouth dry.

In a single smooth movement, Shelley pushed the driver's

side door open, her heart skipping a beat, striding towards Agnes and pulling a silenced Smith & Wesson forty caliber pistol from the inside of her jacket. Agnes had her back turned to Shelley as the first shot hit Agnes's spinal column, her body crumpling in the doorway. She'd never seen it coming.

Shelley glanced over her shoulder left and right and trotted toward the open door. Agnes had landed on her face and was trying to use her arms to scoot her now dead lower body into the room. She glanced over her shoulder, her eyes wide, as Shelley pulled the trigger again, this time taking out the side of her head. Her upper body, which had been functional, now joined her lower body as life left her. Shelley stepped over the body, slipping the gun back inside of her jacket and grabbing Agnes's arms, pulling her inside of the dimly lit room. Once inside, Shelley picked up Agnes's bags and slammed the door closed behind her.

Staring at the dead body in front of her, Shelley realized she was out of breath. She stared at Agnes. It seemed the famous assassin was human after all. Shelley smiled. Agnes, or whatever her real name was, never saw the attack coming. Limping over the body, Shelley looked at her carefully. Agnes's eyes were wide, the brown irises and black pupils unfocused and unmoving, her face spared by the fact that the bullet had entered above her right temple and exited exactly on the opposite side, blowing off part of her left ear.

Shelley knelt on the ground, patting Agnes down. She had nothing on her, save for her clothes, a bit of jewelry, and a bracelet made of cord around her wrist.

Shelley dragged Agnes's body next to the bed. She didn't want to trip over it over the next several hours while she was in the room. She grabbed Agnes's bag and opened it up, going through every item in it.

Much of what Agnes carried was standard airline fare — personal hygiene items, like deodorant, toothpaste and toothbrush, a jar of some sort of cream that had writing on it Shelley couldn't decipher, and a few sets of clothes, basics like jeans, sweatpants and shirts, nothing like the elaborate African dress she was wearing. Shelley pulled everything out of the bag and laid it on the bed, "Well, I expected you to be a little bit better prepared than this Agnes," she muttered.

Examining the suitcase, Shelley realized it seemed that it wasn't as deep as it was wide. The interior lining, thin black, nylon fabric, seemed to be bunched up in a few areas where it shouldn't be. Shelley had worn enough well-constructed suits during her career to know how fabric should lay. That wasn't it. Shelley probed the edges with her finger and then realized there was a hard shell in the back of the suitcase that wiggled as if there was something behind it. "What have we here, Agnes?" she muttered. Shelley pushed her finger in a little bit more to find a series of snaps that could be undone, then a hard piece of plastic – a false back. When she pulled it out she gave a low whistle, "Jackpot."

Agnes had set her up well. She had everything she needed to take out Travis Bishop.

51

The false panel in the back of the suitcase of the woman only known as Agnes revealed a treasure trove of supplies any good assassin would need. Shelley sat down on the bed and carefully lifted each item out, as though Santa Claus had left her a very precious set of presents on Christmas Day. There were stacks of cash in several different currencies — German Deutschmarks, American dollars, and British pounds — in addition to the parts of what looked like at least two pistols constructed of white plastic. The parts included several bags full of projectiles, likely produced on a sophisticated 3D printer, as well as passports, both blank and complete with Agnes's picture, from at least five different countries. Shelley glanced at the body on the ground, "Thanks for the supplies, Agnes," she mumbled under her breath. They would be perfect for her plan.

Those weren't the only supplies Agnes had traveled with. Getting up from the bed, Shelley picked up Agnes's shoulder bag and dumped it out next to the pile of items she'd found in the hidden compartment in the black suitcase. What she saw was exactly what she would expect from someone who had just submitted themselves to a long flight across the Atlantic Ocean. There was a bag of snacks, including pretzels, cheese crackers, and gummy worms, a Chapstick, moisturizing eye drops, motion sickness pills, and a dog-eared book, "Huckleberry Finn," by Mark Twain. The cover and pages were dirty and worn, as though Agnes had read it over and over again. A slip of paper stuck out from the top. Shelley tugged at it, staring. It was a picture, almost as worn and dog-eared as the pages of the Mark Twain book. It showed an African woman with three little kids huddled around her knees. Shelley squinted at it, realizing that the smallest girl, the one on the right with a big smile and two braids was Agnes. Shelley pressed her lips together. She couldn't have been more than three or four in the picture, long before the war tore Nigeria into pieces and turned Agnes, or whatever her actual name was, into an orphan.

Shelley tossed the picture on the bed. It said something about Agnes that she carried the picture of her family with her, but it wasn't enough to make her regret killing the assassin. It was her first kill. She stopped for a moment. She'd wondered if she'd feel anything, any type of regret or sadness. She felt nothing. If there was anything Shelley had learned as a politician, it was a kill or be killed world. "To think all you needed to do was kill Travis Bishop and we wouldn't be here," Shelley said, shaking her head. "But, I guess all good things come to an end, now don't they?"

Shelley picked up Agnes's cell phone and leaned over the bed, casually picking up the dead woman's hand and using her fingerprint to open it. Shelley immediately went into the phone's settings, changed the password, and reset the fingerprint so that she could access the phone whenever she wanted. She would need it if she was going to become Agnes. She scrolled through the texts, finding a particularly whiny one from Tom, "Where are you? We need to get this Travis issue wrapped up!" Based on the time stamp, he had written it only a few hours earlier, likely while Agnes was still on the plane. Shelley's lip curled. Wouldn't Tom be completely amazed to know that his wife, the formidable Senator Shelley Stewart, had killed the world's best-known assassin and was about to take over her identity? That would be remarkable news to him.

She smiled. It was time to get to work.

52

By the time Catherine and Travis landed at JFK airport in New York City, it was nearly one o'clock in the morning. They had tried to make the earlier flight that would have gotten them in around eight p.m. Eastern time at LaGuardia, but they hadn't made it. Losing their identity papers in the bomb blast had set things back a little bit. They'd spent two, very necessary, albeit rushed, hours at MI6 scrubbing the soot and dirt off of them, getting rechecked by Dr. Walsh, and then fitted with new identities, clothing, supplies, and even luggage. By the time they were ready to go, they needed to take the later flight. They had no choice.

There was nothing comfortable about the flight. Sleeping pinned in a cramped seat wasn't pleasant, despite the news that the flight was about an hour and a half shorter heading eastbound due to the jet stream, the pilot reported in a giddy voice as they got on board. After two hours of sitting, despite his best efforts to sleep, Travis's legs began to cramp. After four hours of sitting, he became cranky and by the time they landed, all of the work they'd done at MI6 to get cleaned up felt like it had been for nothing. He felt as dirty and worn out as the moment he'd hit the ground after the bomb blast.

He and Catherine slipped through American customs and immigration without any fuss, quickly grabbing a cab and heading to a Hilton Hotel in downtown Manhattan that someone at MI6 had kindly arranged for them. The young man at the check-in desk, his green hair neatly combed off to the side, his name badge reading Walton, stared at them with bulging eyes, "Mr. and Mrs. Vargas, we have reserved for you adjoining rooms on the sixth floor. Here are your room keys."

Travis didn't say anything, simply scooping up the key closest to him and watching as Catherine did the same. They headed upstairs, both of them silent. Travis scanned the key card on the reader at his door, watching Catherine do the same. The locks popped open at nearly the same moment. Inside, Travis quickly locked the door and strode to the door that accessed the adjoining room, opening it. A moment later, Catherine cracked her door open as well. He stuck his head in. Catherine had put her suitcase on the bed and was in the process of unzipping it. She had dark circles under her eyes. The fatigue of the last few days was starting to show. He was sure she could see it on him as well. Catherine had pulled a few loose strands of her hair over the cut on her forehead Dr. Walsh had bandaged before they got on the plane, hiding the beige bandage. "Let's try to get some rest and get things started early in the morning. Sound good?"

Catherine nodded. "That'll work. Sleep well."

As Travis went back to his side of their rooms, he opened his suitcase, one that had been provided for him by MI6. The tech that had worked with him gleefully handed him a special pouch they'd developed to hide weapons, making it easier for their agents to fly with them. The masking technology was a simple process, he'd explained. A combination of metals and plastics that they used in the pouch created a black spot in the x-ray when the luggage was scanned. The technicians looking at the x-ray would never know that a gun or knife had passed through their scanning technology. It worked like a charm. Travis removed the layers of clothes from the suitcase unearthing the pouch. He unzipped it, finding inside the Glock 17, a holster, two magazines, and extra ammunition that Archie had sent with them. Travis knew Catherine was carrying the same pouch he had. He shook his head. It was amazing to him to think average flyers would never consider contraband was going on a plane with them. MI6, CIA, and agencies like them – not to mention all of the bad actors they were fighting against – had all sorts of contingencies and inventions for getting people and equipment from country to country without being seen.

Travis quickly checked the gun, reloaded it, and set the holster next to it on the nightstand. He went into the bathroom, splashed some cold water on his face, brushed his teeth, and collapsed into the bed, flipping off the light, the smell of freshly bleached sheets filling his nose. He left his door cracked open. Catherine's was too. Her light was already out. Part of him wanted to get up and push her door open and talk to her, to tell her that he was sorry she'd gotten herself wrapped up in the mess he was in. But he knew if he said those words, she would show her stiff British upper lip and say, "Don't be ridiculous, Travis. It's the job."

And she was right. It was her job, but not his.

Staring at the textured white ceiling of the hotel room, he began to think about the ranch and how he wanted to get back to the horses and to being outside. Things that normally annoyed him, like client calls, dealing with the contractor rebuilding the barn, or insurance paperwork sounded good at the moment. As he closed his eyes, he wondered if it would ever be possible to get back to the life he loved and leave the trouble behind. He drifted off, an unsettled feeling covering him as he slept.

53

CIA director Tom Stewart hadn't slept a wink. He'd been up all night, pacing, staring at his computer screen, and waiting for his wife, Senator Shelley Stewart, to come home.

She never did.

At about midnight, Tom had gotten a message from Shelley, "I can't count on you to handle things. Taking matters into my own hands. Don't try to find me."

Those words were the ones that had kept him up all night.

Guilt chased Tom Stewart like a dog nipping at his heels as he checked his Desert Indigo bank balance over and over again, silently hoping that every time he looked at the account it would disappear, that he had imagined the whole relationship. Travis had been someone he'd thought of as a friend. Not only had he betrayed his country and his wife, but he was about to lose a friend, too.

He shook his head, closing his eyes tightly. No matter how much he obsessed about the decisions he'd made, it didn't change a thing.

Regardless of how Tom looked at it, he was jammed up.

Ercan Onan had owned him from the minute that their asset Meset Gul had introduced them in the middle of nowhere in that deserted town in Turkey many years before. It was the perfect honey trap. Ercan had played on what he knew about Tom — his drive to succeed, his insecurity around money, his desire to be at the top of the Washington pecking order. And Tom had made the mistake of falling for it, not putting the pieces together fast enough.

Now his life was in shambles. Ercan owned him. Not only did Ercan know that Tom had betrayed multiple assets over the years, handed him classified CIA intelligence, and caused the deaths of at least half a dozen people that had been recruited by the CIA to provide information, but Tom was in bed with a whole lot of the most notorious terrorists across the globe. The list of Desert Indigo investors was one his CIA colleagues would have salivated over if they had the chance to take even one of them down.

Earlier that afternoon, Tom had locked himself away in his office and done a deep dive on Desert Indigo, something he had been hesitant to do before. Ignorance is bliss, he kept telling himself. And it was. He was just happy for the high returns on his meager two hundred-thousand-dollar investment. Using a contact he had, a black-hat hacker who did work for the CIA from time to time, Tom got a list of all of the investors in Desert Indigo, and all of them shared one single characteristic. They were all terrorists.

Ercan Onan was known for his ability to launder money and move arms. Gonzalo Laguna, another one of the founding members of Desert Indigo, trafficked in oil out of Venezuela, girls, and drugs. The list went on and on. When Tom realized the connection, he sat in his office, his hands shaking, perspiration gathering on his upper lip. He scanned the rest of the list. At the bottom, there was his name, Tom Stewart, Director of the CIA.

Once Tom had seen the roster of investors, it had become blatantly obvious what Ercan and Gonzalo had constructed through Desert Indigo. It was one of the cleverest schemes he'd seen in his time at the CIA. They'd hired the financial genius, Jonah Hudson, to help them launder their funds. Criminal money was notoriously difficult to deal with. Tom remembered when he'd made his first deposit, he'd had to make a wire transfer to a bank he'd never heard of in the Cayman Islands.

Based on what he'd found, Century National Bank, located in the Caymans would accept the money – primarily cash – from the investors no questions asked as to its provenance, quickly diverting it into a Desert Indigo account, at which point Jonah laundered it by buying investments in some of the world best-known companies — companies like Ford, GM, J.P. Morgan Chase, and Disney — the list went on and on. Once the money was in the market, it was considered clean. The investors could buy and sell, moving their funds from the Desert Indigo account, taking their profits and putting them elsewhere, creating nest eggs all over the globe should they ever have to quickly escape the long arm of the law.

Tom shook his head. The worst part? The size of the fund. At nearly half a trillion dollars, Jonah Hudson had a significant amount of leverage with individual companies, other investment managers, and the market itself. But was Jonah Hudson really in control? Or were Ercan and Gonzalo the masters behind their cute little British hedge fund puppet?

As Tom paced the floor that night, the scenarios kept running through his head. He was the one that had called the hit on Travis Bishop, thinking that it would end the exposure he had. Travis had been the only one who had seen him pass information to Ercan. It seemed like a simple process at the time, one that he and Shelley agreed about. Eliminate the only witness and life could go on for the two of them as he expected it to. He'd even thought at one point of retiring and leaving his money with Jonah Hudson. The man had taken two hundred thousand and turned it into millions. Why not keep going? But then as the plot unraveled and the assassination attempts failed, Tom realized there was no escaping it. The damage was done. It was only a question of when things would come crashing down around his head. He was braced for impact.

By four o'clock in the morning, Tom was in a funk. More specifically, he realized, a state of agitated confusion. The facts that seemed so clear when he'd first started down the road with Desert Indigo became muddled in his mind, fear, worry, anger and paranoia all wrapping their tentacles around his thoughts. He felt like his body had been supercharged with electricity. He'd made so many wrong decisions. Wasn't there one he could make that was right?

In a flurry of energy, he picked up his phone and called Travis.

54

The ringing of his cell phone woke Travis up out of a dead sleep. He'd put the SIM card and battery back in the moment that he had gotten on American soil, waiting for an update from Ellie on what was going on at the ranch. He hadn't heard back from her, so he'd left it on, at least temporarily. It didn't seem that having his phone off was providing him any protection anyway.

When the phone rang, he rolled over, slapping at the nightstand with his hand, trying to find the buzzing phone in the darkness of the unfamiliar hotel room. After two tries he managed to snag it, pulling it back toward him. "Hello?" he mumbled.

"Travis, it's Tom."

Travis sat bolt upright in the bed. He swallowed, wiping his eyes, "Tom? What's going on?"

"I'm so sorry. I'm so sorry..." he whimpered.

Travis looked up in time to see Catherine poking her head through the doorway. Her head was cocked to the side, her brown hair fluffy and slightly disheveled from sleeping. She had her arms crossed across her chest, her eyebrows furrowed. Travis mouthed the word, "Tom."

Travis refocused on the phone call, "What are you talking about, Tom?"

"All of it. I'm so sorry, Travis. I don't know what to say."

"Whoa, whoa, whoa. Slow down, Tom. I have no idea what you're talking about."

"The hit on you, Travis. I did it. I'm the one that hired the assassins. I can't stop it. There's nothing I can do. I'm so sorry." Tom's voice cracked.

Travis didn't say anything for a second, trying to gather his thoughts. He had to be careful how he played this. Tom was clearly having some sort of a mental break. This could be the opportunity Travis had been waiting for to get information about what was going on, but he had to be careful. "It's okay, Tom. We all do things we shouldn't. I know I have." Travis tried sounding compassionate, not that he felt any pity for Tom at all.

"Yeah, but you don't understand. I did something really bad this time. Things are really messed up."

Travis hopped out of bed and started pacing. He put the phone on speaker so Catherine could hear. "Can you tell me what's going on? Maybe I can help."

"No. Nobody can. I'm in this alone. But I thought you should know." He paused for a moment. "I was afraid, Travis, I didn't know what else to do. These investors, they have me."

"What do you mean?"

"They tricked me. Maybe they didn't actually do that, maybe they just took advantage of me and I let them. They said they could make me a lot of money. And they have, but I've had to compromise in the meantime. You know what I mean, don't you, Travis?"

Travis nodded. Compromise was espionage lingo for someone who made choices they shouldn't, choices that would put others in danger or exposed state secrets they had no business sharing. Travis narrowed his eyes, "What exactly have you done, Tom?" Travis said, the words coming out slow and measured.

"I can't talk about it, Travis," Tom stuttered, "But if there was a way for me to call off the bounty on your head I would. But I can't. Not now. It's too late."

Tom hung up before Travis was able to ask any more questions. Realizing the call was done, Travis threw the phone down on the bed. Anger surged through his body. None other than the Director of the CIA wanted him dead. He stared at Catherine, "Did you hear that?" Heat built in his chest. Travis had been betrayed by one of his own.

She nodded, "Sounds like a complete admission. Looks like some of the pieces are falling into place."

Travis stood near the bed, staring at the phone, his hands balled into fists, "This whole thing — it's been all about greed."

"I know that, but did you hear him? Tom didn't sound good, Travis. He sounds like he's losing his mind."

"I know. That's what I'm worried about."

55

The call from Tom rattled Travis enough that there was absolutely no point in trying to go back to sleep. Knowing that someone he'd considered a friend at one time betrayed him sent a knot of anger into his gut, the sour taste of bile sitting in the back of his throat. Yet someone else had betrayed him, first Kira and Gus, now Tom.

Travis headed into the bathroom and started the shower, standing under it for a long time, washing off the combination of stale air, sweat, jet fumes, and the frustration he felt after hearing from Tom as best he could. Pulling on a fresh pair of jeans, a T-shirt, and a flannel shirt, Travis dug through the bag he got from MI6 and found the baseball cap he'd requested. He bent the bill on it a couple of times and fitted it to his head. He might not feel himself, but at least he looked better.

By the time he came out of the shower, Catherine was sitting on the end of her bed, dressed and ready to go. She was on the phone with someone. "Yes. That would be fine. Yes, thank you so very much. We'll be in touch," she said as she ended the phone call.

Travis narrowed his eyes, "Who was that?"

"Archie. He's diverted all of the MI6 assets he can spare, plus financial analysts to figure out exactly what's going on."

"Did you tell him about Tom's meltdown?"

She nodded, her lips pursed. "It's unfortunate news, Travis. Archie is going to make some phone calls. I'm hoping that someone can get to him before something bad happens."

"So am I. Can't exactly have the Director of the CIA going off the deep end and exposing classified secrets."

Catherine shook her head. "What do you want to do now?"

"We have to figure out how to end this." Travis looked back toward his room where his cell phone was sitting on the nightstand. "I have a phone call I need to make first."

Travis grabbed his phone and walked to the window, staring outside. It wasn't quite five o'clock in the morning in New York, but there were cars and taxis and pedestrians walking up and down the sidewalks, people heading to work in hotels and law offices and fire departments across the city, getting an early start to their day. New York had the reputation of never sleeping. Travis could see why that was the case.

A fire truck cruised down Washington Street in front of the hotel, an enormous American flag streaming behind it. A lump formed in Travis's throat. The tragedy of 9/11 had happened decades ago, but the city still bore the scars of that day and the pride of getting through it. The flag flapping behind the fire truck was only one of the many hallmarks of what the city had been through. Travis watched as the truck disappeared from his view. He narrowed his eyes. What Tom had done would sully the reputation of the United States among international agencies for years to come. Travis needed to do what he could to repair it.

Travis looked down at his phone. He dialed a number he hadn't used in a while. "Travis? It's mighty early. This better be good."

"It is, Governor. I wouldn't be calling otherwise."

The Governor of Texas, James Torres, had become a friend of Travis's after the debacle at the White House Travis had helped to unravel six months before. "I need a favor."

The Governor chuckled, "I wouldn't expect anything else this early in the morning. What's going on?"

Travis took a moment to explain the circumstances — the first knife attack at the Oklahoma Fairgrounds, how he'd ended up in London with Catherine and Archie, and the confession he'd just gotten from Tom Stewart. "You're telling me Tom Stewart, the Director of the CIA, the most powerful spy agency on the globe, has been compromised?"

"It certainly looks that way, sir."

"Man, Travis, you somehow manage to get yourself in the middle of some humdingers, don't you?"

"I wish that wasn't the case sir, but it does seem that way."

"What do you need?"

"I need contact with whoever you've got that's in intelligence. Someone who's not CIA. We need to give them a heads up."

"That would be Senator Linette Riggs. You'll like her. Former Air Force. Let me give her a call. Luckily she's usually up by now. Soon as I'm off the phone, I'll send you her contact information. Sound good?"

"That'll work, sir. Thanks again."

Seven minutes later, after Travis had paced the length of the room twenty-two times, his phone buzzed. There was no message, only a number. He tapped on it and immediately placed a call, waving Catherine over to him.

A female voice answered the phone, "Mr. Bishop?"

"Senator Riggs? Thank you for taking my call."

"Of course. Governor Torres is a personal friend. He said you had some critical information to pass on?"

Travis sat on the edge of the bed, putting it on speaker once again, "I do. I have MI6 Agent Catherine Lewis here with me.

We've been dealing with this issue for the last several days, but it's time to bring it out into the open." Travis detailed the same information he'd given to Governor Torres about the bounty on his life and then the connection to MI6.

"I'm sorry, Mr. Bishop, I'm not understanding what this has to do with intelligence?"

"Tom Stewart has been compromised."

Travis heard Senator Riggs suck in a breath, "CIA Director Tom Stewart? Are we talking about the same person?"

"Indeed," Catherine said. "It appears Director Stewart was cajoled into handing over some classified CIA information about ten years ago. That indiscretion set the stage for him to get involved with the hedge fund that is being used to launder terrorist money across the globe."

Travis took the next minute, filling in the details about how Tom got sucked into the situation and how the Director had called him the hour before. "Senator Riggs, in addition to handing over sensitive information, Tom doesn't sound himself."

"Are you saying he's been fully compromised and should be relieved of his position? That's a strong accusation, Mr. Bishop, one that I simply can't take lightly without looping in the president." Her words were cold and distant.

Travis didn't back down. "Then I suggest you wake him up."

56

Jonah Hudson was taking his third sip of a cup of scalding hot English breakfast tea with one cube of sugar and a splash of cream when his phone rang. He glanced at the time. It was four minutes after six o'clock in the morning eastern standard time. He raised his eyebrows. Quite early for a phone call, but then again, his clients were demanding to say the least.

He sucked in a breath, letting the phone ring one more time, composing himself. He would've been much happier to have taken the call after he'd at least finished his first cup of tea, but duty was calling. "Good morning, Mr. Onan," Jonah tried to say as cheerfully and professionally as he could manage.

"Jonah. Thank you for taking my call at this early hour. I trust I didn't disturb your morning routine, at least not too much."

Jonah stared at his tea, which was cooling by the moment. Cold tea was not the harbinger of a good day. "No, not at all," he lied. "How can I be of service?"

"Gonzalo and I have been talking. We'd like to make a shift in the way the portfolio is managed. We'd like you to take all of the holdings and simultaneously sell them at three o'clock today."

Jonah's heart skipped a beat. Had he heard Ercan wrong? "I'm sorry? Could you repeat that? You want me to liquidate the entire portfolio at exactly three o'clock today? Take all cash positions?"

"That's correct Jonah. All of it. And exactly at three p.m."

Jonah's hands began to shake. He set the phone down and put it on speaker. "Mr. Onan, I simply don't know if this is possible. We have more than half a trillion in holdings. That type of a sell order would have devastating effects on the American markets, not to mention the ripple effects on the global markets."

There was silence at the end of the line for a moment. Jonah wondered for a millisecond if Ercan was reconsidering his request. Jonah began to stammer, filling the silence, "The hedge fund investment rules are very specific, Mr. Onan. I have discretionary use of the money. My job is to grow it and we don't move it except for twice a year. That window closed yesterday, so it's not possible to do this. Besides the fact that you would basically eliminate all of your gains. There'd be no way to get the top of the market prices for all of the positions that we hold. As we sold them off, the price would necessarily drop, which would cause a cascade of losses across the board..."

"Jonah?" Ercan said slowly, drawing out each sound.

"Yes, sir?" The words came out weak and sad as if Jonah's hand had just gotten caught in the cookie jar.

"Do you have any idea who you're dealing with? You have any idea what I am capable of doing not only to you, but to every person you have ever known or loved, including the family you have left back in England?"

Jonah's entire body began to shake. "I'm sorry, Mr. Onan —"

"Don't question me ever again. Not if you want to live to see the sunset. Schedule the sell orders. And by the way, in case you decide you're going to change your mind, I want you to look downstairs."

Jonah got up from his desk in his Park Avenue apartment and looked down at the street. Two men wearing dark suits with their arms crossed were staring up at his apartment looking at him. "You see those two men, Jonah?"

"Yes, sir."

"Do what I say or you'll be spending a good deal of time with them, time that won't be pleasant, time that you'll wish they would put you out of your misery. Are we clear? Now go to the office and do as you're told."

"Yes…"

Jonah's hands were shaking so hard as he went to hang up the phone he could barely touch the screen to end the call. He sat back in his chair, his eyes closed, thinking about the two men that were standing downstairs, waiting to do unspeakable things to him. Something inside of Jonah knew this day would come. He'd made a ton of money and become a leader in his field, but it came with a steep price. He looked back at his screen, sucking in a deep breath. He had no choice. If he wanted to live another day, Ercan was right. He would have to do what he was told. They owned him.

57

Tom Stewart had gotten back from his run, taken a shower, and was drinking a glass of water, still wondering why Shelley hadn't returned any of his texts or phone calls by six-thirty in the morning when the doorbell rang.

Frowning, Tom assumed that his security detail had a question for him, but as he opened the door, two black-haired men with thick beards wearing jeans and t-shirts shoved their way inside. Tom didn't have time to react. Before he could yell for help or reach for one of the many weapons he had stashed around the house, they'd already grabbed him, cable-tied his wrists together, and forced him out the door, the glass of water he'd been drinking shattering on the floor. Shoving him in the back of a black van parked in the driveway, the door closed. As he was about to demand to be released, a strip of silver duct tape was slapped over his mouth, a black hood draped over his head.

Tom started to shake but sat silently, his CIA training kicking in. Just breathe, he told himself. Just breathe.

58

A half-hour after his conversation with Senator Riggs, Travis got a call back from her. "Mr. Bishop?"

"Senator?"

"Do you have paper and a pen handy?"

Travis walked to the desk in the corner of the hotel room. He'd been busy repacking his suitcase when the senator had called. "Yes, go ahead."

She read off an address in Virginia. "This is the address for Tom Stewart's house. I need you and Agent Lewis to go there right now."

Travis narrowed his eyes. He and Catherine had been planning on spending the day tracking down Jonah Hudson, but apparently, Senator Riggs had another job for him. "What happened?"

"He's missing."

The words hung in the air for a moment. Travis's mind began to reel, remembering the panic and paranoia in Tom's voice from a couple of hours before. "What? How is that possible? I just spoke to him."

"Apparently, his security detail saw him go for his run and

return home. The agent on duty got called back to the office for a meeting. During that thirty-minute gap, something happened. We don't know what. I need you to get there and see if you can figure it out. There's a car waiting downstairs for you. Report back."

"Yes, ma'am."

"This goes no further than you, me, and Agent Lewis. Understood?"

"Understood."

Catherine poked her head in the room, "Everything okay?"

"Tom Stewart has disappeared. Slipped his security detail. There's somebody waiting downstairs to take us to his house."

"Do you think he's on the run?"

"I have no idea, but Senator Riggs wants us to find out."

"Let's go."

Catherine darted through Travis's room and they exited through Travis's door together, striding quickly down the hallway for the elevator and emerging in the lobby a minute later. Out front, as promised, was a black sedan, a young woman sitting inside. As Travis opened the door, he glanced at the woman. Red hair, tied in a ponytail, wearing dark jeans, a T-shirt that read "Good Vibes," and a light jacket over top. On her neck hung a badge. FBI. She glanced at Travis, "You Travis Bishop?"

He nodded.

"I'm FBI Agent Grace Laughlin. Senator Riggs's office sent me. Let's go."

As soon as Catherine closed the door, the black sedan took off. Grace looked at the two of them, "It's a haul down to DC. Would take hours in the car. The FBI Director approved a helicopter so we're headed to the helipad. The FBI chopper will get you there lickity-split quick. Once you land, there will be an agent on the other side to meet you."

Travis nodded. "Thanks."

"Sure enough."

Eighteen minutes later, after battling their way through early morning traffic in New York, Agent Grace Laughlin dropped them off in front of an office building without asking either of them why they were getting VIP treatment. Apparently, her orders had been not to ask. Travis didn't offer and neither did Catherine. "Head to the twenty-second floor," she said, leaning toward them as they got out. "The helipad's up there. They're fueled and ready to go."

"Okay. Thanks." Travis slammed the door to the sedan and then waved at Catherine to follow him. Getting in the elevator, he licked his lips, realizing he had no idea what they were doing. All he knew was Tom Stewart had disappeared and now Senator Riggs was pulling strings to have him help. Was the President involved? Questions pounded through Travis's mind. Certainly by now, President Mosely knew Travis was on the hunt again, but the hunt for what? A CIA director that had gone off the rails? Tom's meltdown still didn't fully explain what was going on. Why the sudden escalation?

As the elevator doors opened, Travis saw the helicopter down a short hallway beyond a double set of glass doors. He and Catherine emerged a second later, running toward the helicopter, the blades spinning slowly above them. The pilot was already in the cockpit, a blue-jacketed FBI agent waving them forward, "Bishop? Lewis?" The two of them nodded. "I'm Agent Holman. Let's go."

Travis waited for Catherine to get in the helicopter and then followed, strapping the seatbelt over his shoulders and waist and then pulling on the headset as the helicopter lifted off the pad on the top of the building. He tried to find an angle to rest his aching ankle as he settled into his seat. It might be the only break they would get for a while. Agent Holman turned to look at them as they flew, speaking into the microphone positioned near his lips, "It's a quick ninety-minute jaunt down to Virginia.

We've got people on the ground. They're waiting for you. Try to relax and enjoy the ride."

Yeah, right, Travis thought. Relaxing wasn't exactly going to happen. If anyone knew he was on the helicopter, he could be looking down the tip of an M4 rocket launcher. As far as he knew, the bounty on his head was still active. Travis stared at Agent Holman, trying to push the thought of getting blown out of the sky out of his head. "Any idea what happened to Director Stewart?"

"Sorry, sir. I've got nothing. Was told to get you down there ASAP. That's it."

59

The helicopter made good time and was able to land a little faster than the ninety-minute predicted travel time between New York and Tom Stewart's lavish home in Virginia. From one of the few times Travis had been invited over, Travis remembered that Tom and Shelley Stewart's house backed up to a golf course. Sure enough, they landed the black FBI helicopter on the manicured green of the seventh hole of the West Woods Golf Course, interrupting several early morning golfers and ticking off the grounds manager who drove away on his golf cart yelling expletives that could be heard clearly back at the clubhouse.

Travis quickly shed the earphones and pulled off his seatbelt, jumping out of the helicopter. He waited for a second for Catherine to join him and they ran across the grass toward Tom Stewart's house.

At the edge of the yard, they met a tall FBI agent, one that moved like she almost had a career in the WNBA, but chose the FBI instead. She had a close crop of dark hair, matching ebony skin, and wide brown eyes. She leaned toward them, looking Travis at eye level, "You must be Bishop?"

Travis nodded.

"I'm Agent Regina Johnson. Nice to meet you."

Again, no questions about who they were or why they'd been sent. Travis pushed the thought away. Someone was keeping a lid on their involvement. "What do we have here?"

Agent Johnson led them to the house, her loping stride eating up the space between the backyard and the side door. "We aren't exactly sure, to be honest," she said, ushering the two of them into the house and closing the door behind them. Travis sucked in a deep breath. He hadn't been in Tom and Shelley's house for probably close to seven years. Other than some minor redecorating, it looked about the same, everything tucked neatly into its place, the wide marble kitchen island taking up the majority of the kitchen, a smattering of appliances on the counter. It was a kitchen that was meant to be seen, not used. He refocused on Agent Johnson, "You'll have to bring me up to speed here, and Agent Lewis too. We got a call from Senator Riggs. She told us to get down here, but she didn't fill in a lot of the information other than Tom is missing."

Agent Johnson pointed a manicured orange fingernail to an agent who was working on a laptop sitting at the kitchen island, "Can you show them the video?"

The young woman nodded, turning the screen toward Travis and Catherine. Agent Johnson spoke as it ran, "We got a call this morning that when the Capitol police came to do their shift change, Tom was gone. Capitol police handle all of the dignitary support for Senators. That's why they were here. Double teaming Tom and Shelley. The officer who arrived noticed Tom's car was still here, and the back door was ajar. It was at that point he called his superiors who called us. We pulled the surveillance video from the interior and exterior of the house, and this is what we saw…"

Travis stared at the video in front of him as the FBI technician pressed play. It showed an image of Tom standing in his kitchen, dressed in slacks, a shirt, and a sports coat, as if he was ready to go to work, when something caught his attention. He walked to the side door and opened it. "It's at this point we see two intruders enter the house," Agent Johnson said, pointing at the screen.

Travis continued to watch as the men quickly grabbed Tom's arms, cable tying his wrists together and then shoving him out the door. Their movements were efficient and practiced; as if they had repeated the process hundreds if not thousands of times. Travis grimaced. The black-bearded men were professionals. Travis refocused on the video. The water Tom had been carrying ended up on the floor. Travis glanced at the side door. The broken glass was still there. It was the only evidence Tom had been in the house that morning.

"Is that all you have?" Catherine frowned.

"No, ma'am. Take a look at this," Agent Johnson said.

The tech switched views, "The exterior cameras captured this. They were in and out in less than two minutes" The video started again, showing Tom being pushed out to a waiting black van in the driveway, the door sliding shut almost immediately, and the van driving away.

Travis shook his head. Whoever had taken Tom was clearly professional. They'd subdued him without any real resistance. That took training. "Any leads? Were you able to get the plates on the van?"

Agent Johnson shook her head, "Unfortunately, no. The van did have plates on it, but there's some sort of a coating on it that makes it impossible for our LPR's to read."

Travis rubbed the stubble of beard on his face with his hand. He'd read an article recently online about LPR technology, or license plate readers. The author had said that the automated technology was only as good as the ability of the camera to capture the image. New counter-technology had been developed, a coating that obscured a camera's ability to capture anything other than the edges of the metal plate. "Any ransom demand? Anything?" Travis asked.

"No. Nothing. He's a ghost. That's why you're here."

60

"Let's split up and see what we can figure out," Catherine said to Travis.

"Sounds good."

Catherine left Travis and Agent Johnson in the kitchen while she walked through the house, getting the lay of the land first. It was the way her mind worked, looking for the larger framework of evidence and then setting the details of what she was looking at on top of it, much like draping a lace tablecloth over a table before setting the dishes on it. In her mind, the process made total sense. She walked into the master bedroom and noticed the bed was still rumpled, but only on one side. Going into the bathroom, she looked around, touching the towels. One of them was damp, the other one completely dry. She walked back out into the kitchen where Travis and Agent Johnson were huddled above the laptop, watching the abduction video again, "Where's Tom's wife?"

"We're not exactly sure," Agent Johnson frowned. "We think she might be out of town at a conference. I've got a call into her office, but I haven't heard back from her Chief of Staff yet. I'll let you know as soon as I hear something," Johnson said, looking back at the computer.

Catherine shook her head as she walked away. Strange that Senator Stewart's own security detail didn't know where she was.

Catherine did another lap through the house, this time looking for more details. She stopped in what looked to be Tom and Shelley Stewart's home office, still wondering where Shelley was. Shelley could be at a conference, traveling the state shaking hands and kissing babies, trying to garner support for one of her bills, or she could have very simply spent the night in DC. Catherine pressed her lips together. Certainly, the Capitol Police knew where she was. Must be a miscommunication, she thought. Most of the government officials she knew had homes in their district as well as homes in the capital as well. It seemed a fair assumption that Americans would operate in exactly the same way.

Sitting down at the desk that was centered in front of a set of built-in bookcases, Catherine started opening drawers. There was the typical assortment of pens, pencils, paper clips, and rubber bands in the top drawer. In the next drawer down, there was a stack of legal pads and an envelope. Catherine pulled it out, looking at it. It was stuffed with small papers. Receipts. They all seemed to be from a gun range nearby, as though someone, either Tom or Shelley, was taking regular firearms lessons. Catherine grabbed the envelope and walked back into the kitchen, "Travis? Take a look at this," she said, setting the envelope down in front of him.

"What is it?"

"It's an entire envelope filled with receipts for a gun range. Was one of them a fan of firearms?"

Travis shook his head, "I don't know. Maybe Tom was trying to stay updated or blow off some steam. You know, being the director is a lot of headaches. It's just like Archie's job."

"Perhaps," Catherine said, wandering back into the office and putting the envelope back where she'd found it. If that was the case, had Tom just been surprised by the attack? Anyone who had spent that much time at the range should have been better prepared, no? Catherine frowned and rummaged through the rest of the drawers, only finding random files that included things like their house insurance, car receipts, and a few bank statements. The desk was a dead end, but she knew there was something to be found. It just might not be at Tom Stewart's house.

On the desk was a laptop. Catherine opened it up and it whirred to life. She stared at the screen, waiting for a password to be requested, but none was. She frowned, "Not too secure for a senator and a CIA director," she mumbled.

After a few minutes of hunting on the laptop, she found nothing. The history revealed frequent searches to the local home improvement store, a few explorations for a new television, and videos of cats doing funny things. Typical, Catherine thought, closing the lid. The computer was barely used, as if it was one Tom and Shelley bought but let sit on the desk, only for shopping or entertainment. There was nothing interesting there.

Frustrated, she got up from the computer and went back into the kitchen. Travis glanced at her as she walked back into the room, "Anything?" he asked.

"Other than those receipts? No. Nothing. You?"

"Nope. It just looks like those two guys, whoever they were, bum-rushed Tom out of the house and into the van. Agent Johnson's people are running facial recognition, but on the first pass, they didn't get anything. They're trying a more detailed run at the images now, but she's not optimistic."

Catherine chewed the inside of her lip. "Seems like this is a dead end."

"I agree."

"I think the real story is going to be in New York, don't you?" Travis nodded. "There's nothing to gain here. I think we need to go have a talk with Jonah Hudson."

"Let's go."

61

"Get out!"

"It felt like hours had passed since the two black-bearded men had snatched Tom out of his kitchen. He'd sat, shaking, with a black hood over his head, his hands bound behind him in a van for how long, he couldn't tell. Thankfully, the initial shock had worn off after a while and he felt at least half himself, even if he'd been kidnapped.

He'd heard a variety of street noises on his trip once he'd calmed down a bit, the quiet hum of the freeway, followed by at least one bridge, the thumping as they passed over railroad tracks and then more pressing traffic, horns honking, the smell of diesel and gas fumes in the air as if the cars were clustered close around the van. He had no idea where he was. His face sagged. Part of him thought he deserved this treatment. So when the van stopped and the door opened, he sat patiently, waiting for someone to tell him what to do. He was a surrendered man, with no fight left in him.

Unable to see, he nearly tripped as he got out of the van, only two sets of strong hands preventing him from falling flat on his face. He shuffled his feet along what seemed to be a dirty concrete floor, only able to see glimpses of the toes of his brown cap-toed shoes as he slid his feet along, the black fabric flapping away from his face just enough to get a glimpse of where the floor was occasionally. The men guiding him didn't say anything, half pushing and half dragging him as they walked. Their grip tightened. They stopped. Tom held his breath as he heard a door open in front of him and then felt himself being shoved inside, the cold steel of a knife pressing against his wrist as the cable ties were cut, the black hood ripped off his head. He turned around in time to see a heavy door close behind him, the room black around him.

He was alone.

62

Ninety minutes later, what Travis could say without a doubt was that CIA Director Tom Stewart had been kidnapped. By who and why still needed to be answered, not to mention how it was tied to the bounty on Travis's head. The feeling that he still couldn't see the full picture of what was going on was beginning to haunt him. He and Catherine were so close, but they hadn't gotten a grip on it yet. They were running out of time.

Travis and Catherine landed back on top of the helipad in New York City to be greeted by FBI Agent Grace Laughlin, the one that had picked them up from their hotel.

"Grace, we need to get into Manhattan, to the Desert Indigo offices. Can you take us there?"

"Grace's taxi service is open for business. That's what I'm here for. Got an address?"

Catherine stared at her phone and then read off the address listed on the website, "11703 East Broadway."

"That's Manhattan. We'll be there in a jiffy."

Travis heard the engine revving in the sedan as Grace pressed the accelerator. She wove her way through New York traffic expertly, a single hand on the wheel, dodging stopped trash trucks and delivery trucks that were lining the streets, all while humming under her breath. Travis looked out the window as they drove. Every inch of New York had been commandeered for tall buildings jutting up into the air, most of them at least five stories, if not taller, which was nothing to say of the Freedom Tower which was the tallest of all of them, a living monument to the losses of 9/11.

Throngs of people walked up and down the streets on either side in groups of ones, twos, or threes. Travis saw a dog walker wearing a fluorescent yellow vest. By Travis's count, the man had to have at least ten dogs with him, a pouch strapped around his waist probably filled with dog treats and waste bags, heavy headphones on his ears, the cluster of dogs traveling together as if they were their own little circus, ready to perform at a moment's notice. Travis rolled his window down, the fresh air mixed with the sour smell of trash, clouds of exhaust, and sweat coming from the people of the city. He shook his head. He'd give pretty much anything to be back in the wide-open spaces of Texas.

Twelve minutes later, Grace stopped in front of a building. "Want me to come up with you? I'm pretty good at flashing my badge," she said, glancing at Travis and Catherine, a grin on her face.

Travis looked at her and shook his head, "No. We've got this. You'll wait here for us, right?"

Grace nodded. "That's my job."

Travis hopped out of the car, waiting for Catherine. He didn't know if Agent Grace Laughlin was new, on probation, or a very solid agent who'd been trusted with carting around VIPs for the day. It didn't matter. They had more pressing matters to attend to than wondering about Grace's career situation. As long as she was there, that was good enough.

Going into the building that housed Desert Indigo's

corporate headquarters, Travis stopped for a second. The brick on the exterior of the building screamed of something that had been built a century before, probably at the hand of Italian or Irish immigrants who had recently made their way into the United States, bringing their tradecraft with them, each brick laid carefully one on top of the other. It was a structure meant to last. He glanced up at the façade. The windows looked like they had been recently replaced, the tint on the glass giving the building a strange old meets new vibe. As they walked inside, there was nothing much to say. It was nondescript, the lobby of one of a million office buildings. The walls had been finished and painted in a muted gray, complementing a no-nonsense matching tile floor, perfect for the sloppy winter weather in New York City. Travis pointed at a placard on the wall. "It says Desert Indigo's on the sixth floor. You ready?"

Catherine's expression hardened. They strode toward the elevator, pressing the button for six as they stepped inside.

As the doors opened on the sixth floor, Travis stared. There was no hallway, no additional entrance or exit doors. The elevator opened directly into the Desert Indigo offices, as though they had been dropped in the middle of the operation. A tingle ran down his spine. Anyone off the street could march themselves right into the office space. Maybe it was meant to be that way, but something about it didn't make sense to Travis, not for an organization that managed nearly half a trillion dollars in wealth for its investors. A young woman wearing glasses and a high bun approached them, "Can I help you?"

Catherine stepped forward, straightening her shoulders, "We'd like to speak to Mr. Hudson, if possible."

The girl, as if confused by the request, blinked and then looked at them, "I don't know if he's available. You have an appointment?"

Travis was just about to answer when Catherine laid her

hand on his arm, "We don't, but could you be a dear and show us to his assistant? Perhaps she could give us some help?"

The girl nodded, as if what Catherine had said made a lot more sense than the request for a meeting.

As they walked through the offices, Travis found himself surprised at how basic they were. For a company that managed the amount of money they did, he expected to see some sort of opulence, but there was none. The carpet was commercial grade, short nap, and highly functional in a dark, charcoal gray. The walls had been painted a soothing tint of bluish beige, images of the New York City skyline placed every now and again artfully on the walls. Offices, some of them occupied, some not, were placed at regular intervals along the hallway. The center of the room had been carved out into an open work area. Not cubicles, but large, long tables outfitted with a wide array of electrical connections that looked like they could accept everything from a laptop to a cell phone. Extra monitors were placed judiciously along the tables, some of which were in use by the staff, others that were dark, the tangle of unconnected cables trailing on the surface like black snakes.

Travis checked the time on his cell phone. It was nearly lunchtime. They'd spent the entire morning going back and forth between Virginia and New York, checking out Tom's house, which had netted nothing. Hopefully, their visit to Jonah would give them more of a sense of what was going on.

"She's right over there," the young woman with the bun on the top of her head said. "Her name is Cynthia. She's very nice, at least most of the time. Today's a nice day, I think. I'm sorry, I have to get back to work. Mr. Hudson is expecting research from me."

Travis raised his eyebrows at the young woman's inability to help them and her comment about Cynthia having a "nice day." What did that mean? Travis shook his head.

In front of him, seated at an L-shaped desk, was a young

woman with blonde bobbed hair, wearing a navy-blue blazer. She was working furiously on her computer as if pounding on the keyboard would make it cooperate better. Travis narrowed his eyes. She glanced up at Catherine and Travis and said, "Hello, may I help you?"

"Are you Cynthia?" Catherine started.

"I am."

"I'm Catherine Lewis," Catherine said, pronouncing the words very slowly.

Travis watched as a flicker of recognition passed over Cynthia's face. Catherine said they had an asset at Desert Indigo. Was it Cynthia? "I realize we've just dropped in unannounced., but we'd like to see Jonah Hudson, please,".

Cynthia's face flushed, "I am so sorry. I'd love to be able to introduce you to him, however, he's been on calls all morning and is backed up with paperwork. He asked not to be disturbed. Could I ask what this is in regard to? Are you interested in becoming investors?"

Travis only believed half of the words that were coming out of Cynthia's mouth. Something was going on. He could feel it in his gut. "We're here now, Cynthia. And we'd like to see him..."

"As I said, I am so very sorry, but Mr. Hudson is —"

Travis didn't wait for her to finish the sentence. He glanced up. The office door directly behind Cynthia's desk read Jonah Hudson, Manager. He crossed the distance before Cynthia could intercept him, turning the door handle. It was locked. He glanced back at Catherine who cocked her head to the side. No objection. In one move, Travis lowered his shoulder and aimed it into the door, pushing off on his bad ankle which sent a wave of pain through his body. He didn't care. The door ricocheted off the hinges, banging against the frame. Travis shoved it open and stepped inside.

The first thing he noticed was the breeze in the office. A door had to be open somewhere. As Travis scanned the space, he saw a door to a balcony was open, bright sunlight streaming in. There was a figure outside, a small man with blond hair. He had one leg over the railing and was staring back at them, his eyes wide. Catherine charged ahead of Travis and ran across the room, screaming, "Jonah, no!"

But she was too late.

By the time she and Travis made it out to the balcony, Jonah Hudson's body had already landed on the sidewalk six stories below, his body twisted and mangled, a pool of red blood seeping out from the back of his head staining the concrete. Travis turned to look back at Cynthia, who was standing in the doorway, her hands clamped in front of her mouth, her eyes wide. Travis strode back to her and put his hands on her arms. He looked her square in the face, "I need you to go call 9-1-1. Tell them what happened. Can you do that?"

Cynthia nodded slowly and turned and walked back toward her desk. From where Travis was standing, he could see a few more of the Desert Indigo employees standing, frozen where they were, their attention drawn by the clatter of Travis breaking through the door. A low murmur started rumbling throughout the office, people hugging and crying, shock setting in at the loss of their beloved leader.

By the time Travis turned back to the office, Catherine was already at the bank of computers on Jonah's desk. She was typing frantically, glancing at the screen every second or so, "It's not working. It's locked out. Something's wrong with the system!"

Travis ran to her side and looked at the screens. There was gibberish all over them; as if the system had been completely corrupted. "It looks like he released a virus. Torched his own system."

Catherine shook her head, whispering, "What did he do?" Travis scanned the desk, pointing to a piece of paper that had fallen on the floor, probably from the breeze of the open door, "Look at this," he said, picking it up.

It was a single sheet of cheap white copy paper, as nondescript as could be, with the thin lines of a blue, ballpoint pen scrawled across it, "I'm sorry. I had no choice, Jonah."

"He had no choice about what?" Catherine stared at Travis.

"I have no idea."

By the time Travis and Catherine got downstairs, Grace was on the phone, the wail of sirens nearing them. She hung up from her call and looked at Travis and Catherine, raising her eyebrows, "I know you two are intimidating, but she didn't need to scare the guy to death."

Travis shook his head.

"Too soon?" Grace smiled.

Travis nodded, "Maybe." He was familiar with the grim humor that came with law enforcement. He'd seen it in the military too. It was the only way to mentally protect yourself when your job was seeing death and dismemberment all day long, every single day, month after month, year after year. Before Travis could say anything else, Grace looked down at her phone. It was ringing again. "Excuse me, I gotta get this."

Travis watched Grace as her face wrinkled into a frown, "What? Where? You're kidding! No, I'll bring them right over."

Grace looked at Travis and Catherine, "We gotta go. They've spotted Director Stewart."

"Where?" Travis asked, running for the sedan.

"The New York Stock Exchange."

63

The weight of the vest that covered Tom's upper body was heavy, heavier than he would ever have imagined was possible. He'd worn weighted vests to run in, but this was different. Crushing, the vest dragged down on his shoulders, rubbing against his collarbones.

An hour before, his captors had given him a glass of water. He was told to drink it. By the time he had two sips down, he was already feeling groggy. He'd woken up to find Ercan standing over him grinning, a suicide bomb strapped to his chest. "We have a little job for you, Director Stewart."

Still a little wobbly, the men had stood Tom up and forced a bright green T-shirt on over the explosive-laden vest. Once they had it on him, they wove his arms into his sports coat. Ercan stepped forward, adjusting Tom's tie, surveying his look. "We don't want you to seem out of place, now do we?"

One of the men grabbed a wire that was hanging down from the sleeve of Tom's sports coat, glancing at Ercan. Ercan shook his head, "We'll take care of that in the van. Let's go."

An eight-minute drive later, traveling at gunpoint, Tom sat stock still, paralyzed by fear, feeling perspiration run down the side of his face. His lips were parted, short pants of breath going in and out of his mouth. He looked down to see his hands, which were placed on each one of his knees, shaking. If Ercan had handed him a pencil to hold at that point, he wasn't sure he would be able to hold it. "Where are you taking me?" Tom mumbled, his throat dry and scratchy.

"You'll see in just a moment," Ercan called from the front of the van where he was perched next to the driver.

The van pulled up right in front of the main doors of the New York Stock Exchange. The man in the back of the van put his gun down and grabbed an ID badge that was hanging on a hook nearby. He slung it around Tom's neck. It was a picture of Tom, a string of numbers and letters, a bar code, and the name Desert Indigo printed on it. The man grabbed Tom's right hand, telling him to hold a small red tube that had a black button on it, in his grip. "Don't move." Glaring at Tom, the man lifted Tom's shirt and reached around the side fussing with the vest. Instantly, a few red lights lit up on the front of the bomb vest but were quickly dimmed when the thick T-shirt was replaced over it.

The man arming the bomb looked at Tom, "Hold the switch down." Tom did as he was told. The man scowled at him, "If you let go of it, the bomb will go off. Do you understand?" the man said in a thick accent that Tom had a hard time placing. Albania? Turkey? Armenia?

Tom didn't say anything.

Ercan turned from his spot in the front seat and stared at Tom, an amused look on his face, "It's called a dead man's switch, Tom. If you let it go, you're a dead man. Pretty simple, right?"

Tom nodded weakly.

Ercan's face got more serious, "If you are hoping to survive this little exercise of ours, then there's only one path forward for you. I've told Jonah Hudson to make some rather radical sales this afternoon, changes that will impact the course of history. Since you are such an important man, I've chosen you to be on the floor to ensure they go through. If they do, once everything is done, you walk right back out here to this van and my associate will disarm the bomb. If they don't, then kaboom. Do you understand?"

Tom nodded slowly, "Make sure the trades go through then come back to the van."

"Excellent. Now go," Ercan hissed.

64

The first few steps out of the van were the hardest, Tom decided. He felt his legs steady as he started to move closer to the doors of the New York Stock Exchange. Tugging the sleeve of his jacket down over his right hand, he shoved the dead man's switch into his pocket. He'd done a million missions before, he reminded himself as he stepped inside, the cool of the air conditioning pressing against his damp skin. The fog in his mind cleared a bit. A group of people wearing serious blue and black suits, a combination of women and men were walking out the door on the other side of him, one of the men holding it for Tom as he entered, "Thank you," Tom mumbled, avoiding eye contact.

There was a security kiosk in front of him along with a magnetometer. If he stepped anywhere near the scanner, it would surely go off. He didn't want that. Watch for the trades, then go back to the van. The words Ercan said rang in his head. Tom waited for a moment, watching. He saw another group of people who had credentials like his. All they did was scan their barcodes at a kiosk nearby and went right in. Tom followed along, doing the same.

As Tom walked out on the trading floor, he thought to himself how much smaller the room seemed than what he'd seen on television. Perhaps it was just the panoramic cameras that gave that impression of the market as a sprawling space. Above him, he could see the podium with the New York Stock Exchange logo in front of it where the market was opened and closed each day, the old-fashioned bell that used to be rung on a stand off to the side. The market now used an electronic belt to start and stop trading, the old one gathering dust, a relic of times past.

There was a low hum of voices in the room, as a few hundred professional traders walked from desk to desk, placing in-person trades in the pits, their hand signals telling the story of purchases and sales they intended on making. Although traders still littered the floor of the NYSE, much of the trading was done online now, handled by gargantuan servers kept in New Jersey, only a few miles away.

Tom scanned the area, trying to figure out how he would know when Jonah's sales were taking effect. He watched the people moving from desk to desk, the low murmur of voices in the room, feeling the cool filtered air of the ventilation system drifting down washing over the people and the computers that ran the stock exchange. His heart pounded in his chest as he looked up. A giant board took up one entire wall of the New York Stock Exchange, showing constantly updated statistics on the Dow, the S&P, and the NASDAQ, plus many of the world markets including the EURONEXT, the Nikkei, and the London stock exchange as they constantly updated.

Tom swallowed. His mouth was dry. If he'd been at the stock exchange any other day, he would have marveled at the way that the economic machine ran the way it did. Even a child with a single dollar could participate in the building of a democratic free market economy right alongside professional investors like Jonah Hudson. A tingle ran down his spine. Ercan told him to watch for a dramatic change in the market. What would that even look like, Tom didn't know. He started to walk, not sure what else to do.

65

"What do you mean he's at the New York Stock Exchange? What is he doing there?" Travis said to Grace, his eyes wide. She had the lights and sirens blaring as she drove the black sedan through the streets of Manhattan. Grace was no longer humming.

She shook her head, nearly avoiding a dump truck that was coming out of an alley, swinging the car wildly to the left and then to the right to avoid an oncoming bus, "I have no idea. I got a call from the NYPD. We put a BOLO out on him. They caught him on one of their cameras."

Travis shot a look at Catherine as they pulled up in front of the stock exchange. His hands were gripped into tight fists, his knuckles white. No part of this was good. Tom showing up at the New York Stock Exchange wasn't a move he'd anticipated. Not by a long shot. Flying out of the country? Yes. Running for the Canadian border? Sure. Taking a tour of the NYSE? Nowhere on the list. It had to have something to do with his abduction that morning. As they jumped out of the car, Travis heard Grace behind him yelling into her phone, "Yes, set up a perimeter! What? Are you kidding me? Now!"

Travis didn't wait to see what Grace was doing. He ran inside, Catherine on his heels, and was quickly stopped by one of the security guards. A voice behind them called, "Let them through,"

Grace had followed them into the building. She was still yelling into her phone, but she'd had the presence of mind to flash her badge. She looked at Travis and Catherine, "Go in and see if you can find him. See what the problem is. I gotta go back out and wait for the cavalry."

The security guard who was blocking their path moved to the side, his eyes wide, but he didn't say anything. Travis and Catherine took off at a fast walk. They needed to find Tom, but they didn't need to spook anyone else in the process, especially Tom. Maybe Tom had always wanted to see the landmark and decided to visit. Travis shook her head as they made their way down the hallway onto the trading floor. He hoped it was that simple, but his gut told him that there was no way that was actually the case. Something bigger, way bigger was going on, especially if Jonah had jumped to his death. Travis didn't believe in coincidences.

As Travis entered the trading floor, he looked around. There were a variety of different kiosks with monitors bolted to the top of them, graphs and numbers, and pricing for the various stocks represented on the market flashing everywhere. Travis grabbed Catherine's arm and stopped for a second. He looked at her, "Something's wrong. I don't see Tom, but everyone seems concerned. See the looks on their faces?"

Catherine nodded. She glanced up at the big board and pointed. The Dow was plummeting. A trader was about to run by them when Travis reached out and grabbed his arm, "Excuse me, what's going on?"

The man shook his head, his eyes wide, "We don't know. It looks like somebody placed a ton of sell orders. If this doesn't stop, the market is gonna drop through the floor. I'm not even sure the automatic system is going to be able to shut it down."

The man didn't say anything more, running off. Catherine stared at Travis, grabbing his arm, "We have to find Tom, now."

As they started to walk around the kiosk that was closest to the door, they spotted him, standing near a wall, his lips parted, his eyes vacant. "Tom?" Travis said, walking slowly toward him, holding his hands up in front of him. Travis stopped, narrowing his eyes. Something didn't seem right. Tom was pale, sweat running down the sides of his face. Tom turned toward Travis, but held a single hand up, "Travis, stay there. Don't come any closer."

Travis tried to keep his face relaxed and his voice calm, "Why? What happened to you?"

Before Travis could ask another question, Tom reached down with his left hand and lifted the thick green T-shirt he was wearing. Travis sucked in a breath. A bomb vest. "Oh my God," he whispered. He looked over his shoulder at Catherine, "Get these people out of here right now."

Catherine nodded and started waving people out of the building. Travis stared at Tom, holding his hand up, "It's all right Tom. We will figure this out. You stay right there." Travis glanced over his shoulder looking for Catherine. She was at the doors, motioning for people to leave, making a call at the same time, likely to 9-1-1. Her quiet movements weren't getting people moving fast enough. Travis calmly walked over to the nearest wall where there was a fire alarm. He pulled it, immediately seeing the red lights start to flash and hearing a siren scream overhead, an automated voice repeating, "Emergency. Leave the building immediately. Emergency." The people who were left on the trading floor, already concerned about the drop in the market, looked even more concerned with the alarm ringing, but started flooding to the doors. Catherine jogged back toward him, her eyes wide. "He's wearing a bomb vest?"

"Yes. Go out and tell Grace. Tell her exactly what's going on. Go now!"

Catherine glanced at Tom and then at Travis, "I called 9-1-1 already. I don't want to leave you here by yourself."

Travis shook his head, "Not now, Catherine. Go. I need you to talk to Grace. Tell her we're going to need a bomb tech, a containment unit, and a three-block perimeter, at least. Have them evacuate the neighboring buildings." Not knowing exactly what kind of explosives were in the vest, that was the best Travis could do.

Catherine didn't say anything else. She ran toward the exit, disappearing amid the throng of people that were exiting the building.

Behind Travis, he could hear crying and whimpering. A woman with jet black hair and black glasses who had seen the vest on Tom was huddled near the corner of the wall, her arms up over her face. She curled herself into a little ball as if that would save her from the bomb. Travis backed toward her, keeping one eye on Tom, "Ma'am, I need you to go."

"I can't! He has a bomb!"

"Ma'am, you aren't safe in here," Travis said, grabbing her arm and pulling her up into a standing position. He gave her a little shove, "Go!"

As the woman ran out, a few more stragglers ran past Travis. A couple of them saw Tom and screamed.

Then the market was quiet.

The only noise left in the building was Travis's sharp breathing, the beeping of the Dow as it tumbled, now down nearly five thousand points and continuing its descent. Tom pointed at the numbers, "Ercan told me to watch for something like this. He told Jonah to do something, I don't know what, but he said then I could go back out to the van and they would take this thing off of me. So, that's what I'm gonna do," Tom said in halting language, sounding like a child who was trying to remember a string of instructions, but couldn't.

Travis shook his head and held his hand up, "No, Tom, you can't go outside, not with that bomb on you. And Jonah's dead."

"What?" Tom said, his eyes wide. "What happened?"

"He committed suicide about an hour ago. Jumped off the balcony outside his office. Do you have any idea what's going on?" Travis knew it was a risk to ask Tom, given his mental state, but it might be the only chance Travis would have to get answers if the bomb went off.

Tom shook his head, his face going even paler, "I... I'm not sure," he stammered. "After I got off the phone with you this morning, I went for a run. I got showered and was ready to go to work. I couldn't find Shelley. I still haven't heard from her. She's been gone since yesterday." He glanced up at Travis, his eyes tearing. "Maybe they have her too?" He shook his head as if he were trying to dislodge the cobwebs. He closed his eyes for a second, "Like I said, I was ready to go to work. I was having a glass of water when two men barged their way into the house and took me. They kept me in a dark room for a while and then put this bomb on me." Tom's face sagged, his mouth open, "I don't understand about Jonah?"

Travis glanced up at the big board. The market had already fallen seven thousand points in the space of ten minutes. He gritted his teeth. Weren't automatic stops supposed to be in place to protect the market? Why wasn't the market shutting down? "I don't know about all that, Tom —"

Before Travis could finish his sentence, a shot rang out, clipping Travis in the shoulder. Travis immediately ducked down, running for the closest kiosk. He saw Tom do the same. Who was shooting at them? Hiding behind one of the desks, he looked at the wound. It felt like he'd been stuck with a hot poker. Luckily it was just a graze. A few inches to his right and it would have hit his heart. Travis glanced around, the breath catching in his throat. His heart was pounding. Tom was loose in the New York Stock Exchange with a bomb strapped to him and someone was shooting at Travis. His eyes were wide, his mouth dry. Had Agnes tracked him as he followed Tom?

Travis moved out from behind the trading desk, only to feel another shot whiz by him, this time a couple of inches to the side of his head. Where were the shots coming from? Travis took a deep breath, trying to calm himself. Based on the direction of the shots, it seemed like whoever was shooting at him was positioned above him. The balcony.

Travis ran out toward the open area where he'd been standing when the first shot came at him. Maybe he could draw out the shooter and get a line on where they were. As he did, he saw Tom hiding behind one of the other desks, across the stock floor from him. Travis held up his hand telling Tom to stay put. Tom started to walk toward Travis, his eyes glazed over, as though he'd lost any confidence in his ability to survive. As he did, words came slowly out of his mouth, like he was drunk. "I'm sorry, Travis. I'm sorry for everything. You should never have gotten dragged into my mess." As the last word came out of his mouth, a shot rang out, hitting Tom right in the forehead, his body crumbling to the ground.

Instantly, Travis went to his knees, waiting for the bomb to go off. He'd seen the dead man's switch in Tom's hand. Was Tom somehow still holding onto the switch? A second later, he realized the bomb hadn't been triggered. Travis glanced at Tom, wondering if it was a dummy bomb, just meant to scare him. Before he could investigate, Travis heard a noise in front of him as if someone was running. He glanced up to see a figure lumbering down the hallway with a pronounced limp. The shooter. He pulled the gun out of his holster and started to chase. As soon as he got around the corner, he saw it was a small woman with brown hair caught up in a ponytail. He'd seen that limp before. Just outside of the stock market doors, as he was about to yell for Shelley Stewart to stop, he felt the bomb go off, the heat and concussion so powerful it knocked him off his feet.

Travis's body skidded on the concrete sidewalk in front of the New York Stock Exchange, his head bouncing against the hard surface. Glass and debris rained down over him as he scrambled to his feet. The line of NYPD cruisers, black FBI SUVs, and ambulances in front of the building were covered in soot and smoke. Travis didn't have time to see if everyone was okay. He glanced to his left, the ringing in his ears deafening him, his head pounding. He saw Shelley Stewart disappear down the street and dart into an alley. Travis ran after her, nearly stumbling, but righting himself at the last moment, the pain in his ankle surging.

At the corner of the alley, Travis slowed down, his ears still ringing, his heart pounding in his chest. The roar of sirens off in the distance was the only thing that he could hear, that plus a whoosh of blood through his ears as adrenaline surged through his system. Everything else seemed to be muffled, all covered in a wad of cotton, from the blast.

Travis held his gun up in front of him, positioning himself behind his sights. He moved slowly, rolling his feet from heel to toe, making his way carefully down the alleyway. He'd gone about ten feet when another shot rang out. Shelley Stewart had emerged from behind a pile of wood and packing crates that had been left in the alleyway and then started running again, more of a lope with her limp. "Shelley! Stop!" Travis yelled. The ringing in his ears made his own voice sound muffled.

"This is all your fault!" She turned toward Travis, her face contorted by rage, holding a gun up in front of her, aiming directly at him.

Travis couldn't wait any longer. He pulled off two shots from the Glock 17 Archie Elliott had given him, landing one in her stomach and one in the middle of Shelley's chest. She dropped to the ground, the gun clattering away from her. Travis ran to her side and knelt by her. The wound in her chest was bubbling. Catherine ran up behind him, "Travis? Are you okay?"

"Get an ambulance," he growled. "Now!"

Travis looked down at Shelley, pressing on her wounds. He glanced at her, "Why, Shelley?"

"This is your fault, Travis. You were the only witness. You were the tainted asset. We had to get rid of you," she hissed as the life drained out of her. Her eyes went still.

Travis stood up, took off his flannel shirt and laid it over Shelley's face. He started to walk away as Grace and Catherine led a team of EMTs down the alley. Travis shook his head and walked away. Sadness flowed over him. He was the tainted asset no more.

EPILOGUE

"It's been a rocky week for investors on Wall Street," the announcer on the business channel Travis was watching, said, "After a bomb went off on the NYSE trading floor, the Dow lost nearly thirty percent of its twenty-six trillion-dollar value overnight, almost eight trillion dollars, with global markets reacting sympathetically. The markets reopen today under limited trading only. From a statement by the New York Stock Exchange Board, we understand they expect to have full trading restored within the next seven to ten business days. Personally, I think that's optimistic, but stay tuned, folks. This is an evolving story."

Travis was sitting on the front porch of Bishop Ranch as he watched the clip on his phone. As he shut it off, his phone rang.

"Hello, Archie."

"Travis! I hope it's a lovely day in Texas," he boomed from halfway across the world.

"It is. It's good to be home."

"And I trust you're healing adequately?"

Travis nodded. He'd gotten checked out at the scene by some of New York's finest EMTs, who patched up the bullet graze on his shoulder, told him he had a concussion, and suggested he go to the hospital. He didn't.

As he left, he waved to Catherine, gave a brief statement to the NYPD, and then let FBI Agent Grace Laughlin deal with the rest. It was a federal investigation anyways. With the help of Senator Riggs, Governor Torres, and Travis suspected the President himself, Travis had gotten himself on the next flight out of LaGuardia and back to Dallas where he'd rented a car and drove to Austin.

The hearing in his left ear was still humming a little. He knew from experience it might take a few days or weeks for it to go away. But it would. Just like the rest of his injuries. He spent the first day or so just hobbling around the ranch, taking time to check all the horses, making sure he and Ellie had enough supplies for the next few weeks, ordering a load of hay, and returning phone calls that had been stacking up. A new client was bringing in two more horses for training the next day. Whether he liked it or not, he'd have to get back to work in short order. The horses, and more importantly the clients, weren't going to wait much longer.

"Yeah. I'm feeling okay. Hoping to be back in the saddle again tomorrow."

"That's wonderful news, Travis. I'm happy to hear it. I had a few follow-up items for you, if you don't mind."

"Sure. Shoot."

Over the last week, Travis had learned to appreciate Archie's directness. In another time and another place, he wondered if he and Archie would've been friends. They were completely different, that was for sure, but there was a boldness about Archie that Travis respected.

"I'm sorry that Catherine hasn't been in touch. She's been on the move, tying off the last bits of this operation."

"Ercan Onan?"

"Yes, it includes Mr. Onan. He's come to a rather inauspicious end, courtesy of a joint operation between the Yankees and the Brits, along with many of his other Desert Indigo investors. It turns out that the Stewarts were part of Desert Indigo. Given the fact that Tom and Shelley are now deceased, we may never know how they got drawn into it."

Travis frowned, "That would explain why they went after me. I was one of the only people that could tie Tom to Ercan through Meset Gul."

"That certainly does appear to be the case, but with both of them dead, it will be a more difficult situation to prove. I do have some good news, though," Archie said, his voice brightening.

"What's that?"

"A few hours ago, I was notified that the terrorist assassin formerly known as Agnes has died. From what we've been able to piece together, Shelley Stewart tracked her using her contacts at Homeland Security, ambushed her, and killed her at a seedy motel outside of New York City in a small berg called Floral City. Shot in the back. Never saw it coming, the poor girl."

Travis frowned. Shelley had taken out Agnes? "So the bounty on my head is gone?"

"That's correct. You are a free man!"

"Thanks, Archie. I appreciate everything."

"You take care of yourself, Agent Bishop. MI6 is always available if you need us."

"Thanks. No disrespect meant, but I hope we never talk again."

Archie chuckled. "None taken."

As Travis hung up the phone with Archie, a trail of dust appeared on the driveway. He sat, watching it. A minute later, the pickup truck stopped, rolling down the passenger side window. Ellie. "You gonna sit there all day or are you gonna come give me a hand with all these horses?" she said, smiling.

"Yes, ma'am," Travis said, pushing himself up to standing. "I'm on my way."

CIA assets compromised in war-torn Ukraine. The Agency has given up protecting them. Can Travis recover their identities before more innocents lose their lives?

Click here to check out the next book in the series now!

If you'd like to join my mailing list and be the first to get updates on new books and exclusive sales, giveaways and releases, click here!
I'll send you a prequel to the next series FREE!

A NOTE FROM THE AUTHOR

Thanks so much for taking the time to read *Tainted Asset*. I hope you've been able to enjoy a little escape from your everyday life while joining Travis on his latest adventure.

If you have a moment, would you leave a review? They mean the world to authors like me!

If you'd like to join my mailing list and be the first to get updates on new books and exclusive sales, giveaways and releases, click here! I'll send you a prequel to another series FREE!

Enjoy, and thanks for reading,
    KJ

TRY THESE OTHER BOOKS BY KJ KALIS...

Check out these series and add them to your "to be read" pile today!

Investigative journalist, Kat Beckman, faces the secrets of her past and tries to protect her family despite debilitating PTSD.
Visit the series page here!

Intelligence analyst, Jess Montgomery, risks everything she has — including her own life — to save her family.
Visit the series page here!

Former detective, Morgan Foster, is on the run from the people who tried to kill her, until trouble comes knocking at her door.
Visit the series page here!

Printed in Great Britain
by Amazon